The Veil

by M. Saban-Smith

Copyright © 2013 M. Saban-Smith

All rights reserved.
This book or any portion thereof may not be reproduced
or used in any manner whatsoever without
the expressdp written permission of the publisher except
for the use of brief quotations in a book review.

This book is a work of fiction.
Any similarities to real people, living
or dead, is purely coincidental.
All characters and events in this work are
Figments of the author's imagination.

First Edition, 2013

ISBN 978-0-9928037-1-1

Published by M. Saban-Smith
Hampshire, UK

See more and contact the author online:
Web: www.msabansmith.com
Twitter: @msabansmith
Facebook: www.facebook.com/msabansmith

Acknowledgements

I began to tell people that I had started to write a book in 2011. Some people were very enthused and excited for me, whilst others were more dubious. Rightly so, I suppose. For those that know me, know that I have a track record of not completing some things I set out to do...This time was different. The remainder of the book, some 70,000 words was written from the middle of August 2013 until 18th December 2013...So for those of you who ever doubted me, with good humour, I would just like to say *'I told you so!'* Whether The Veil sells well or not is yet to be seen, but never-the-less, I have written the book!

As with any book, I guess, there are hundreds of people to thank, but these folk have really stood out to me in the last couple of years.

Firstly, I need to say thank you to my Facebook friends and Twitter followers who have helped spread the word about me as a writer and also about the book. They read the excerpts I put on the website and gave me some great feedback. Notable followers are Eileen Nockles, Jenny Kenyon, Rebekah Abbott, Richard Brand, Gillian and Sheila Daglish, Tammy Gowers and Simon Evans for their constant encouragement and comments on Facebook.

Carole Samuda, thank you for keeping my head as straight as it can be!

Not only for their personal support, but also for their unerring belief that I could actually pull this off: Janice Horrocks, Toby Reynolds, Richard McNick, Jodi Hill, Sam Hays and others at the High Sports Climbing Wall in Alton and the Alton Sports Centre in Hampshire where I work. They all read excerpts from the book and commented constructively. Sorry it made you cry, Janice!

I couldn't have finished the book without the honest feedback from the few that read The Veil before I did! Charlotte Feldon (sorry it made you cry too), Sally Smith and Steve Nash. Their comments made me rework some large portions of the book - thank you. If it wasn't for you, then the story would not be as full as it is now!

Jane Cuff, (who is a great children's author!) has supported me from the very beginning. I remember telling her about the basic story line about years ago and showed her the very first draft of chapters one and two in December 2011. Thanks, Jane for your ideas, encouragement and advice, and thanks to Nathan Cuff too for advice on publishing!

Charlotte Parkins has been a good friend for at least eight years now, and I am very grateful to her for superb professional advice on book editing and casting her critical eyes over various chapters for me. Thank you, Charlotte.

My parents, Sally and Graham. They've listened to the story develop and grow since August and mum now needs to read it again as parts of it changed when I edited it. Thank you for your patience and understanding. Your help, as quiet or as vocal as it may have been has been amazing.

Finally, my children, Xander and Clara. They were excited for me writing a book since I started it some two years ago. They enquired after its progress many times when they came to stay with me, and I wish I could have told them more about it, but it is not a story for young ears. One day, they will be old enough to read it for themselves, and they will find out why Daddy was a bit cagey with the details! Their excitement, and their pride in their old man spurred me on. Thank you, kids...I love you both so very much.

For Sarah,

*'I still believe in God,
But God no longer believes in me.'*

From *'Wasteland'* by The Mission, 1987

17th October

The most difficult thing Naomi could think of was how she would be able to carry on without him. Her day had been dull and uninteresting, as all the days had been since he had gone. She had spent most of her time numbly gazing through the window at the street that seemed every bit as dull as her days were turning out to be.

Her tea had gone cold, forgotten about as her mind wondered through random thoughts, her fingernails tapping tunelessly on the mug, not hearing the sound. She saw the people outside going about their business, totally oblivious to the eyes watching them.

Just as the clouds moved across the sky, the shadows of the people and buildings moved round too as the day went on. How long she had sat in that chair she did not know. The entire day had passed her by without her even noticing. She was too lost in her head to care. What had she achieved today? Nothing. What had she resolved to do? Nothing. What was she going to do tomorrow? She dare not think about it.

Retiring to bed long after the sun had gone down, she had laid there, staring for what seemed like hours at a point in space half way between the sheets and the ceiling listening to the traffic noise had died away to a distant hum from the busy main road a few streets away. The neighbourhood cats had stopped fighting and the late night pub goers had gone to bed too. She finally fell asleep.

She lay, dreamlessly cuddling a pillow for comfort. She nuzzled it, gently rubbing the corner against the side of her nose and cheek. She could be mistaken for a child sucking its thumb if it wasn't for her long hair with a grown-up cut and her clearly womanly features.

Somewhere in her mind she missed feeling Aiden breathing warmly along her back as he lay spooned-up behind her. But this was the tenth night he had been absent. Her back felt cold and exposed. Her man, making her feel so safe and secure with his arms wrapped round her body had not come home.

-|-

He walked in through the open bedroom door, bringing with him a slightly cold, breath of stagnant air. He moved round the bed, closely observing Naomi as she lay bathing in the orange street-light glow. He watched the bed clothes move slowly up and down as the delightful woman before him took shallow breaths and let them go again, repeating the same rhythm. She had no idea he was standing over her, watching.

Kneeling beside her, he looked at her eyes, hoping she was dreaming, but they remained still behind the recently cleaned lids. There was a faint aroma of cucumber coming from her soft skin from where she had washed that beautiful, precious face before climbing into bed. He didn't really care what the smell was, he was never any good with feminine cleansing products in the first place, and that was not the reason for his being there.

Naomi was still unaware that he was there.

What am I going to do now? It seems a shame to wake her at this hour, the man thought to himself. *I'll just do it and get it over with, but it would be nice if she was awake when I do it.* She continued to lay still, unmoving, save for the rhythm of her breathing under the bed clothes.

He moved his head closer to her face, the feint smell breath causing her to wrinkle her nose with the slight change in the air's fragrance. She moved her hand to scratch her nose, the pillow must have tickled it. She took a deep breath through her mouth, not quite a yawn and let it out with more like a regretful sigh than anything else. Her eyes began to move behind the clean, cucumbery lids. She began to dream.

Deep in her subconscious, she heard Aiden tell her that he loved her. She loved him so much. Her eyes screwed up as if she were holding back tears. *Can you cry when you are asleep?* He thought.

"*I love you, Naomi.*" he whispered, his face so close to hers now that her minty breath sent a shiver through him. Her breath on him was electrifying. It enveloped his soul, making his heart feel bright and alive. He adored her lying there.

Nothing. She didn't move. Her eyes relaxed and stopped moving. Maybe he didn't whisper loudly enough.

"*I love you.*" he tried again, a little louder this time.

Nothing.

"*Naomi? I love you.*" he said for a third time, this time nearly as loud as his normal voice.

Nothing.

"*Naomi? Wake up. I love you. Open your eyes for me, my love. Look! I'm home.*" He was beginning to sound a little desperate. Why wouldn't she open her eyes? He leaned back, sitting on his heels, running his hands though his tousled hair.

"*Naomi! Its me!*" he smiled nervously, voice waivering "Please wake up, I haven't got long, then I have to go again."

He wasn't prepared for this. He expected some movement, an acknowledgement of his presence. He wanted her to open her eyes, look at him with the sleepy smile he loved so much. But she gave no impression of wanting to wake at all. He needed to see her eyes, feel her arms around him, her fingernails down his back. Why wouldn't she wake up for him? He got up and paced round the room, gazing longingly at her from around the bed. She looked so peaceful there, curled up innocently under the duvet.

Analysing what to do, he held his chin, fingering his lip whilst his other hand was tucked beneath the opposite elbow. He muttered to himself, confused. He wanted to touch her, feel her skin against his fingers again, one last time perhaps, but she was so beautiful that to wake her by touch may startle her. He continued to watch her, puzzling over what to do next.

Finding a louder voice, but not too loud to scare her, he tried again as if he had just entered the room. He knelt down again. *"Naomi..."* he said cheerfully with a smile and wide eyes. He waited, his smile slowly vanishing from his lips.

Nothing.

"Naomi! Wake up! It's me, Aiden! Please wake up!" His voice grew louder with frustration, peaking as a near shout at the end. Was she drunk and had passed out? No, he thought, her breath did not smell of alcohol. Drugs? Sleeping pills? No, it couldn't be. She had never been into those sorts of things and she could always get to sleep well.

He stood-up and raised his voice, as if projecting it into an auditorium with arms out stretched. *"NAOMI!"*

Nothing.

Feeling anger rise inside him he began to lose control. He felt like he was panicking. Why couldn't he wake her up? He was told that he could. Just once, they had said, *'but then you must return.'* He remembered the words. But if he couldn't wake her up to tell her, did he have to leave then? He hadn't been told that. No, he'll stay until he could say what he felt he had to say; the one thing he was allowed back to say, 'I love you.'

He screamed again and again that he loved her at the top of his voice. Tears ripping their way from his eyes, such was the desperation he now felt at her for not being able to hear his feelings. Somewhere inside him, the dormant memory of his teenage years burbled its way from the pit of his stomach to his head. The feeling of a teenage boy so head over heels in love with a girl at school that he had to tell her no matter what that he loved her, only to find her in someone else's arms when he arrived at the park.

There was an uncontrollable rage now. He screamed with all his might at her. He could have bitten her nose, but she remained still and silent with just a tiny wisp of hair moving from her fringe in a barely perceptible breeze as he shouted himself hoarse at her. He missed the hair move, his eyes blurry with tears. He also missed that when his tears dropped from his eyes, they never landed on the bed or the floor. They simply vanished.

He flung out with his arms violently at the bottles and assorted items on the chest of drawers to scatter them noisily across the room to try that. Nothing. Nothing moved at all. His arm passed straight through everything leaving the smallest amount of condensation where he should have made contact.

Stunned by the lack of movement or noise from his efforts, he staggered backwards looking at his hands in disbelief.

Confused, desperate and suddenly feeling dreadfully alone, Aiden fell to his knees, the realisation of what he was dawned upon him. He sank back onto his heels, shoulders rounded, his head hanging heavily to his chest. All the life he thought he had suddenly fell away. He was a ghost. He was somewhere between this world and the next. *How can this be? I thought I could come back? I thought I would have a body I could use to touch her.* He felt betrayed by his own stupid belief that he could come back with a physical body.

The memory of what had happened to him escaped him. It was all a blur, a bit like a very drunken night out. There were sketchy memories, but nothing concrete. All he could remember was being taken somewhere by someone or something and pleading to be let go and be allowed to return to his beloved Naomi. He did not see anyone when it happened, not that he could remember anyway. There was no bright light for him to walk to. What had happened? The only clear memory he had was being told that he could go back to tell Naomi that he loved her and then to return on the first of November. Nothing more.

Standing hunched over by Naomi's bedside table he felt the rage begin again. Boiling hot and rising up from the deep within him, his anger at this injustice overflowed in what would have been a terrifying act of violence in that room, if only anyone could see or hear it.

Aiden stood alone, lashing out at everything, trying in vain to pick things up and throw them around, but his hands passed through everything like a drunkard trying to pick a fight and missing with every stumbling punch. He kicked, shouted, screamed and let everything out of him all at once in a fit of frustrated, angry rage.

There was nothing left in him. He had failed. The only effect his desperate out-flowing of frustration had achieved was to move the air around in the room a little like a summer breeze coming through the window.

Aiden was spent. He gazed longingly at Naomi sleeping soundly in the bed, unaware that less than an arms length away, Aiden's heart was agonisingly tearing itself out of his chest to be with her again, tears streaming down his face. He would stay with her now and never leave her side, no matter what happened. He would be there for her. He had always believed in guardian angels, and now was his chance, although he never imagined it would be him that was doing the guarding.

Wiping the tears from his eyes, Aiden composed himself. *"I love you"* Her eyes tightened again, as if holding back more tears, then relaxed.

18th October

Naomi awoke with a disgruntled huff and a puff. She rolled herself out of bed, straightened up her nightdress (who for she didn't know, but did it anyway out of habit) and wondered to the kitchen, already beginning to dread what lay ahead of her that day. Coffee. What a good idea that was. Simply the best way to start the day. She caught a glimpse of herself in the hall mirror on the way. She was a wreck this morning: bags under her eyes combined with dark circles, her hair looked as though she had spent the night in a wind tunnel and there was the imprint of her hand on her chest. *How attractive* she thought as she shuffled her way to the kitchen.

As the kettle boiled, she took her place at the table, which was now her viewing platform out onto the world. Her eyes wondered round the scene not knowing where to rest their gaze.

It must have been early as there were few people about. The scene was almost the same as last evening. Few people, few cars, but those that were present were going in the opposite direction, and the sun was in the opposite side of the sky. A reversal, a repetition of these peoples daily routines. She thought about life and how it is a never ending cycle of to-ing and fro-ing from one day to the next.

Click. The kettle had done its job Barely perceiving the noise, Naomi lumbered to her feet again and fumbled around the cupboards for the coffee and a suitably large mug. Then to the neglected fridge. It was empty apart from the usual things you would find: a couple of eggs, half a pint of nearly off milk, cold pizza and something that may once have a vegetable or two. Draw. Spoon. Good.

With the various articles required to make her caffeine fix, Naomi drowsily made her drink. It was a bit stronger than normal and she enjoyed the bitterness of it. *Reminds me of how I feel. Bitter.* She thought. Taking her coffee back to the bedroom she slumped herself back onto the messy bed, not wanting to have to get dressed for the funeral.

Somehow she would have to find the strength to face her friends and family in a few hours and she wasn't sure how she was going to do it. Heck, she had enough trouble looking at herself in the mirror. She felt the all too familiar lump in her throat making her feel sick and the sting behind her eyes like a wasp repeatedly digging into her. *Bugger, not again.* She put her coffee down, slopping some of it onto the bedside table, next to the photograph of her and Aiden taken last year on holiday. They looked so happy. They were so happy. Not a care in the world. Oh, to be back there again. She would gladly trade everything she had to go back to there. Her smile in the picture was amazingly wide and her eyes looked so alive and full of joy, almost child-like. Aiden's smile was smug and his eyes were almost sleepy.

At that single moment, she had never been more in love with anyone.

Her chin began to twitch and her shoulders rose up, hugging her neck. She wrapped her arms around herself and began to let go the tears that were forcing their way out of her eyes. She looked down through and let them drop, making a small salty pond where her arms touched. They soaked into her nightdress too. She didn't care, there was nobody there to see her cry or to witness the pitiful mess she was in this morning anyway.

Aiden had seen everything though. He had not slept at all, but then again why would he? He was no longer alive. He felt he should have done, or at least tried, but fatigue didn't seem to take over. He felt fleetingly tired after his angry rampage around the room, but then he felt fine. Instead, he spent the night on his knees, praying almost, but watching Naomi sleep. He must have looked like a guard dog keeping vigil at his master's bedside.

Seeing Naomi weeping as she was, filled his heart with love for her. All his angry thoughts had vanished for the moment. He stood and then sat on the bed next to her without making any of the covers move. Then he moved closer, watching her and feeling the bed move slightly as her shoulders shrugged up and down. He felt so far away, yet unbearably close, unable to communicate with or touch her. He sighed and moved closer still.

Naomi shuddered slightly and goose bumps erupted at the top of her right arm. She rubbed them back down without pausing for thought on the cause. Aiden looked lovingly at her as Naomi's tears began to subside. She sat still and quiet now staring again at everything but nothing. Her once beautiful eyes looked older now, tired and salt-stained. There was a redness to them, sore from hours of crying, the rubbing and wiping away of tears with toilet roll and tissues. She had clearly been through the emotional ringer of late and she didn't seem to be all the way through yet. Why though? How much more must she endure before she would smile that knock-out smile again that he had gone cuckoo over and kissed so many times in the past?

He missed kissing her. Those lips, so sumptuous to the touch. Her tongue, searching for his in the dark of the bedroom and gently licking his lips like they were the most fragile and tasty ice cream at the seaside. They drove him insane and he would gladly let her explore his mouth with hers until the end of time. Every little flick of her tongue was like a shot of luscious venom shooting around his body, paralysing him and leaving him totally under her control.

With a 'humph' and a sigh, she stood up and walked purposefully into the bathroom. Aiden followed silently down the hall feeling like a puppy trailing its owner everywhere.

Naomi flicked on the shower and closed the door, allowing the air and water time to warm up. She studied her face in the mirror. Bags, rings. She was going to need more make-up on today if she wasn't going to arrive at Aiden's funeral looking a mess. She felt she needed to be strong, but inside she was quaking with nerves. Her stomach was already a bag of butterflies and she was beginning to feel sick again. Her deep eyes stared back at her, looking deeply into her own soul to find the strength to get through the day. What she saw did not fill her with confidence. All she saw was a black future, tinged with a deep grey at the edges. It held no fixed shape and was moving, twisting around itself. Black summed up how she felt about the whole situation.

She couldn't bare to see herself falling to pieces any longer and looked away from the mirror. How much more misery could she face? *Let's just get today over and done with and then move on tomorrow,* she thought.

Aiden was standing in the doorway looking at her in silence, she turned and looked right at him, but through him, without seeing him. He smiled at her, forgetting his own position in all this. He used to smile at her like this when he watched her in the bathroom.

She moved to the door and closed it in Aiden's face jerking him back to the reality that he was not actually there.

Stepping through the bathroom door, leaving a condensation outline of his body. He saw Naomi drop her night gown to the floor. Her body, lean and curvaceous stood in front of him; she was an object of their pleasure, passionate nights and something so beautiful to behold. He moved forward to be closer to her, reaching out to feel her skin beneath his fingers, but drew them back quickly, too scared to make contact. She stepped into the shower.

Aiden watched through the foggy glass. Naomi stood under the water in silence, letting it fall all over her head and down over her body. Her hair was hanging down as she looked between her breasts to her feet. She felt like shit and it wasn't even a hangover. If it was a hangover at least there would be a good night to remember to make the banging head almost worthwhile. But no, this was just a banging headache created by the constant emotions that come with the sudden loss of someone you love; The injustice that it should happen to you, the anger that can't be released anywhere because there is apparently no-one to blame. It all gets bottled up and then slowly leaks out over time, but is never fully satisfied. Who can you shout and scream at? God? No, certainly not.

She turned round in the shower and let the hot water splash all over her face. She grabbed the soap and a sponge and began to furiously wash herself as if trying to rub away the thoughts going through her mind, and perhaps even rub away the memories of Aiden altogether so she would not experience this crippling pain any longer.

Aiden watched from inside the shower now admiring the body he loved so much. She would so willingly share herself with him whenever they wanted and he devoured it with his gaze regularly; undressing her in his mind whenever he saw her. His fiery passion for her often took him by surprise as he felt he had to have her constantly. She never used to mind as her sexual appetite was every bit as voracious as his.

When they were together, their union was often rough, brutal even; she wanted him deeper inside her all the time and he felt that he could always seem to manage another inch to satisfy her. She would scratch him and he would bite her. And then, just as often, the couple would take a long time over each other, exploring each other's bodies for hours as if it were the first time they were together.

But now, Naomi was in the shower so urgently cleaning herself that Aiden didn't know what to think. It looked for all the world like she was feeling dirty and cheap; an unexpected, accidental whore. She never, ever washed with such a sense of purpose. She would take her time with her eyes closed and hands wandering everywhere, imagining Aiden standing behind her, as naked as she with his erection planted firmly between her buttocks, ready and eager.

What Aiden was seeing this morning was very out of character. He was worried now. He had no idea that today he would be invisibly escorting Naomi to his own funeral.

Naomi looked up, allowing the warm water to run through her hair and she looked straight into Aiden's eyes. He could not believe the pain he saw. Her pitiful face looked as someone may do when facing an executioner; begging their innocence but knowing no-one is listening. The corners of her mouth were drawn back in agony and her teeth were clenched tightly together. She closed her eyes, flung her head forward as if waiting for the axe to fall. Angry, Aiden stomped out of the shower through the door, leaving his outline flooding down the glass but was covered again as the steam rose.

He stood outside the bathroom listening to the haunting noise echoing from the bathroom. It gripped him tightly round his heart. How can he possibly comfort her? How can he put his arm around her shoulders and let her know for certain he was still there? He was right there, waiting for her to realise it. He heard the water switch off and he looked in to see Naomi step out of the shower like a beaten woman; shoulders rounded, slumped almost as she stood on the mat and reached for a towel. She threw it round her chest and tucked a corner in under her arm. It hung down like a mini-dress, tantalising short, but not quite short enough for Aiden's liking. She grabbed a second towel and wrapped it round her head like a pink turban.

The phone in the living room began it's shrill ringing, urgent and persistent. The noise startled Naomi. She dripped quickly out of the bathroom to answer it, drying her listening ear as she went.

"Hello." her voice was resentful, low and dark. She paused, listening to the response.

"No, Dad, I'm not ready yet. I've just got out of the shower. I know when the car is coming for me, I've got plenty of time. Please leave me alone." she snapped back. At the other end of the phone, her father's face looked solemn for her. His forehead creased with worry. Naomi heard her mother say something in the background, probably from the kitchen. "Tell Mum I'm OK will you and I'll see you a bit later. Sorry Dad, I need to sort myself out. Bye." her voice had softened like an apology. She hung-up. Time to get ready.

Aiden was racking his mind as to why she would need a car to pick her up.

Slowly, the realisation of what was happening dawned on him. The feeling overwhelmed him making him feel incredibly lonely.

She was going to his funeral! Today, in a few hours, his beloved Naomi will be going to say goodbye to him for the last time. Shocked and stunned at the thought, Aiden sat on the bed next to where she had thrown a black dress and tights.

His emotions were sinking lower by the minute as he watched her get dressed for what would be a very difficult for them both. The skin on her bare shoulders needed to be touched, comforted and to have some colour put back into them. They looked grey, older and tired. She was as low as he in her mood, and who could blame her? Soon, she would have to stand, without him there to comfort her at the funeral of the very man she breathed for and who she thought would never leave her.

-|-

There was a gentle knock at the front door. Naomi was sitting at her regular place in the kitchen watching the world go by, coffee cup sitting in a dried out ring of brown caffeine on the table though she didn't see the black car pull up outside. She wasn't seeing anything at all. Her mind was numb at the thought of the events to follow. Both she and Aiden snapped their heads round to look towards the front door. Aiden had been with her all the time, never more than an arm's length from her, and now it was time.

She stood up, straightened her dress and hat, picked up her small clutch-bag and walked calmly to the door. She looked like a goddess in black. She was composed now, strong and single-minded. She was going to see this day through with dignity, for him. For Aiden.

"Morning, Miss, the car is waiting for you" said the chauffeur with a reassuring smile and black cap tucked beneath his arm. "Are you ready? Is there anything I can help you with?" he continued with an air of genuine concern.

Naomi she hesitated "No, thank you. Let's go." She clearly forced the words out, convincing herself that she was OK. She had packed tissues, eye-liner, lipstick and various other cosmetics into her bag earlier and Aiden was amazed at how much she had managed to pack into such little space.

Outside, the air was chilly, biting at her sore eyes as the chauffeur opened the back door to the car. Naomi grabbed hold of the top of the door, looked around nearly choking on the fear she felt inside. She saw the window of the flat she and Aiden had shared. Somehow, it felt very empty now without him waving her off to work in the morning. The children in the park nearby were quieter than usual. They must be there somewhere, but her mind was so far away that the world could have been on fire and she would not have noticed. She was so removed from everything other the funeral that nothing mattered any more. Only the thought of Aiden lying cold and alone in a thin wooden box occupied her mind.

She stepped into the car and Aiden joined her, feeling every bit as nervous as she.

It would be fair to say that Aiden had not yet come to terms with his own demise. It must have happened quickly or Naomi would hopefully not be so distraught at the prospect of this unexpected goodbye. If he had died of some debilitating, long term disease then they would have had time to say a proper farewell.

Precisely what had happened at the end, Aiden still did not know. But he wanted to find out. There were no marks on the spirit body he had now. It was just as it was when he left. He felt strong within himself, but he seemed powerless in this world.

Perhaps that is what happened when you died; any injuries or diseases that crippled your body at the end vanish when you enter the afterlife. All cuts, bruises and abrasions went away, all cancers where removed and body parts repaired. He did not know. What he did know is that death does not heal the living so quickly. They had to live with the memories of the departed, no matter how painful. His love, Naomi was sitting next to him, trying to deal with the end of him and the beginning of her new life, alone.

Perhaps it was the fact she had resigned herself to the day's events that she held herself with such dignity, such poise. A picture of grace. Perhaps the thin black veil across her face was hiding something.

Inside though, Naomi was going through Hell. Her stomach was tying itself up in knots, pulling tightly, making her feel like she needed the toilet. Her skin was crawling with fear and oddly, hatred of Aiden. She knew this was not true, but when dealing with situations like this, there are all manner of conflicting emotions to deal with. One minute it would be overwhelming hate, the next, the most powerful unconditional love. But she knew that if she were to carry on with her life after today, she would have to remember what she and Aiden had had together before he left her.

She hated him now. He had gone forever without so much as a goodbye! He had left without any permission or agreement, leaving her with all this shit to deal with. How the fuck dare he go like that? The bastard. She swallowed hard, trying to push the hate away. She was confused.

As her car drew up to the funeral directors chapel, she saw the hearse gleaming black in the autumn sunshine. It was empty and being buffed by one of the undertakers. She was touched by the efforts they were clearly going through to make Aiden's final journey one of dignity and respect. She cocked her head at the sight before her and for a moment, she forgot about what she was doing there. Her mind was rapidly going into lockdown, a self-defence mechanism people go through when facing times of huge stress and emotional upheaval. She sniffed as the chauffeur opened her door. "Miss, Naomi," the man said as he held out his hand for hers. "Your family are waiting for you inside."

The chill in the air caught Naomi's breath as she stepped from the car. It flooded her lungs and brought her round to reality. The first few steps she took made her knees feel weak, but the closer she got to the door, the stronger she felt. She had to be strong for her family, and for Aiden's.

Their parents stood by the door to the chapel as if welcoming people to the funeral in the way a Groom welcomes guests to a wedding. A wedding? Oh, how delightful a wedding to Aiden would have been. She would have been a picture of loveliness and he, tall and dashingly handsome. The guests would be drinking Pimms on a warm summer's day somewhere, and they would be laughing and joking and enjoying themselves. Naomi and Aiden would be holding hands, walking round the pretty garden talking to everyone, exchanging kisses and hearty, back-slapping man-hugs.

All the guests for today's event though would be gathering now in the solemn garden at the crematorium, sharing quiet conversations and memories of the deceased, aware that soon, their friend would be arriving for his big day. Not the kind of big day that he and Naomi had dreamed of but rather, the day that should not be happening for many years. He should have been old, wrinkled and grey; a couple of kids, and perhaps a handful of grandchildren. That would have been ideal.

The door to the chapel of rest opened smoothly and quietly. There was near silence inside and Naomi felt as though she had interrupted a secret conversation between her family and Aiden's. The assorted family members all stopped talking and looked at her, heads bowed slightly, handkerchiefs in hand or carefully blotting mascara.

"Hello, love", her father said, walking over to her and touching her arm. His lovely round face looked pained for his little girl, for he, like everyone else despised the fact that she had to go through this.

"Hi Dad,' she replied in a whisper, trying to choke back the tears now banging in her eyes to be let out. "How are you?"

He ignored the question, perhaps not even hearing it.

"Aiden is over there." he whispered back to her, pointing with his other hand towards a small stained glass window beneath which lay the coffin flanked at the head by two lit candles. It looked serene.

Naomi took a long intake of breath and started to walk towards Aiden's body lying cold in the silk lined box. Her father took a couple of steps with her until she gently removed his hand from her arm. She would not be helped like an old lady to say goodbye. She wanted to go alone. Everyone watched her, following her down the aisle with their eyes like a bride dressed in black, their hearts going out to her as her footsteps echoed on the stone floor.

A rush of emotion engulfed Naomi as she neared the coffin. She could not see inside from the end of the aisle, but the closer she got, Aiden's body came slowly into view. First she saw his hair, and then two steps later, she saw the face she had kissed so many thousands of times that now looked peaceful and creamy grey in the glow of the window and candles.

Aiden walked with her down the length on the chapel from the end of the four rows of seats, too scared to come face to face with himself lying there lifeless. He too was a concoction of emotions, all spinning themselves within him.

It felt like an age before she arrived at the coffin, and

Aiden's side for the final time.

With her eyes closed and knuckles white as she gripped the side of the coffin, she bowed her head.

"Hello, Aiden." she mouthed quietly.

Aiden joined her on the opposite side of his new home, mirroring her pose, looking at her. *"Hello, darling."* He said as a light film of condensation formed where his hands were. Again, Naomi did not notice. She wanted desperately to be alone with him in her thoughts. She wanted to close her eyes and make her memories of him stronger in her mind but also wanting to keep them open to see last sight she will ever have of him.

From her bag, she pulled out a small photograph of them together. It was a copy of her favourite picture of them together. Hands shaking slightly, she reached over, gently lifted an arm slightly and tucked the picture under his fingers in a manner a mother would tuck a sleeping child's arm under the covers at night.

"I brought you this, my love, to remind you of our time together." She shivered at the waxy feel of his skin beneath her fingertips as she touched his face as she had done hundreds of times before. She frowned at the unfamiliar chill. Leaning over, she kissed Aiden's forehead for the last time, her eyes closed, battling back the tears that were fighting to be set free. Holding her composure for just a while longer, she swallowed and touched her cheek to his.

She wanted her words to be last to enter his ears before they locked him up. "I love you Aiden. I love you, I love you, I love you." As she stood up, the painful tears defeated her resilience and one tear dropped onto Aiden's closed eyelid and ran down towards his ear. It made him look like he was crying too.

Leaving her hands on the side of the coffin, she sank to her knees. She dropped her head down between her shaking arms, as if praying. Her painful sobs filled the chapel with the sounds of love ripped away, torn from this world in an unjust, unpredictable and desperately unfair incident.

Naomi's mother stood dumbstruck at the end of the aisle, barely able to comprehend or react to what she was seeing before her. The vision of her daughter so distraught at the side of her love bore into her eyes, she could not decide what to do fast enough - Run and hug her or run away. She looked at her husband, open-mouthed and fearful of her own indecision. Naomi's father walked down the aisle and joined Naomi kneeling on the floor. He put his hands on her shoulders and rested his head on hers.

"I'm so sorry, sweet heart, so sorry. It's time to go now. Please. It's time to go." He gently rubbed her shoulders, encouraging her to go with him. Petulantly, Naomi resisted, not wanting the final moments to come.

Although Aiden was lying dead, these last moments were precious, so precious that she wished the world would grind to a halt and allow her all the time she needed to say goodbye properly.

"Naomi, please." her father gently pulled at her shoulders. "It's time to go." She shook her head and sniffed.

"No, daddy, I can't leave him. He's cold and I want to keep him warm on his journey. He looks so lonely. I can't leave him, daddy." She squeezed the sides of her head with her arms as more tears fell. Her father's face softened even more, his brow rose like a church spire. There was nothing he could do for his little girl now except be there for her and hold her.

Aiden knelt down beside her and was every bit as sad as she. He was angry too. Angry that he could not tell her that he was there for her, always to be by her side from now until she was ready to come to him at the end of her own life.

He was angry at how unjust the entire scenario was. They were both young, talented and bloody good at their jobs.

They were talking about getting married in a year or two, then they would start a family. But now look at it; Their dreams had been smashed to pieces.

A tall, gaunt man and three other, equally sombre looking men entered the chapel and walked slowly towards the coffin in pairs. They were dressed smartly in black tails, without hats and each as focused as the next. They did not show any emotion, just a respectfully emotionless face in the presence of the deceased and his family. Naomi could hear their footsteps, echoing out a slow pace coming towards her. She held on to the coffin, trying to pull her dignity together that her nails dug into the silk lining, tearing it slightly as she dragged herself to her feet, shaking all the time.

With head down, hiding the tears from the pallbearers, her father took a supportive hold of her and lead escorted her carefully back down the aisle.

Aiden stood by and watched wringing his hands anxiously as he suddenly felt painfully very alone. There was no-one who could help him in this world. He didn't know how thin the veil between his new world and theirs was, or how easy it could be to tear given enough anger. At the moment though he felt more afraid than anything else.

The men around his coffin were now preparing to place the lid on the top and screw it into place with what looked like four brass butterfly-nuts.

Just as Naomi and her father got to the front door, her mother opened it for them. She offered Naomi a handkerchief. For the first time in her life, she felt completely hopeless. What can she possibly say to her daughter? She could not speak from experience as her man was still with her. Naomi would have to start again after they had said goodbye to Aiden. *But how long would it be?* She thought.

As the shadow of the coffin lid passed over Aiden's lifeless face, he let out an enormous shriek, like he was dying again, trying to cling on to his last possible seconds of existence. Outside, Naomi turned round and glanced back at the door as if deep in her soul, she heard the scream as it was silenced by a slamming door. She frowned and turned back.

The finality of the lid being sealed was unbearable for Aiden to witness. He did not want to believe he was dead. He would not believe he was dead. There was so much more to do, so much more to see, so many people to meet and so many years of happiness ahead of him with Naomi at his side. He wanted to grow old with her. But now she would grow old without him and he would have no choice but to stay out of sight and watch her carry on until it was her turn to die.

Another man dressed in black tails stood by the hearse as Aiden was brought out by the four pallbearers. The coffin was almost completely level as they made their way to the the car. Carefully and with a well rehearsed motion, they lowered Aiden onto the shiny silver rollers in the back and slid him gently in. They locked the coffin into place and just as gently laid the flowers around him as if to comfort him for the journey.

Naomi stood by and watched the entire scene with tunnel vision, light headed and woozy. She felt like she was watching reality TV, but with all the proper emotions thrown in for good measure. She was certainly not sitting curled up on the sofa today with a cup of coffee and her thick house-socks on. Today, this drama was for real and she apparently was the very reluctant star.

Aiden stood close by, watching with a numb apprehension of what was to come. Where would they be going? Church probably, but then where? A cemetery or crematorium? He began to feel sick at the thought of the journey.

-|-

Naomi was lead quietly to another black car with Aiden's parents and her own. They had been together for years and in many respects they were already married so the two families had formed a strong bond. She loved Aiden's mother and father and hoped they would not become strangers after today. But why would they stay in touch? There were no grandchildren for them to dote on, and no ring on her finger to legally bind them. Aiden was their only tie to Naomi. It seemed inevitable then, that today would probably be their last day together. It felt like today was the end of many things.

Thinking more positively though, Naomi thought that nothing has an end, just a new beginning or a change in direction. Aiden felt the same too as he invisibly sat in the spare seat diagonally opposite Naomi watching her intently. He noticed how she was looking out of the window at the world going by, going about it's business, unaware of the misery passing slowly by in the highly polished black funeral car.

Stopping at some traffic lights, Naomi's blank eyes latched onto an elderly gentleman shuffling down the street. He would have been quite tall without his little stoop and dressed as most old men she had ever seen; light brown pressed trousers, pulled up too high with a brown leather belt and fake gold buckle, an off-white pressed shirt neatly tucked in, a vest, clearly visible above the open neck of the shirt, a brown jacket with brown shoes. It seemed like the standard uniform of old men. She grinned inwardly at her own harmless stereotypical view.

The old man stopped and looked at the hearse with the large wreath in the back lying along with coffin saying 'Aiden'. He then looked suddenly uncomfortable as he caught Naomi's eye. She held his gaze, almost pleading with him to take her away from today. He removed his flat cap and bowed his head slightly and lowered his eyes. Just as the lights turned green, he looked up and gave the stranger that was Naomi a supportive and sympathetic smile. His eyes looked genuinely sad for her. She mouthed 'Thank-you' and smiled back at him. He nodded appreciatively and the hearse moved onward.

All the way to the crematorium she did not look inside the car at the other inhabitants. She was not even aware if they were talking, or just sitting there with their heads bowed, selfishly getting on with their own misery. She continued to gaze out of the window and day-dream about seeing the old man at the traffic lights. It simultaneously filled her with gratitude for the respect he had shown her as well as sadness for the future she and Aiden would no longer share. They wouldn't shuffle down the street together all wrinkled and drinking tea in the cheap little café on the high street. They wouldn't be able to give the grandchildren back to their kids at the end of an exhausting weekend and they would never go on a cruise round the Med', ballroom dancing and drinking sangria on the lido deck. God, she loved him so much. And today would be the end of it all, the end of the dream and the beginning of the nightmare getting over him. *"Bugger"* she thought to herself, *"how much worse can things get?"*

The hearse rounded the corner and turned again into the ornately pruned garden-drive of the crematorium. Aiden gulped to himself as he saw the solitary building at the bottom of the drive. He looked over at Naomi who had straightened herself in her seat and carefully adjusted her veiled hat. She was biting her lip, her eyes were closed and slightly scrunched holding back the inevitable tears but she determined not to let them loose until she was on her own again; A tall order given the length of the day planned.

Outside the building, the assembled friends, family and colleagues of Aiden ceased talking, turned silently and drew a collective inward breath. They seemed to form a line for the hearse to park alongside. The trees stopped swaying in the breeze and even the flowers seemed to stand still in a silent salute. It did not go unnoticed by some of the mourners. They glanced at each other at the strangeness of the event. It was like the world knew that Aiden had gone and was paying it's own tribute to him. The hearse drew to a halt along the line. People moved back to allow the passengers to alight.

Naomi took a deep breath and stepped graciously out of the car when the door was opened by one of the men in black tails. She stood up, straightened her skirt and hat once again and moved aside.

She looked simply amazing in Aiden's eyes as he stood closely behind her right shoulder; a figure of pride and elegance. Even on a day as hard as this for her she managed to keep herself composed, upright and frankly, in better shape than most of the others. Perhaps she was putting up a mental block on the situation and just going through the motions of the day like the television program she imagined back at the chapel of rest.

-|-

Aiden looked her up and down. God, she was a fit woman. She was strong, lean, tall and had a figure any man would dream of taking to bed. And she was his. *"Was"* being the main word he thought to himself. How many times had he looked at her like this? Hundreds? Thousands? And now, he was looking at her with different eyes, the eyes of a former lover and wishing with the jealous temper of an ex-partner. *"My God, she is the most amazing thing I have ever seen"* he said under his breath, forgetting knowing no-one could hear him.

Naomi turned slowly at the breeze in her ear. She thought she felt something on the wind, but there was nothing. Aiden saw she that she had she heard something, or was it something else that caught her attention? He had no idea, but now the coffin was being removed from the rear of the hearse, he lost his train of thought as his body began the last leg of its final journey.

As the coffin was carefully removed and placed on the shoulders of the pall-bearers, the hush of the mourners grew deeper still as the reality of the scene settled among them like a fog. It was painful for all of them, but most of all Naomi and Aiden's parents. Aiden's mother broke into a packet of tissues and began to dab her eyes. *"How typical,"* Naomi thought. *"She couldn't even bring a proper handkerchief to her son's funeral."* Whilst Naomi loved her would-be mother-in-law, she had always had reservations about her. Why was she always so prim and proper? How can she be so stuck-up one minute and downright cutting the next? Sometimes she seemed to have no sense of decorum at all and would cut someone down with a well-timed comment of distaste, almost loathing. Naomi was sure that today would not go by without her offending someone somewhere, somehow and may or may not actually mean what she said. It could be very embarrassing at times.

From inside the crematorium, Pachelbel's 'Canon' began to emanate from the now open doors. The funeral director respectfully ushered the mourners into the building to allow the ceremony to begin. At the request of Naomi, she would escort Aiden's coffin down the aisle to the catafalque where she would then take her seat nearest to him. She was standing by the door to the building and smiled sweetly at each of the people reluctantly went in to take their seats. Some smiled sombrely back to her or offered a hand to her shoulder gently as they passed, each silently wishing they were not there and that the events to follow they would not have to witness for another fifty or so years. Heavy hearted, they cleared the outside, leaving just Naomi, Aiden and a collection of supportive funeral service men doing their bit with professionalism and utmost respect.

Returning, the funeral director stopped in front of Naomi and, touching her shoulder said "We're ready now. If you follow Aiden down the aisle, your seat is there for you on the right." His old, soft voice was reassuring to hear and something that Naomi clung to as the coffin was brought forward towards the door. Pachelbel went quiet for a moment, and then the familiar guitar sound of The Kink's 'Days' filled the space between her ears and that was all she heard as she followed her love down the aisle. She heard no sniffles or cries of the ladies in the pews. She heard no coughing of sentimental men struggling to keep emotion from over-flowing, protecting their pride and manliness.

"Thank you for the days....those endless days, those sacred days you gave me"...Naomi sang along in her head as she walked slowly behind Aiden, not daring to take her eyes of his box. She looked for all the world to the congregation like a bride walking down the aisle to marry the corpse. She held herself with pride and walked upright and strong, the teary eyes of the assembled upon her.

Aiden followed Naomi down the aisle from the left side of the building, walking along the edge of pews, along the wall. He was in awe of her. So strong in her walk yet he sensed in her and himself a rising panic that it would all be over soon and she would be getting on with her life without him. How long would it be before she found someone else to look after her? How long before someone came along and bowl her over with his wit and charm, good looks and bedside manner? It didn't bare thinking about at the moment.

Naomi's heart was racing and her mind was overflowing with thoughts and emotions. She felt like she was about to leap forwards and rip the coffin from the men carrying it, pull the lid off and throw herself into Aiden's cold and beg him to take her with him. She was longing so much to see him that her heart felt heavy and black. So black that anger began to rise in her too. So much anger and love thrown together that the feeling was confusing and terrifying at the same time. She felt her hands tremble as the feeling grew tighter in the pit of her stomach. The questions running through her mind were tripping over each other as they clambered for her attention. Why? How? Where? Why me? Why Aiden? She began to blink as the first tear dropped from her eye. She was losing the battle to keep her composure. The music echoed round her mind and her eye blurred, making the coffin look like she was seeing it through a bathroom window. She lost track of where she was down the aisle. The funeral director took her gently by the arm and led her to her seat.

The coffin was placed on the catafalque as the final verse of the song rang through the room. *"I bless the light....You're with me every single day, believe me"*... then, silence just as the wreath saying 'Aiden' was laid beneath the cold platform on which the coffin stood, alone.

Although Naomi was sitting just a few metres from Aiden,

he seemed a million miles away as her head reeled in the occasion. She felt dizzy with desire to see him again. It was a longing so great that the urge to tear the lid from the coffin was only kept at bay by the knowledge that he was dead and this was her final time to say goodbye. It would do no good to follow her desire and would only upset everyone, anyway. Instead, she sat stock-still staring at the coffin in front of her.

A shiver went down Naomi's spine as she saw David rise from his seat, and place a hand on the coffin as he passed. He took his place to officiate the ceremony and looked out at the bleary eyes now watching him.

Where had that shiver come from? It wasn't a shiver she had expected to get today. It felt like a kind of electricity shooting from her head to her legs. How odd. David stood at the lectern and began to read.

"Ladies and Gentlemen, it is a real privilege for me to stand here before you, and Naomi, to lead us all in saying goodbye to our much loved friend Aiden. Please forgive me if I find the things I have to say a little difficult and I must thank Naomi and Aiden's family for asking me to speak to you all today. They have encouraged me and helped me with what to say to make sure Aiden is honoured in a way we can all be proud of."

He surveyed the faces in front of him. Ladies with hats over their eyes hiding their tears, men looking at him blankly with bloodshot eyes, holding back the tears they were too ashamed to let go of. He coughed a little, bit back his own tears, and looking over at Naomi, across the top of the coffin and held her gaze as she looked at him with pride and gratitude.

Aiden had known David since they were children and they were the best of friends. They had skinned their knees together falling off bicycles and climbing trees. They were virtually inseparable until Naomi had come along and took Aiden away from him. David had been gracious enough, but deep inside he felt jealous of Naomi having the attentions of his best friend. She would often go out with them and entertain the string of David's girlfriends and sing his praises at pubs and clubs. She would comfort him when it all went wrong and offer advice for the next in line. He was a strikingly attractive man with piercing icy eyes and uncontrollable hair. His face looked like it had been carved by Michelangelo himself, and although the years had put a little weight on him, he carried it well. She stared intently at him, admiring his stature and pride at being given the honour of officiating his friend's funeral.

"Well, thank you all for coming." David continued after clearing his throat "We are here this morning to pay our last respects and bid farewell to Aiden, but also to honour and pay tribute to his far too short a life. We all loved and held admiration for him."

From somewhere in the middle of the room, a stifled cry broke the silence of the mourners. David choked of his grief and Naomi bowed her head, waiting for the ceremony to continue, wishing it would end now and at the same time wishing it would never end so she could at least remain close to Aiden, even though he was in a box just out of arms reach. David's voice echoed again.

"We have all been deeply hurt by Aiden's death, and though he was taken from us far too early, we must try in the short time we have here this morning to make this occasion a celebration of his life and to express our thanks for having known him and loved him."

David's words swam round Naomi's head as she glanced up at the brown box containing Aiden's body. Inside he lay motionless and cold. She loved every bit of him so much that the pain and longing in her heart made her want him more with each passing second. She had no idea that he was standing next to his coffin, right in front of her, looking down at her with his beautiful caring eyes, his face every bit as full of sadness as everyone else's. Without knowing why, she looked up and caught a glimpse of him standing in front of her, wearing the clothes she last saw him in. She gasped and brought her hand up to her mouth, her eyes instantly filled with tears. She whispered his name through her fingers as if she was calling to him to get his attention. And then he was gone again.

David paused and looked down at Naomi who was sitting, staring at something, focused solidly on a space next to the coffin. He frowned and continued. "...glad that you took the opportunity to do some of your grieving in the presence of others who have known and loved him."

Looking across at Naomi again, David stumbled over the

next lines, confused at what he saw. Naomi seemed to be looking at someone. Her hand to her mouth, eyes pouring tears and staring intensely. At what? Nothing it seemed. Her father had his arm round her shoulders, comforting her.

"There is no, er...church Minister here this morning. It's only me...and though I know that most of you will be familiar with an alternative form of service, I hope we can agree that our shared love of Aiden is far more lasting in importance than those matters which may divide us in this respect." His voice trailed off, concerned about Naomi. She turned and looked at him, giving him the confidence that everything was alright to continue.

Naomi's mind was spinning. She had just seen Aiden, as bold as daylight in front of her. Was she seeing things? Had he seen her? Wait, no, that was stupid, of course he hadn't seen her, and he's lying dead in the box. He can't be there.

But Aiden had seen her. He'd been watching her, watching all day. He was there and he had been watching her when she saw him. He saw her eyes focus upon him. His heart had leapt up when he saw her looking at him and as he reached out to her, but it was obvious now from her expression he had gone from her sight again. She looked lost again and glanced round the room to see if anyone else had seen him. How could be make her see him again? How could he make her believe he was there with her? It was nothing he did that made her see him, it was her doing, surely. Is all she had to do was want to see him so much and he would be there? Surely not. She must have wanted to see him any number of times today or last night. He had been there all along, so why now? Maybe it was because this was the last time she will get to be near him, near his body. Or maybe it was because she was saying goodbye. Aiden stood still where he was, his hand upon the edge of the coffin lid, a small mist of condensation forming underneath his fingers. He looked down at Naomi again, and at the others gathered in the room. No-one else appeared to have seen him. Naomi was looking at David again.

"At the time of his death, Aiden did have a small religious faith, so I will ask you now out of respect for that faith to say The Lord's Prayer." David bowed his head but watched Naomi out the corner of his eye. There was a shuffling of feet, sniffs and sobs as the room adjusted itself for the prayer.

"Our Father, who art in heaven," Naomi's head felt heavy as it hung down, the final minutes of Aiden being in her world tick-tocking away.

"Hallowed be thy name." She was acutely aware that she had just seen Aiden in front of her, motionless which was unlike him, unless sleeping. David looked at her, concerned.

"Thy Kingdom come," He had come to her. She wanted to believe it so badly that, with her head down, eyes wide open, searching the floor for answers, she caught a glimpse again of Aiden's shoes out of the top of her eyes. She snapped her head up again, only to see him for the tiniest of seconds..."Aiden, I love you" she whispered, her voice seeming to plead to any listening God to let him come home forever. David heard her quietly beneath the prayer and wanted to go to her.

"Thy will be done," he flickered into view again, right before her eyes and then vanished again. She was wringing her hands in agony as she saw him come in and out of view again. He looked a bit like an old movie with broken frames; slightly jerky movements and flicking on and off as he raised his hands to her and took a step forward, then vanished again from her sight. She felt like she was going mad as she sat in stunned silence, the words of the prayer a million miles from her conscious mind. All she wanted was to see Aiden again. He was right there in front of her a second ago, his face looking pained. Was it pain he was feeling from his injuries or the pain of missing her?

"On earth as it is in heaven"

"Give us this day our daily bread." Naomi's heart felt like it was being stabbed by thorns. They randomly stabbed with every thought, every memory of Aiden. Biting back the tears as hard as she could, she closed her eyes tightly until they hurt from the squeeze, but it did not subside. It grew and grew. She exhaled long and hard, trying to suffocate the feeling.

"And forgive us our trespasses,"

Naomi's father put his arm round her again and pulled her into his chest to comfort her, but she sat herself up again and looked round to see if anyone else had seen him. All the heads were either bowed for the prayer or hanging in grief. She could hear nothing.

"as we forgive those who trespass against us." Naomi turned back to the front and saw nothing. Aiden had gone again.

"And lead us not into temptation,"

"but deliver us from evil." Despite the pain, Naomi felt the incredible irony in that line. *"Deliver us from evil"*, she thought. ,*"It must be pure evil that allowed Aiden to be taken away from me."*

"For thine is the kingdom, the power and the glory, for ever and ever." Bullshit.

"Amen"

Naomi looked blankly round the building for another sign of Aiden for the rest of the ceremony but saw nothing. She looked into the eyes of the others there and saw nothing, just an enveloping sadness that they all shared with her, but was nothing like hers. That's what sympathy is, she guessed; a shared emotion, but on a lesser plane than that of the person you have sympathy for. How could any of these people even begin to understand what she was going through? Many had lost friends or mothers or fathers. But this? No, this was the most acute pain imaginable. She felt angry at them for not feeling as she did. Felt resentment for their being there, sharing her sorrow. Until it happens to them, they would never know. She almost hated them.

Aiden in the meantime had been listening intently to the kind words being spoken about him. 'An upstanding fellow', 'a right good laugh', 'caring and thoughtful'. He couldn't agree more. Then David said that he was a "loving and devoted partner to Naomi", at which point, Aiden turned and looked at his love. She was absent. Not physically, but he could see in her eyes that she was not there. Her senses apparently had shut down, devoid of emotion, like a robot. She just sat there, scanning the room, expressionless. He felt for her. He moved down the steps from where his coffin lay and stood next to her. He so wanted her to look at him, to reach out and touch him.

Without thinking, he reached out and touched her shoulder. She shivered and moved her gaze back to David. He was nearly finished now. It was nearly the end. "Time to say goodbye, Aiden." She muttered under her breath, her eyes beginning to weep again.

David spoke solemnly and with heartfelt words. "Aiden suddenly and unexpectedly died on Saturday the sixth of October. He will be remembered among other things, for his honesty his sense of humour and his compassion." He clenched his eyes tight for a moment and brought his hand to his mouth, obviously trying to hold himself together. His mind running riot with years of friendship and the memories they shared. "And far, far above all else... for his undying love for his beautiful Naomi." He loved Naomi too. He had loved her as a surrogate sister ever since she and Aiden got together. Aiden never knew how he felt, but he felt a different kind of pain. He desperately felt for her loss, but he could not put his arm around her and comfort her just yet.

Naomi turned white at the crushing realisation that now really was time to say her final goodbye. David's words had hit her straight where Aiden now lived, in her heart and soul. Just like Cupid's arrow had struck her those years ago when she first fell in love with Aiden, it was there again, but now it was being torn away, ripping her heart apart as Cupid reclaimed it.

David continued, as if trying to prolong the agony for everyone, but Naomi didn't want it to end. The longer Aiden remained intact and within touching distance, the end could not come. "Our friend Aiden was a flame that burned so brightly. He was extinguished without so much as a flicker and a puff of smoke and all we have left is the memory of how brightly and vigorously it burned for his time with us."

"Let us now spend a few moments in silence, so we can each remember Aiden in our own special way and those of you without a faith may like to wait quietly for a few moments whilst we share together a simple prayer for Aiden, Naomi and their families which we hope will bring them, and perhaps the rest of us, some form of comfort and strength in the coming days, weeks and months ahead, as we all adjust to our lives without Aiden."

There was not a breath of noise as everyone retreated within themselves. No sniffles, weeps, cries, coughs or sighs. No noise from outside; no rustling leaves or cats or dogs. No cars, no planes or people. The world was as still as the mourners in silent reflection of Aiden, preparing to say goodbye. It could have been that the world did not matter at that moment for anyone there. Their thoughts and cares were elsewhere entirely. Maybe if you stop and think hard enough on something, then everything else simply ceases to exist for a brief moment, allowing you complete focus.

"Father in heaven, we thank you because you made us in your own image and gave us gifts in mind, body and spirit. We thank you now for Aiden and the time you gave us with him, and what he meant to each and every one of us. As we honour his memory, make us more aware that you are the one from whom comes every perfect gift, including the gift of eternal life through Jesus Christ."

There was a low and appreciative 'Amen' from the friends and family of Aiden. This time, there were some ruffles of clothes as arms were wrapped around shoulders in a vain effort to offer some moral support to those most visibly upset. Naomi's hearing had become hyper sensitive now and she felt she could hear every movement, every breath and every tear drop from of every person. Each rustle of David's papers was as loud as if it were coming through a speaker. Perhaps she was stretching her hearing to see if, by some last chance and the grace of God that Aiden would wake up and start scratching at his coffin lid to be released. Scratching in panic, she would rush to him, open the lid and pull him into her arms, like a drowning child being pulled from the waves. Then everything would be alright, she would have her man back.

Aiden's last chance to escape eternity had arrived.

"Everyone, please stand for the committal" David's voice was wavering heavily. Naomi didn't know what, or how to think; her mind had left her just when she needed it to try to keep her heart from bursting out of her chest. Should she feel sorry for him, or grateful for taking on such a difficult task of seeing off his friend? Neither, she did not have the strength to feel anything for anyone else at the moment other than her Aiden who was about to be taken away from her forever. *"Please Aiden, please wake up."* She thought to herself through clamped-shut eyes. *"Do it for me. Please."* She was pleading inside her mind now, begging him to come back to her, to break out of the coffin and for it all to have been a sick joke. She opened her eyes again and as David began to read the poem, Aiden appeared before her, once more standing next to the coffin, looking at her sorrowful and worried, beaten and with rounded shoulders. His tall figure was as bold and vivid as always and standing right there in front of her again. Then he was gone again. Naomi stood in shock, gazing straight ahead, her heart reeling through what she had just seen again, scarcely able to believe her eyes.

"Into my heart an air that kills

From yon far country blows:

What are those blue remembered hills?

What spires, what farms are those?

That is the land of lost content,

I see it shining plain,

The happy highways where I went,

And cannot come again" David's voice trailed off into silence, hardly managing a whisper for the final lines. His heart was breaking too.

Naomi bowed her head and managed to graciously bring her handkerchief to her eyes. "Aiden...." She pleaded out loud. "Aiden, Aiden, Aiden...sleep well my darling." She choked hard as everyone present choked at hearing her softly spoken words. They all felt the same and, for the next few moments sank to the lowest depths of grief to join Naomi at this most final of times.

"Now is but a moment in time, I dedicate the next few moments to every single precious memory we shared with Aiden." David turned and faced Aiden's coffin for the final time. And, finding an inner strength, locking everything inside, began his final act as friend and confidant for twenty three years; sending him away. Forever.

His voice was strong, loud but soft. "To everything there is a season,"

"Please no. Not now, not ever. Dear God, bring him back to me. Please bring him back." Naomi was falling to pieces as the coffin began to sink into the catafalque. Her father's grip on her shoulders, and now her hand tightened as he felt her body begin to shake under his loving, fatherly embrace. He tipped his

head to hers, allowing them to touch, and he closed his eyes too, not knowing how painful this moment was for her. No-one should lose a partner at this age. There is too much life to live for two people so in love to be parted like this. His daughter looked on in dumb silence as slowly and silently Aiden began to vanish.

"A time to be born . . . and a time to die. Here and now . . . in this final act . . ." David was continuing despite Naomi's thoughtful protestations. His voice remained resolute and determined.

"Come back Aiden! Don't let them take you. I love you. I love you so much. I don't ever want to be without you. You can't leave me, not now!" Naomi wanted to scream out loud, at the top of her voice, for all the world to hear her desperation. She was feeling weak. She could feel her knees trembling, hardly able to keep her upright. Her father, stifling his own grief held her gently, supporting her how only a daddy can for his daughter. Her mother was weeping quietly, and Aiden's mother had her face buried in her husband's shoulder, not capable of watching her son being taken away from her. Yet still, despite all the love in the room for Aiden, he was slipping away from them all, right in front of their tear stained eyes.

"in sorrow but without fear . . . in love and appreciation . . . we commit the body Aiden Williamson to be cremated."

And then he had gone, to his eternal silence.

Naomi imagined the catafalque having a huge stone lid closing down over it, trapping him inside with a deafening bang followed by an echo sounding like thunder reverberating round the room. Her insides were in painful knots, she felt nauseous and angry. The room was quiet.

The peace was broken by David's voice.

As he spoke, Naomi came back into the room. Where she had been she didn't know, her mind was black and empty. She had thought of nothing, blanked out for a moment or two. "Please be seated" said David calmly.

He coughed gently, composing himself and trying to lift the atmosphere from the depths of sadness.

"Let us remind ourselves that the dead do not reside in the grave, or an urn, but in the hearts and minds of the living.

And that is surely where Aiden is with us all now." He was struggling again with his words. His eyes were red as he looked at Naomi with a look of such pity for her, that for the first time, her heart went out to him. He had been so brave to do this for her.

"Look round the room, the town, the country and the world and there can surely be no-one like Aiden. He still lives on in our memories. And although he is no longer visible in our lives, he must still remain a member of our families and circle of friends through the influence he had on us, and the special part he played in our lives."

Aiden looked on aghast. He was sitting now on the steps next to the catafalque where his body had been moments ago. He was determined to remain an influence on his family and friends. In his mind, he wasn't dead yet. Whilst he still roamed this earth, whether visible or not, he would make sure that somehow he would be able to influence those dear to him, and to finally find a way to tell Naomi that he loved her more than anything this world or the next could throw at him. He looked long and hard at Naomi, sitting just feet away from him but an eternity distant all the same. The veil between them was very thin and he was convinced he could make it back through, just for a moment or two to tell her how he felt. He was beginning to feel calmer now the ceremony was coming to an end and that Naomi could start a new life with him, her invisible guardian angel never far away. If only she knew.

David's voice sounded again. "We are nearly at the end of the ceremony, but before we go, Naomi would like to play the song that she and Aiden first danced to. 'Your Song', by Elton John. It is a song greatly admired by many people here and says many things about Aiden and is very appropriate for today, I think." David paused for a moment. "Naomi, and Aiden's parents, Jack and Anna Williamson would like you to join them afterwards at a celebration of Aiden's life at their house. You are all most welcome."

Somewhere in the back of Naomi's mind, she heard a piano start playing and she drifted off into a day dream of her first dance with Aiden. She closed her eyes and smiled a secret smile, just for her. This memory was one she would never share with anyone, it was so precious to her.

Peter and Jane's wedding reception had been a long day, and everyone had had plenty to eat and drink. The ladies were dancing round handbags and the gents had shed their jackets and ties. The children had crashed out in the hotel reception. The tables were a mess with the debris of party poppers, empty wine bottles, beer glasses and napkins. Naomi was sitting alone fiddling with a spoon when he approached. The song had just started and she looked up at the handsome Aiden for the first time.

"I've been looking at you all day" he said in a quiet, shy manner as he carefully sat down beside her "and I wondered whether, as it's nearly time to go home, I may steal a dance with you." He smiled.

Naomi didn't speak. She couldn't. She had been watching him all day too; this enigmatic stranger whose mere presence in the room made her shiver with nerves. He was amazingly handsome, and at the reception all alone! She held up her hand with a thankful smile and he lead her to the dance floor quickly, so he could have her in his arms for as long as possible. There were only a few couples left dancing now. It was long passed midnight.

Aiden stopped in the middle of the dance floor and turned to face Naomi, looking her straight in the eye. She was magnificently attractive, even after God knows how much wine they had been drinking all day. Taking her round the waist with one arm and the other on her ribs, tantalisingly close to her breast, Naomi took a deep breath and stepped in. His body was warm and lean, strong. She instinctively put both her arms around his neck and rested her head on his shoulder. She thought she could hear his heart above the music. It sounded as excited as she was. They didn't so much dance as stand still gently swaying to the music.

"I've been watching you all day too." She said, looking up at him. He looked down at her, their noses touched and their mouths were so close they could feel each other's breath on their lips, warm and moist. Aiden turned his head and kissed her gently. The lightning that shot through Naomi's body during that first kiss was mind-bending. It was as if someone had plugged her into a generator and given her a huge boost of mind, body and soul. Instantly she felt brand new and so alive that her hair tingled and her lips just melted at the touch of his. She pushed her tongue through her lips to catch a taste of him. She felt him shudder under her arms as she caught his lips with her tongue. He responded slowly, but very deliberately. She dissolved into a heady *feeling and she felt her breathing deepen and she explored his mouth and lips. 'God, he's good' she thought to herself. Aiden pulled way and looked deeply into her eyes, searching them.*

"You are simply beautiful" he whispered, and kissed her again. Then, as the song finished, they sat in the hotel reception for hours talking, drinking with arms round each other, falling slowly in love.

Back in reality, the song echoed round the hollow expanse of her mind. Her body felt cold without him to hold it and her arms felt weak without him to wrap them round. The mourners were leaving; she was aware of that, but unaware that she was expected to leave with them. She had totally lost herself in one of the happiest memories of her life on the saddest day of her life. The song finished, and with memories of their first dance, she stood-up, looked around at the empty building and the catafalque where Aiden had been taken from her and walked towards the waiting funeral director. She felt it was a last, slow dance coming full circle, that song started their relationship, and now it ended it. Quite fitting, she supposed.

Outside, with her mind back where she felt it should be, she walked round the floral tributes left outside. She read the cards as her friends made pointless small talk about anything else other than what was happening. Naomi just smiled and pretended to care what people said, but all she wanted to do was talk about Aiden and how great he is. Was.

-|-

At the gathering back at Jack and Anna's house, they had laid on a large buffet of all the traditional fare; sausage rolls, sandwiches and the like. There was plenty of booze too. In conversations, everyone meant well of course, but Naomi couldn't help but feel a little bit lost; she was the bereaved girlfriend, but not quite the widow to whom someone could talk to like an old friend. *"Never the bride, never the widow"*, she smiled wryly to herself at her dry wit. She was somewhere in the middle perhaps. It was all very strange, and there was one overwhelming thought that kept coming into her mind as she stood at the window looking into the garden at the bench she and Aiden used to sit on in the summer. *"What the hell am I going to do now?"*

Aiden was still reeling from the shock of attending his own funeral as he sat on the bench in his parent's garden, contemplating the event and how it had affected Naomi. She would have to continue her life now without him. The day was fast running out of hours; the sun was beginning to set and the shadows were creeping across the garden, enveloping everything in the darkness of night. They looked like fingers wrapping themselves round the bushes and shrubs, up the trees and round the back of the shed. Tomorrow was a brand new day, the first day of Naomi's new life alone.

He stood looking at the house. It was red brick with a clay tiled roof. Modest in size with two windows at the top, one of which was his old bedroom and the other was the guest room. What were his parents to do now also? They were not of an age where another child would be a possibility. He had no idea. Perhaps they would just grow old together, sad in the memories of that Saturday in October when it all went so terribly wrong. It then dawned on Aiden that he still did not know how he had got to this point. The manner of his departure from life was not mentioned at the funeral and he heard no-one talking about it, not that he was paying much attention to anyone except Naomi, and she had certainly not said anything to anyone about it. He would have to find out, but for now he had to do something to stop himself feeling so hot.

-|-

At the crematorium, Aiden's coffin had been loaded into the furnace and the heat was beginning to eat away at the sides and bottom of it. The thin wood was beginning to tarnish and the tough plastic handles were starting to soften and sag. In the garden outside the wake, Aiden felt the burning on his back. His body stiffened and eyes closed with the agony of the rising heat. He lay on the grass as if in the coffin.

Back inside the coffin now, Aiden opened his eyes to the blackness and the heat. All he could hear was the blasting of the burners outside. They were slightly muffled, but the cracking of the wood beneath and beside him was a sure sign of the relentless, hungry flames. He tried to move away from the heat, but his body wouldn't move.

The interior of the coffin began to glow orange and the

first flames broke through the blackened wood with flickering fingers, looking for the body to wrap around and devour. A horrific sense of panic rose in Aiden as more and more of the wood around him allowed the flames through to the body. The temperature on the gauge outside read nine hundred and sixty seven degrees centigrade. He flailed around as the sides caved in and the coffin lid disintegrated down onto his chest, face and legs.

No matter how he struggled, his body remained motionless, allowing the flames to lick his blackened clothes and work their way onto his skin. The temperature continued rising inside the furnace and Aiden's howls of utter agony could only be heard by him. He was refusing to die again. He was crying out to Naomi, willing her to come and rescue him from the excruciating pain he was suffering. The one woman he loved with all his heart and mind could not be there. She had already said goodbye and was miles away now, mourning him. He was dying again in this blackened carcass, this vision of hell in the crematorium furnace.

All of his nerves withered away and he was left in a rapidly charring and vaporising body, but he could still feel everything happening to him. As the fluid evaporated from his muscles, he could feel them tense as they dried, pulling tightly on the joints. Then slowly, as the flesh crumbled away, his bones began cracking in the immense heat and Aiden could feel every one of them pop and splinter like dry sticks, sending his spirit body into twisted, broken and writhing shapes above the growing pile of ash.

Seemingly from nowhere came a memory of him and Naomi. They were walking down a London street somewhere a year or so ago.

Hand in hand in December, wrapped up in their coats and scarves, walking briskly against the winter wind they laughed. They laughed hard down the streets, getting lost in the labyrinth. With their noses red and heads swimming with wine, they hailed a cab and spent the ride home kissing and fumbling in the back seat whilst the cabby smiled to himself glancing at them in the rear view mirror.

He could see how in love they were and it made him think of his own younger self, and the wife he left at home every day. He loved her too. But this young couple were so in love it warmed the heart to see on a cold winters evening like this.

Arriving at home and with the cab driver paid, Naomi and Aiden hardly waited to get inside the flat before trying to get their clothes off. Scarves came off before they reached the other side of the road, and coats off half way up the stairs.

Giggling like teenagers Naomi fumbled with her handbag to find the key as Aiden was rummaging his face in her neck, his cold nose sending shivers across her shoulders, but the warmth of his lips and tongue tingling that artery in her neck. He knew that that spot was a sweet one.

Flicking on the light in the hall, they continued to undress, the tension rising between them, and their cold hands brought goose-bumps to their flesh. Virtually naked, they jumped into bed and under the covers, and the mood changed. Suddenly Naomi turned serious. She put a finger to Aiden's lips and he stopped still instantly.

"What?" said Aiden in a whisper.

"I love you so much" Naomi replied "We'll always be together, won't we?"

"Yes, or course." came Aiden's reply, and he lowered his head to kiss her, and he felt her body arch into his to gain as much contact with him as possible.

Aiden screamed again as he felt his jaw fracture from the heat and his face distorted as if hit by an iron pipe. The memory of London in December evaporated as quickly as it arrived. The parts of his skull, so intricately joined together since he was a child split apart and fell over the remains of his shrinking brain charring more as they went. His eyelids, like the skin on his face had burnt away leaving his lifeless eye sockets staring up at him. He could feel his face collapse inward as the contorted spirit that he now was wrenched his head round to see the result of the burning beneath him.

After almost an hour of the most horrific agony of the promised second death, the body was virtually complete ash, laying hot and in piles in the furnace, bone fragments laying where they fell. The flames from the burners died down slowly and in the middle Aiden knelt, head in hands, allowing his frustration and anger to build inside him. He embraced it as it filled him. It felt good and he almost felt alive again. Now that his earth-bound body had been destroyed, his spirit body had somehow returned to the image it was before; a handsome healthy man with the world at his feet.

The pain of the burning had subsided. What was absolute pain had turned to a numbness that was almost as agonising. But this was an emotional numbness; the kind of numbness brought on by total loss and he could feel it rise and erupt from within him. He felt strong and at the same time completely empty. Empty of all feelings except a unconditional love for Naomi. He could never let her go. Never.

His loud cry of desperation echoed around the furnace. He felt like a phoenix rising from his own ashes. He had to prepare himself now to keep away from those who said he had to return to them after this second death and keep as close to Naomi as possible in order to fulfil his self induced duty as her guardian angel.

-|-

Slowly getting out of the car, Naomi closed the door with a heavy thud. She stood at the side of the road in the evening drizzle and looked up at the flat with a deep sigh and a sense of foreboding. She examined the window she was looking through just a few hours ago and wondered how different her life would be now she had to start it all over again. It felt like she was either too old to start again or too young to carry on until her own inevitable demise.

Her feet patted through the water on the pavement up to the front door of the flat. She put the key slowly into the lock, not sure if she wanted to go in on her own. Although Aiden had been gone for nearly two weeks, the flat now felt totally empty with no hope at all of it being filled with his laughter and gregarious nature. As the lock turned, she thought she heard an echo of the key in barrel, like the door to a vast cave being opened for the first time in hundreds of years. The door silently opened and slowly she took a step in and closed the door behind her.

She looked up at the stairs and had the same memory as Aiden had when he was in the furnace. That night in December and the undressing on the stairs. She smiled a tired smile to herself and felt the now all-too-familiar sting behind her eyes. She hoped she wouldn't start crying again as she couldn't have many tears left for today must have finished them off.

The stairs were illuminated through the small window above the door by the orange glow of the street lights outside. Aiden stood half way up, invisible to Naomi, like a spiritual door she would have to pass through. He looked peaceful, but desperately sad. His shoulders were heavy and low, his neck looking longer than usual, his arms hanging down by his side. He looked exhausted. He too was thinking again of the night in December when they had undressed each other on the stairs in fits of laughter brought on by love and far too much to drink.

Naomi flicked on the hall light, and for the briefest of seconds, Aiden became visible. She caught sight of him out of the corner of her eye. She took a sharp intake of breath and held it for a moment as she gazed at the step he was standing on, but he had gone. She thought she had seen something. No, she knew she had seen something, but she quickly dismissed it as a shadow and a tired mind. Her heart was pounding loudly in her ears. The stairs and the flat upstairs were silent as they had been for the last eleven days.

Making sure the front door was closed securely, she made her way lazily up the stairs. Aiden stood still before her.

Just as she went passed the step where Aiden was standing, the air turned to a deathly chill and Naomi shivered for a second. The hair on the backs of her hands and neck stood to attention and her shoulders shuddered with the breath of cold. For the shortest of moments, she felt anger, jealously, frustration and a spilt second of utter rage. And love; she felt complete and utter unconditional love, but it wasn't the kind of love she was used to. It was strange, she felt like she loved herself, but then everything passed as she took the next step. She paused momentarily but carried on, barely noticing what had happened, choosing to ignore it as being damp from standing outside.

At the top of the stairs she flicked on the hall light, and the stairs one off, as if keeping the creeping darkness at bay and the light moving with her as she moved through the flat. She felt that the dark should stay away from her, that Aiden was in the dark now and that was somewhere that she really didn't need to be right now.

What she did need right now though, was a drink. Coffee or Baileys? Both? She didn't prepare either. Instead she threw off her coat and slung her bag on the chair in the kitchen after turning one light on, and the other one off. She remembered that she had taken her hat off at Aiden's parent's house but thought it could just stay there. At the moment, she wanted to be by herself, to come to terms with the day's events and begin to figure out what she was going to do now.

Sitting at her spot at the kitchen table, she gazed blankly out at the scene below the window. The drizzle down the window pain looked like her face from earlier: streaked with tears. There were very few people out and about now. The street lights shone down on the wet pavement, lighting the way for no-one and his dog. The odd car shooshed its way along the road, tyres kicking up spray and wipers flicking away the tears of rain. A cat darted out from beneath a parked car, perhaps fed up of sitting there for hours and was now hungry, so decided to make a dash for home. Litter stuck to the path, clinging on to the kerb against the easy wind that blew up the street. The steady drizzle stood out against the street lights. It looked like it was lazy rain. Not quite hard enough to be rain, and not quite light enough to not worry about. It just came down relentlessly, drenching everything in an uncaring way. A man walked along the road with his collar turned up and his head down, looking at the pavement. The leather of his jacket glistening with wet. His black trousers had a damp sheen to them and his hair matted on his head revealing a bald spot on the crown that would not be too evident if his hair were dry. His sodden shoes looked more black than brown and would take days to dry out properly. He looked like she felt. Another car went passed, shooshing again with wipers going.

Leaning back in the chair, Naomi looked to the ceiling and sighed again. Put the kettle on, she thought. Standing and moving to the kettle, running her hand along the back on a chair, somewhat aimless in her movements, she picked up the kettle and filled it with water from the tap, put it back in it's stand and switched it on.

She didn't know what happened in the next five minutes. They vanished in her thoughts, and her mind only came back to the kitchen when the kettle clicked off. It made her jump slightly.

Half heartedly she made a cup of coffee. Looking in the fridge she found the questionable milk and noticed how bare it was of food. The thought of having to go shopping filled her with dread. What if she saw someone she knew at the shop and they ask about the funeral? Grabbing the milk and hurriedly closing the door to the emptiness, she evacuated the thought of shopping from her mind.

Living room light on, kitchen light off. She slumped herself down on the sofa, not bothering to close the curtains. The silence was penetrating every fibre of her conscience. It was incredibly quiet now, but her head was talking loudly with random thoughts of progression and keeping hold of the memories of the funeral.

Aiden stood watch over her from the corner of the room, hidden in the shadows. If Naomi could see him, he would look menacingly obscured. He looked at her with a longing in his eyes. He didn't know what to do to show himself to her again. He knew she had seen him at the funeral, and he was sure that she felt him as she walked up the stairs. He would have to try different things to see if they worked.

-|-

Out of the silence, the phone rang loudly, startling Naomi back into the living room. She had been somewhere between asleep and awake with her mind enjoying a happy daydream. As her body flinched, she looked around the room for what had made the sound. Confused by the noise, she stood up cursing and grabbed at the phone. Seeing the caller ID as being her long time friend Jane, whose wedding she was attending when her and Aiden first met.

"Hello, Jane." Her voice sounded tired, strained and not really wanting to talk.

"Hi Naomi, so sorry for calling you. I'm worried about you. Are you OK." Replied Jane, concerned.

"Yeah, I'm fine" Naomi lied badly "I've not been in long. It's been a pretty bad day, don't you think?"

Jane didn't know quite how to respond. "Er, yes, it has been a pretty bad day, but the ceremony was a nice as it could be I guess. Do you want to talk about it? It's not too late, I could come over and see you, if you like." Her caring attitude towards her friends was evident and she would always put herself out to lend a hand or a shoulder to cry on.

"Um. I don't know. Thank you for asking. Perhaps I should be alone for a while." Naomi paused, looking round the lonely flat that seemed twice the size it was than when she came home. "Actually, yes." Her voice sounding a little lighter now "Come round. This place is really quiet and maybe some company will cheer me up a bit."

Aiden smiled at her. *"That's a good girl,"* he thought. *"A bit of time with Jane will be good for you now."* It would be interesting to hear what they had to talk about. It's not often a man gets to hear all the chit-chat of two females who think they are alone.

"OK" said Jane, with a spring in her voice. "I'll be round shortly."

"Thanks. See you soon. I'll put the kettle on again." Naomi hung up the phone and huffed at the thought of having to entertain a visitor after the shitty day she had had. "Her heart's in the right place, I suppose" she said to herself as she walked in the kitchen, flicking the light on.

Filling the kettle once more, she looked out of the window. It was very dark now and the drizzle continued to fall from the flat black sky. Looking around for the time on the front of the microwave, she saw it was not even eight o'clock yet. The street was as quiet as it would be after midnight. She felt like she had been home for hours, but it couldn't have been more than one as her coffee on the table in the living room was still warm so she knew it couldn't have been that long.

Looking round the flat, she thought it was tidy enough to accept a visitor. She didn't really care that her room was a bit of a mess and the living room hadn't been lived in much recently. Most of her time was spent gazing out of the window in the kitchen, and that was a bit of a mess. Empty and half empty coffee cups partially filled the sink and the draining board, a bottle of milk sat empty on the side and a packet of stale biscuits lay opened near the empty bread bin. *"I hope Jane doesn't want anything to eat."* Naomi thought to herself. In fact, Naomi hoped she didn't want more than one cup of tea as there wasn't enough milk for more than one drink each. *"Pitifully poor show."* she continued to think.

With another huff as the kettle boiled, Naomi made Jane a cup of tea. She knew exactly how long it would take Jane to get to her, she had been doing it for long enough.

-|-

Just as the last drop of milk finished off the tea and coffee she was making, Naomi jumped at the sound of Jane banging on the door. She never used the bell. Coming out of the kitchen, she checked herself over in the hall mirror. She muttered something under her breath about looking a lot better before and then plodded downstairs to the door.

With a deep breath and a very fake smile, she opened the door to a damp Jane standing huddled in the rain. She had only walked from her car to the door, all of seven or eight metres and she made it look like she had walked all the way from her house.

"Hi. You really didn't have to come, Jane. But thank you. I appreciate it." Naomi felt like she had lied to her friend, but in fact she really was pleased Jane had come and that the extra body and voice would help fill the void, even if it would only be for a couple of hours.

"Don't mention it, Naomi. I thought you could use some company this evening. Are you OK?" Jane replied with a caring but inappropriate over enthusiastic tone. "I brought a bottle with me. I thought you might like a drink!"

It wasn't unlike Jane to be over zealous, but this arrival with a bottle of wine seemed more like an entrance to a party rather than comforting a grieving girlfriend.

"That's nice, Jane. Thank you. Come in, you look cold." Naomi tried to sound as enthusiastic as Jane, but failed.

Understandably, Jane thought, Naomi's normal spring in her step had faded to a slow walk up the stairs. She followed the shadowy figure to the living room where she sat down whilst Naomi fetched a couple of glasses from the kitchen.

The atmosphere in the living room seemed dank, oppressive almost, like there was a lingering smell. The feeling was almost tangible to Jane who sat on the edge of the sofa with the bottle of wine in front of her on the table. It made her feel uncomfortable, scared almost and wary and she looked around like a deer in the woods looking for an unseen huntsman. Quiet, and unnaturally still, everything in the flat just seemed to have stopped, just hanging in time waiting to be kick-started back into life. A bit like Naomi perhaps.

As a group of friends, Jane, Peter, David, Naomi and Aiden had spent many evenings here with other friends dining and having terrific thirty-something fun over many, many bottles of wine.

In the kitchen, Naomi felt like she was disintegrating for the third or forth time that day. Although her friend coming to see her and comfort her was a very kind gesture, all she really wanted was to be alone. She gripped the kitchen worktop and hung her head down towards her elbows, eyes tight, breathing deeply, holding back the prickly tears.

With one final deep breath, Naomi reached into the cupboard, grabbed two wine glasses and went back to the living room. Smiling falsely she beamed "Everything alright, Jane?"

Jane snapped out of her uneasy feeling and equally beamed a confirmation of her being alright, but could see in her friends eyes that everything was indeed, not alright. Naomi's eyes were sunken and reddened, more so now than when she arrived a few minutes earlier. It didn't take more than two minutes to collect two wine glasses for the kitchen. She must have been crying, Jane supposed.

Trying to gloss over the uncomfortable silence that now sat between them, Jane struggled to find a conversation starter that didn't relate in same way to Aiden's funeral. She poured the wine in silence as Naomi took her place on the sofa looking and feeling just as uncomfortable.

The two women looked at each other and exchanged little smiles as if two strangers on opposite sides of a train carriage had briefly made eye contact, and even this, between two old friends felt uncomfortable. Jane began to wish she had not come, and Naomi wished the same, but she was deep in thought about the day and was summoning up the courage to tell Jane what she thought she saw at the catafalque.

"Jane?" her voice sounded uneasy.

"Yes" she said, placing her already half drained glass on

the table.

Without hesitation, but after a deep gulp of breath, Naomi made up her mind to tell her. "Do you believe in ghosts, Jane?" Aiden's ears pricked up in the corner. He listened more closely.

"Dunno," she said "Never seen one." She took a mouthful of wine, dreading, but knowing what was coming next. Jane had lied. She had seen several in her time but deemed this a bad time to admit it.

Naomi paused for a moment, reconsidering her decision. "I think I saw Aiden today. He was standing next to his coffin looking at me." Her voice was flat but certain and she stared out the window as she spoke.

Jane's silence allowed Naomi to continue.

"He tried to reach out to me but just as he did, he disappeared again. I think I saw him again when I got home earlier."

Naomi was speaking like she was making a statement and not wanting a response. She knew what she saw and hoped that Jane wouldn't dismiss it as an upset girlfriend either making it up out of hope for the lost, or her mind hallucinating from exhaustion and grief.

From the shadows in the corner, Aiden moved a little closer to listen more. He was so proud of Naomi and how she had composed herself for his funeral, and hearing this coming from her now, so soon after the ceremony was a sign that she had indeed seen him there next to his coffin.

Jane had taken her wine from the table and was draining the glass. She could see that Naomi wasn't joking even though she was looking away. She put the glass down again, shuffled over on the sofa and gently took Naomi's hands in hers, comforting them like a daughter would do her ageing mother's in the last moments of her life. She looked down and squeezed their hands together.

"You poor thing. Are you sure you saw Aiden there?" Jane's eyes were looking deeply into Naomi's now, searching for something there that would give her a clue to the truth. It was absurd. How could she have seen Aiden? he's dead, she thought. Naomi nodded. "Naomi, really? How could you have done?"

Turning to face her friend, Naomi looked straight into Jane's eyes, all sorrow gone from her mind for the moment. Inside her heart, she had a feeling of hope that she would see him again. "I don't know, I have no idea. He was there right in front of me, Jane. As plain as day. Standing still, looking right at me and then he reached out to me, then he was gone. I was crying and my vision blurred quite quickly, but it was him, Jane. I know it was, there was no-one else there, and David was standing on the other side. Am I being silly? Do you think I saw him?" Jane looked a little shocked and poured another glass of wine and topped up Naomi's.

Aiden had moved out of the shadows now and was standing in front of them both by the table, listening to the women's conversation. He was amazed that Naomi had seen him, but now confused as to why she should now be doubting what she saw.

Jane regarded her bereaved friend with caution. She didn't want to give her any hope because there mustn't be any. Aiden was dead and although Naomi knew that, love sometimes does funny things and leads people to do irrational and stupid things, neither did she want to shatter the illusion. She sat quietly for another moment, considering what to say. "I don't know." She said "You've been under a lot of pressure lately, and I think you probably saw what you most wanted to see. It could have been him, but he must live in your heart and memory now. He'll never die there. Maybe your heart brought him back to you for a moment, as a reassurance that he's still with you. I don't know."

Aiden enjoyed hearing this from Jane. He was indeed still with her and had no intention of ever letting her go. At least, not until she joined him from her death bed, probably many years from now. He would be waiting at the foot of the bed, excited at the prospect of her terminal breath and then they would be together again, for ever this time. He instantly felt envious of Jane. She had those years to share with Naomi and he would simply be an invisible onlooker from the shadows, living only in the hearts and memories of Naomi and their friends. He had to find a way of letting them all know that he was still with them. He thought he may try something to let them know she wasn't making it up or daydreaming through hope.

Naomi stared into her glass of wine, knowing that Jane was right in everything she said. The wine swirled slowly in the bowl of the glass, gently agitated by the slow movement she was giving it. "I know it's really soon after his funeral, Naomi, but in a week or two, it will be time to carry on with your life, you know? Life is for the living." She paused and stroked Naomi's hair behind her ear. Her voice became quieter now, more caring and almost a whisper "Remember the dead, but at the same time, you mustn't forget the living. Give it a couple of weeks, then start moving forward with Aiden firmly in your heart and memory."

Taking a sip of her wine with a shaking hand, and holding back more of those blasted tears, Naomi gave a little smile and a sniffle. "You're right, so right" she said. "Maybe it was just my mind playing with me." She shivered slightly as Aiden sat down beside her, on the arm of the sofa, and leaning down on his knees explained that it wasn't her mind playing tricks, even though she couldn't hear him. It was him there at the funeral, that he was with her throughout the ceremony, and the night before, and he was here now, never letting her go and that he would be her guardian angel until her dying day.

-|-

Both women sat in silence for a few moments with Aiden, unseen on the end of the sofa. Jane was thinking about what to say next. Something to lighten the mood and Naomi was thinking about what she had just said and what on earth Jane must think of her now. She probably thought she was a little neurotic and not willing to let Aiden go. She guessed it would be fair of her if she did, but at the same time, why shouldn't she grasp tightly at the memory of the man she loved with all her body, heart and soul? It's not her fault she loved him so much. If anything, it was partly down to Jane and Peter for inviting them both to their wedding in the first place. If they hadn't invited one of them, they may never have met and never fallen in love, and then she wouldn't be feeling like this.

Aiden felt the uncomfortable silence between them and wished he could do something to break it.

No sooner had he thought that, the quiet was broken by

the sound of the phone ringing. Naomi left it for a moment longer than usual to see if they would hang-up, but the incessant ringing continued. She got up to answer it. Just as she got there, the voice mail collected the call. "Hi, thanks for calling Naomi and Aiden"

"I need to change that" she said looking back at Jane with a wry smile and a break in her voice.

"We can't take your call at the moment. We might be out or we might just be ignoring you! Anyway, please leave a message after the tone. Bye!" the happy voice mail message fell silent, waiting for a disembodied voice to begin talking. For several seconds, there was nothing. Naomi looked at Jane again, wondering what on earth was going on. Given the conversation they had just had, the eerie silence put Jane on edge too. Her eyes returned to the startled deer look they had when she was sitting alone in the living room whilst Naomi was collecting glasses.

"Hey. Naomi. It's David. If you're there, can you pick up. I'd like to see if you're OK" He paused, and Naomi paused too, looking at the phone, her hands confused as to what to do with the call.

David was sitting at home, alone in the living room, thinking about the day and looking forward to the following day. He'd had it rough today. He never had had such a tough job to do for anyone before, and he was grateful that he managed to hold it together till he got home. Then he sat in racks of tears, and with no-one to comfort him, he cried for what felt like hours. He needed Naomi to be there with him, to hold him and tell him everything would be OK. He felt like they had a shared grief in the loss of Aiden, but he needed her there for another reason too.

Quickly, after David's silence had gone on for long enough, Naomi snapped up the phone. "Hello. David?"

"Oh, Naomi, I am so pleased you're there." His voice sounded harsh and broken. "Are you OK? It's been a hard day and I wondered if everything is alright with you."

"David, that's very sweet of you. Thank you." She blushed a little and turned her back to Jane. "I'm fine, thanks, and thank you so much for what you did today, I'm very grateful.

You did Aiden and his family proud." Her voice began to break a little too.

"How about you, Naomi?"

"You did me proud too, David. You really did, and I'm sure Aiden would have, er, enjoyed it. No, that's such the wrong word." Aiden, now standing next to the phone smiled at her faux pas. "I meant to say appreciated. So sorry."

David chuckled though his watery eyes. "That's OK" he said "Aiden would laugh at that!"

"I have Jane with me at the moment. We're sharing a bottle of wine."

David was just about to ask if she wanted him to come over, but on hearing that he was too late, he sank deeply into the sofa and put his hand to his forehead, rubbing it as if smoothing out the furrowed lines from todays emotions. "No problem" he lied, badly. "Can I call you tomorrow?" He so badly wanted to hold her, to comfort himself as much as her. He had admired her for so long from a distance and each hug she gave him squeezed a little more love into him for her. He had been envious of Aiden for all these years and he didn't want to blow his chance with her, but thought he had to at least see her soon, to remind her that he was still there, before she moved on with her life. And if she did that, there was every risk that she would move away and properly start again with a new place to live, new job and new friends. After all, there were so many reminders of Aiden everywhere, a move would be a sensible thing to do.

"Sure, of course you can. It will be good to talk to you. Bye." She slowly hung up the receiver and sat down with Jane again with a slightly wider smile on her face. She let out a slight cough, to break her mood, into her wine glass.

'Well?' said Jane 'What was that about and why the hell are you blushing?' her tone was a mixture of agitation, humour and concern.

Naomi frowned at the comment. "That was David. He would like to speak to me tomorrow, and I would like to speak to him too. Is that a problem?"

"I'd guessed it was David. It's not in itself, no. But why are you blushing?"

"I'm hot, that's all."

"Rubbish. It's chilly in here. Has been since I arrived. You've got a crush on David, haven't you?" Naomi was silent for just a little too long and Jane was on her. "Jesus, Naomi, you've just buried Aiden and you're blushing like a schoolgirl because your crush has phoned you, and it was HIM who conducted the ceremony. For fuck sake, finish grieving before you move on. Please, just make sure you are ready to move on first. You don't need a rebound relationship, and certainly not with him." Her tone lessened.

Ignoring the attack on her, Naomi considered her feet for a moment, like a guilty schoolchild. "It's not what it seems, Jane. Really, it's not. David and I are very close. You know that. I've always had a soft spot for him. You have too. He's been like our big brother for the last few years, don't you think? Both Aiden and I are, sorry, were very fond of him. He would have been the best man at our wedding, were we ever to have one. We spoke about it a few times. We were together long enough to get married, don't you think?" She paused again, considering what she was missing out on.

"Well, yeah. OK."

"Good, then please don't accuse me of having a crush. It's not like that. I think I need to go to bed now." Naomi finished the last of her wine and Jane took this as a most definite sign that she ought to leave.

-|-

After Jane had left with a slightly sharper 'Bye' from Naomi than was maybe necessary, she closed the door and began her bedtime routine.

Aiden watched her again as he had done the night before. Tomorrow would be the beginning of a new life for Naomi. A life he desperately hoped would not be a lonely one, but at the same time, he hoped that she felt she could love no-one again and be content only with a group of friends. Eventually though, they would marry-off and have children, and he didn't know how he would feel if Naomi were to fall in love again.

He had been concerned that Naomi was blushing over David's phone call. Was there, or could there be something going on between them? Of course not, she and he were too in love for her to play away, and there was too much respect between him and David for him to go behind his back. But now though, with Aiden gone from the living, there would be nothing to stop David making a move on her in time. The thought did not bear thinking about and he pushed it from his mind. He felt a twinge of jealousy run through his body and he clenched his fists, a reflex to the surge of emotion.

The flat was silent. The drizzle had given way to a fog which absorbed the sounds of what traffic there was going by. Naomi's bare feet on the floorboards quietly broke the silence as she made her way round her evening ablutions. She didn't talk to herself, barely looked at herself in the mirror. She knew she looked rough just by feeling her face as she yawned. Her skin felt a little tight. Dried up tears had left a thin layer of salt on her cheeks and she could feel it. If her skin was tight, then her make-up had probably run a bit too. She must look like a clown in a feak show, so instead of looking in the mirror, she just washed her face blindly in the basin, and then looked in the mirror. Still not great, she thought, I'll be less puffy in the morning.

Pounding the pillows on the bed that now felt too large for one person, Naomi wearily climbed in, her body heavy with the subsiding emotions on the day. Now she was alone, she felt she could be the person she needed to be today, and that was a weak, vulnerable and emotionally wrecked woman who had no desire in life other than to see the one person she loved so completely with her entire body and soul. She lay there, still, looking at the photograph of her and Aiden, the larger copy of the one she gave him in the coffin all those hours ago. She felt comforted by it. His smile beamed out of the frame reassuringly at her in the orange glow of the street lights. Despite herself, she couldn't bring herself to say goodnight to him. *"He's not here, so what's the point?"* She thought. Feeling a bit like Scarlet O'Hara, she closed her eyes, sighed deeply and believed that 'tomorrow is another day'. Tiredness overtook her and she fell quickly and deeply to sleep.

Sitting on the floor with his back to the wall, Aiden began his eternal vigil of watching over Naomi. Like a loyal family dog, he sat patiently and watched over her, ready to protect her, suffer with her, guide her through the hard times and smile with her through the good times.

-|-

Jane felt like she had been told off, and rightly too, she thought as she sat in the car. She looked up at the flat she had just left and began to worry about her friend. David and Naomi had always been close. Too close perhaps for her liking, but each to their own, she supposed. She didn't like the way David had called her on the evening of the funeral like that, but quickly dismissed it as being a silly idea. He was only calling to see if she was alright, wasn't he? They had been friends a long time and it was only natural he was concerned about her wellbeing. But could he be harbouring feelings for Naomi that he shouldn't be revealing?

Shaking her head, Jane started the car and with one last glance up at the flat, loosely hoping to see Naomi standing at the window looking for her, she saw that the lights had been turned out and all was dark. She could only dream of the pain her best friend was going through right now. She knew she would be just as shattered if she were to lose her husband, Peter. The pain would be unbearable and she knew that she would need her friends around her like Naomi should have done. They were all there for her, but for some reason, she turned most people away.

Naomi's voice-mail was full of unreturned calls from friends concerned for her and offering shoulders to cry on and evenings of self-pity over a bottle of wine. She hadn't wanted any of them, preferring her own company. She had wanted to allow herself to fall apart completely over Aiden and then, when the time was right, pick herself up, rebuild a new her and move on. She thought her friends would try to keep her together and prevent the self destruction she felt she needed. If Aiden was gone, then her own world should be destroyed alongside his. That way, part of her would die too and go with him wherever he had gone. He could take it with him to remember her by, and keep it close to his heart.

25th October

A week on from Aiden's funeral and Naomi was beginning to feel like her old self again. The spring in her step had begun to return and life started to be a little more normal. She had developed a routine for herself which helped keep the reminders of Aiden at bay. She had changed her morning routine to something completely new, as well as her evening routine. The living room had been rearranged, and her bed was now against a different wall. Her mother and father had come to help her do it a few days previously. They were pleased to be able to help. She was so independent normally and kept her feelings very much to herself, that to be allowed in, let them feel needed and appreciated. They had had a pizza delivered for dinner that evening and had enjoyed the time together. Over a glass of wine, Naomi and her mother discussed what was going to happen next. How was she going to move on, and her father listened in with a pint of water. When those two got together and started their mouths going, he had learnt to keep his own mouth shut and let them get on with it. Naomi wasn't the only one missing Aiden.

Now though, Naomi was pushing herself up the road against the stiff, cold autumn breeze coming straight into her face. She was wrapped up in a knee length woolen coat with a scarf wound tightly round her face and ears. She had had to remove her hat to save it from blowing away. The sky was perfectly clear and faded from a firey orange behind the buildings to the deepest blue above her head. The brightest of stars began to show through the darkening sky and Naomi admired it as she made her way to Mr Gorshani's little shop and newsagent on the nearby high street.

The shop wasn't the biggest in the world, and it certainly wasn't the best stocked, but Mr Goshani carried most of the everyday essentials, almost every day. Naomi peculiarly enjoyed going there for something important and finding Mr Gorshani didn't have any and then returning home with something else instead.

As the pages of the remainder of the day's newspapers blustered open as Naomi entered the shop, Mr Gorshani called to her in his normal happy way. "Good afternoon, Miss Naomi. How are you today?"

"I'm well, thank you Mr Gorshani. How are you?" Naomi flashed him a beaming smile that made the slightly aged gentleman clasp his hands together in front of his chest.

"I am very pleased to see you. It seems a long time." He had come towards the front of the shop to stand with her. "Mrs Gorshani and I were very sorry to hear about Aiden. Such a lovely young man. We've been thinking about you."

"That's very kind of you both, Mr. Gorshani. Thank Mrs. Gorshani for me, won't you?" Naomi was surprised at how well she had handled comments so far. This was the first time she had been out properly since the funeral and was dreading seeing anyone she knew just in case they mentioned it. *"This is a promising start."* She thought.

"What can I get for you?"

"Oh, Mr Gorshani, that's very kind of you. Er, milk, eggs, tea bags, coffee. A couple of microwave meals, because I can't be bothered to cook at the moment," she laughed "and a loaf of white bread. Thank you."

Mr Gorshani grabbed a basket for the shopping and collected it all for her. He was a sucker for Naomi. She was so pretty and so polite, he couldn't help himself treating her differently to all his other customers.

After paying for her shopping and allowing Mr Gorshani to squeeze past her up the aisle between the tinned goods and magazines so he could open the door for her, she stepped out into the chill of the late afternoon wind.

From out of nowhere she remembered that David had called a week ago and she hadn't returned his call.

"Bugger" she exclaimed loudly as the wind caught her face.

"I beg your pardon, Miss Naomi?" Mr Gorshani thought she had stubbed her toe or forgotten some shopping. He look surprised at her curse.

"Mr. Gorshani, I'm sorry. I remembered I had to do something I should have done days ago. Bye for now."

"Goodbye. See you soon." He closed the door behind himself and rubbed his hands on his arms, giving a loud 'Brrrrrrr' as he went back to the counter.

-|-

The front door to the flat swung open with the wind as Naomi arrived home from Mr Gorshani's shop. Her hair was a mess and hanging in strands down her face as she pushed the door shut against the weather. "Must phone David back." she said to herself. She had been reminding herself all the way back from the shop. She felt bad that she hadn't done so already as it had been a week since he rang.

Hurriedly unpacking the shopping and putting the kettle on, Naomi groped for the phone in her handbag. There was a text message from Peter waiting for her. She hadn't heard the notification. 'Hi Naomi. Fancy dinner at our place sometime?' it read. 'Yes, thank you. That would be lovely.' Naomi smiled as tapped out the reply. It will be good to get out and about again and get into some kind of social routine again.

Naomi had been living as a virtual recluse since Aiden died. She had not wanted to see or communicate with anyone, preferring to be alone and think about the situation. Her friends had all rallied round her but were held firmly at a distance and only allowed in when Naomi felt comfortable enough to do so, and not in what she thought was a pathetic mess. She appreciated them making the effort to come and see her, even when she didn't open the door. Her voicemail had been busy with messages enquiring after her, offering to buy some shopping for her and that sort of thing. She had ignored most of them and only called her most trusted and closest friends when she felt she could.

Now though, Naomi was rediscovering herself and was looking forward to getting on with her life.

Finding David's number in her list of contacts, she clicked the little green telephone icon next to his photograph and took a deep breath. Quite why her heart was fluttering so much, she didn't know. It was nice. It felt like butterflies.

She could hear it ringing and ringing. "Come on David, pick up." She didn't understand why she thought her call was so urgent. She was only returning it from last week. There was nothing urgent about it at all.

"Hey, Naomi! Good to hear from you!" David's voice sounded excited and genuinely pleased to receive the call.

"David, hi! I'm glad I caught you. How are you? So sorry I haven't returned your call yet." To her own surprise, she sounded almost as excited as he did. Things were obviously looking up for the state of her mind.

"I'm good, thanks. All the better for hearing from you." David flirted. "I was just calling you last week to see if you were OK. You sound it now though, which is good. Do you need anything?"

Naomi had the phone tucked between her cheek and shoulder putting the last items away, banging doors shut as she went. This was much more like the old Naomi. "That's sweet of you. Thanks. I'm alright, I've actually just got in from the shop. The cupboards were completely bare so I've been stocking up."

There was silence now. "David?"

"Yeah, sorry. I was miles away."

"You said you would ring me back the next day after the last call. You never did." Naomi was teasing him now.

"I did, didn't I? So sorry. I must have forgotten all about it."

"Not to worry, David. I've got you now."

David thought to himself that she had no idea about how much she did have him. He would gladly give himself to her at the drop of a hat. All she had to do at the moment was ask him and he would be there for her. Until then though, he would have to play it cool, giving her the time and space he thought she needed. Then, when the time was right, he'd make a gentle move to test the water. He had it all planned out.

"Yes, it appears that way, doesn't it?"

"I guess so."

Another awkward silence.

"How have you been since last week?" Naomi asked quickly thinking how to break the quiet.

"Not too bad, I suppose. Been a bit up and down to be honest. I keep thinking about it. Work hasn't been very productive. How about you?"

"Much the same. More down than up, but feeling much better today. It's nice to have woken up this morning without dreading the day and how many times I'm going to start crying at the slightest little thing. It's good. I might go back to work next week. I'll get this weekend over with, get some sleep and go into work on Monday."

"Really pleased to hear that, Naomi. Well done. If I can help, let me know?"

"Of course I will."

The silence this time was longer. Both Naomi and David wanted to say something they weren't sure they should, and were both holding there tongues, fearing the reaction. Naomi wasn't sure if she should even be thinking about inviting David out for coffee next week, and David was not sure if he should even be thinking about asking Naomi if she fancied a night out. Naomi looked around the room and the ceiling trying to find something to talk about whilst David simply looked blankly out of his window.

As if their minds plucked up the courage to speak at exactly the same time, they both spoke each other's name. Both of the blushed and chuckled at the silliness. "You go first, David."

"OK." He said, knowing that he had to get it out now, despite the fact he was screwing his stomach up in knots at the thought. "I was wondering if you fancied going out for a drink next weekend. Just as friends."

"That's nice of you, David." He feared the worst. That sinking feeling of asking a girl out and her saying no had suddenly engulfed him.

Before giving Naomi a chance to finish what she was saying, he butted in, keen to save as much of his pride as possible. "Sorry, Naomi, I shouldn't have asked so soon after the funeral." He stuttered the apology a little and blushed even more.

Naomi smiled at him, even though he couldn't see her. "If you let me finish, David." She said sternly but with a playful intonation. "It will be as friends, yes. But I was thinking more along the lines of meeting up for a coffee and a chat. And yes, it is too soon to be asking me out for a drink, if it is to be just you and me going out. Maybe later."

"Excellent!" He David sounded excited and Naomi could hear the relief in his voice.

"OK" she said. "Third of November. Two thirty at the coffee shop on the high street. The usual one. I'll see you then. And thank you for asking." She smiled sweetly at the end of the sentence. She was grateful, and she was certainly not quite ready to go out for a night on the town with David. The risk of bumping into other of their friends was too great, and she didn't want them thinking she had moved on so quickly from Aiden. Coffee was the right thing to suggest. Yes, she was sure of it.

"Sounds perfect. Third of November. Two thirty. I'll see you there. I'll look forward to it. Bye for now."

"Me too, Bye."

Naomi hung up quickly before David could say anything else. Putting the phone down on the kitchen table she giggled a girly giggle and finished making her cup of tea.

Aiden, who had been standing behind her the whole time, was not impressed.

28th October

Feeling desperately alone, so close to everyone but a terminal breath away, Aiden's frustration was beginning to get the better of him. He was feeling increasingly angry at not being able to communicate with Naomi. He would follow her round almost every day, watching her going about her business, which at that moment was not a lot. She had sat and half watched the television and gazed out of the window for almost eleven days. She had not eaten properly, the cupboards were virtually bare. He worried about her. She didn't look very well. Her features were drawn, her eyes were much darker than normal and the radiance that she always had exuded had faded. This heap of a woman had slumped herself on the sofa in her dressing grown and hardly looked like the woman he fell so deeply in love with.

Yesterday though, Aiden was amazed to see her get up and actually look positive about the day. She was up and dressed and tidying the flat before lunch time. Her energy was returning and she had finally seemed to have pulled herself together enough to try to get her life back on track.

She still had no idea he was there for her. She couldn't see him at all, or feel his presence. Perhaps she had to believe in ghosts to see one.

He had tried many different ways to contact her; Shouting didn't work, trying to appear in the bathroom mirror like in the movies didn't work either. Neither did trying to write a message on the shower door or moving things like a poltergeist. Clearly, being a ghost wasn't as easy as Hollywood made it out to be. He wasn't a ghost anyway. He had thought about it a lot in the last ten days, and he much preferred the title of Guardian Angel. He felt it suited him better anyway. Ghosts? Whoever believed in such things? He did. Now at least.

The world Aiden existed in was neither here nor there. He knew he was dead, but there seemed to be nowhere to go to. No bright light to follow, and neither was there a hole to dive into. He felt just like he was between worlds, which he guessed was right. No Heaven. No Hell. Just here.

There was no-one to talk to, no-one he could depend on. He couldn't sleep, there was no need to sleep. He didn't feel hungry, there was no need to eat. *"So, this is what love is?"* he thought. Just like when someone first falls in love; They can't eat, sleep or think straight. They feel like they can thrive on the emotion alone. That's what Aiden had to do now. Eternity is a long time.

He had almost resolved himself to spending the rest of Naomi's life following her and trying to find a way that he could help her, guide her. Hopefully, for her sake it would be a long and successful life. But for Aiden, possibly sixty years without being able to talk to anyone would surely drive him mad. He had to find some way to communicate. Until then though, he was resigned to observing only. He didn't like that idea at all.

What would he do when she found someone else who loves her? And what if she loves him? What if they get married? How would he feel then? And how would Naomi feel if he did manage to make contact with her and all these happen? The conversation she had had with David a few days ago had worried Aiden. It sounded very much like he was trying to ask her out. She had looked coy enough for Aiden to know that something was up. He didn't like it, and he didn't like being able to only hear half the conversation. Perhaps there was a way to listen to both sides.

"David is supposed to be my best friend! How could he even

begin to think he was allowed to make a move on Naomi? That's not respectful, it's bloody treachery." Aiden could feel the familiar anger building again through his thoughts. It doubled in strength and kept getting stronger when it could not be released, so it sat dormant in him. It could be suppressed, but not released. Not yet anyway. Aiden had not yet found out how. He could not let David take his girl from him. Naomi was his.

Naomi needed him. She had told him so on several occasions. This was his chance to prove to her that he would always be there for her.

-|-

"Aiden." A new voice came into the room.

It was a voice Aiden had not heard before and he span round to see a tall, emaciated person standing in the doorway. He, at least Aiden assumed it was a 'he' as its features were masculine but at the same time erring on the feminine, filled the doorway from top to bottom, but not side to side. He was painfully thin, almost skeletal and pale blue veins ran up his hands and disappeared into a long bright white shirt. Or was it a blouse? Aiden couldn't make up his mind. He didn't feel at all threatened. Surprised? Yes, because he was being summoned by someone or rather, some-thing, that could quite evidently see him. He felt calmed, serene.

"Who are you?"

"My name is Samael, Aiden. I have a message for you. Please, come with me now. Naomi is fine. Nothing will happen to her whilst you are gone." Samael's voice was slow, calming and quite monotonous. He held out his hand for Aiden to follow.

Pausing for a moment, Aiden looked down at Naomi. She was sitting quietly and looked comfortable. Not really wanting to leave her alone in case she spoke to David again, Aiden reluctantly followed Samael out the living room door.

Without any warning or sense of movement, Aiden found himself standing by the river with Samael at his side, looking towards the Houses of Parliament. He looked up at Samael who showed no emotion at all.

The late autumn sun was shining off the water, spattering Aiden's eyes with pin-pricks of light. He felt warm, but the wind was quite bitter. Londoners walked by them both without seeing them but every-so-often one of the passers-by would look directly at Samael and Aiden and hastily walk across to the other side of pathway looking down at the ground until they had passed. They looked scared at what they could see. This tall, thin skeletal being with no definite skin tone, long white hair and monotonous voice clearly made some people very nervous indeed.

Aiden was confused. Some people looked right through them whilst others avoided them completely. "Who are those people that keep looking at us?" Aiden asked, fearing he already knew the answer.

"They are dead too, Aiden. Just like you, they are waiting to be collected by Us or by Charon, The Ferryman."

"Dead? So I can talk to them? Who are Us, and what was your name again?" Aiden sounded like a child asking too many questions at once about something new and potentially exciting. He leaned on the concrete wall and listened for the answer.

"Yes, Aiden. They are dead too and you can talk to them if you can find them. They look just like everyone else, and they are just as scared as you. They may not want to talk to you, and you certainly don't want to talk to all of them." The monotonous voice sounded soothing despite the warning. "My name is Samael. I am a member of the Principium Angeli. I have been sent by Gabriel to give you a message, and a warning."

"Oh." Said Aiden dejectedly "And what are they?" He turned and leaned on the wall, facing The London Eye and saw more and more people walking by with their eyes averted from Samael. As far as he could see, there were more dead than living in London at the moment.

Samael considered the message in his mind for a moment. He just stood, quite still, looking towards the great building and the Queen Elizabeth Tower that housed Big Ben. "Many things are decided there, aren't they?"

Aiden looked over his shoulder. "Yes, I guess so. Why?"

"You have a decision to make, Aiden. And it is one you should not make lightly."

"And that is, what? Your message?"

"Yes. When you died, you begged us to be allowed to come back to Naomi, even though it was your time to die. We gave you until the first of November to complete what you felt you had to do and return to us. Your time runs out in three days."

"Who are 'we', here, Samael? The Principium what?"

"We? The Principium Angeli. The Principle Angels. We collect souls and deliver them where they need to be. We gave you a chance where others were denied. I hope you won't abuse what we have given you."

"And who are you in the Principium Angeli?"

"I am the severity of God, the angel of death."

Aiden looked ashen at this and began to shuffle his feet. He looked up at Samael who was still looking at the Houses of Parliament, his face pale in the glow of the sunshine, the veins running blue where they could be seen. This 'angel of death' didn't seem that frightening "And what is the warning, Samael?"

"If you do not come with us on the first of November, Aiden, we will give permission for Charon to collect you himself."

"Oh." Aiden laughed nervously. "And who is 'Charon'?" he mocked the name and Samael turned and looked at him directly in the eye. Aiden could see, all of a sudden a million deaths in the eyes of Samael. This angel had seen more than Aiden could ever dream of. His eyes were nearly black, but behind them, somewhere was a soul of souls. A collector for the others in the Principium.

"Charon is the Ferryman. He is the one who will collect you and take you across the River Styx to Hades. And that, Aiden, is where you will reside for eternity, a million deaths away from your precious Naomi. You will die again and again in the agony of a thousand fires." Samael paused, allowing this to be comprehended. "Should you come with us though, you will not see Naomi again until her own time is ended. And then you will be together for eternity."

Aiden looked around at the passers-by. Some looking at him whilst others, those still living busily went about their business, unaware of the presence of an angel.

"Hell?" said Aiden darkly. "This, Charon will take me to Hell?"

"Yes."

"I come with you, and everything will be alright?"

"Yes."

The significance of Samael's bringing him to the Houses of Parliament was sinking in. The choice he faced was so obvious. He should clearly go with Samael and the Principium on the first of November and wait for Naomi to die. Then they would be together, as the cliche goes, forever. But could he face sixty or more years without him being with her? He missed her enough when he was alive and she went out for just one night. But sixty years without looking at her, smelling her, watching her would be too much, surely.

Aiden felt his love for Naomi was powerful enough for him to dig himself up from Hell to be with her if he had to, even if Charon ferried him across the river Styx a hundred or more times. His love for her must out-weigh anything the universe could throw at him.

Samael placed a hand on Aiden's shoulder. "You and Naomi were meant to be together, Aiden, and you were destined to die when you did. Your death will make Naomi the person she was born to be."

"What? You're telling me that no matter what happened, I would have ended up with Naomi anyway and died when I did, and there is nothing I could have done about it?" Aiden was angry. It sounded very unjust to him.

"Yes, Aiden. Everyone has a place and a purpose. And if that purpose is to die to make someone who they were born to be, then that is their destiny, my friend."

Aiden was dumbstruck. He rifled through his emotions trying to find a suitable one to feel, but he drew a blank. There was nothing he could feel at that moment. Everyone's entire lives are pre-written? Destiny will always draw you to where you need to be, in order for that destiny to be fulfilled? It just seemed preposterous.

Samael continued. "Everything you have ever done,

everything anyone has ever done for you or to you, all lead you to this point, Aiden, just so Naomi could become who she was born to be."

"But what about me?"

"Everyone has a purpose, Aiden. And that was yours. David came to you, Peter and Jane came to you, purely so you could meet Naomi. All four of them were your destiny, Aiden. And in turn, everyone you ever met, you changed slightly and made better, and they changed you too. And by dying, you have changed Naomi. Knowing you has made her a better person."

"Naomi is now who she was born to be, because of me?"

"Not yet, Aiden. She has to discover it for herself first. She will meet others and fall in love again. And when she does, she will know who she has to be. And when she does, it will be because of you, and she will know it."

Aiden felt abused by fate. He felt like he had achieved nothing in his life at all now. It had all been for other people. Those he loved most, Naomi, Peter, Jane and David had all driven him to his death, although they didn't know it. Yet.

"But what would have happened if I had gone to a different college or University?"

"You would have met other people, Aiden, of course. But ultimately, whichever pathway you chose to follow, they would all have lead to Naomi and the others. They were your destiny."

Aiden felt resentment now. The emotion he couldn't find a moment ago had surfaced. He resented them all. He loved them all, but resented them for how they had treated him. Naomi, Peter, Jane and David had no idea that every one of their actions would have ultimately lead to his death, but nevertheless, his closest and dearest friends had killed him for the benefit of one of them. Where is the justice in that?

"This can't be true, Samael? There's no such thing as destiny." Aiden was protesting, begging almost. Feeling the resentment and anger build again inside him tears of hopelessness swelled in his eyes.

"Don't be so sure, Aiden. All of life is pre-written. There is nothing any mortal can do to influence it. From the moment of your conception, to the moment of your death, everything that happens to you is foretold and is the destiny for something or someone."

The frustration and anger overflowed and Aiden lost his temper, pacing heavily along the pathway towards Westminster Bridge and then back towards the London Eye. "But why couldn't Naomi become who she was destined to be with me alive? It's so bloody unfair! I love her, Samael, can't you see that?"

"Yes, we can, Aiden." Said Samael calmly. "And that is why we let you come back, so you could tell her one last time."

"But I want to tell her I love her every day for the rest of her life! Why did I have to die, Samael? Why?"

"Quite simply, because it was your time to. Any earlier or later and Naomi would miss her own destiny. Dying that night was yours."

"How? How did I die? And how exactly did my death at that moment ensure Naomi's destiny?"

"Aiden, what concern is that of yours now? You do not need to know."

As Aiden was about to speak, he turned to see that Samael had vanished. He had not told him what he wanted to know. He left without a goodbye or anything, leaving him near Westminster Bridge, in the middle of London and a long walk from home, and Naomi.

-|-

How long it would take Aiden to walk back home he had no idea. *"Why am I worried how long it takes to get home? It feels like I've got eternity to get there."* He thought.

Clouds had rolled in slowly and the sky had turned a grey brown colour. They looked busy, like London on a busy Friday evening before Christmas. They were laden down with rain as a shopper would be with bags of presents; getting on as quickly as possible against the tide of the other shoppers, each trying to go in their own direction but inexorably drawn in the same direction as everyone else. Swept along with the crowd.

The sky grew darker and soon, the pavement was speckled with spits and spats of rain as the beginning of the downpour became intent on washing the streets clean of the daily grime. Aiden lifted his shirt collar to protect himself from the deluge.

He did it out of habit, he supposed. He couldn't get wet. On his side of the veil, he could see the rain, but not feel it.

Before too long though, he stopped and as he turned his face upwards to have his face cleaned as well, the droplets didn't appear to be touching him. They passed straight though him to the paving slabs beneath. *"Of course, I can't get wet."* He thought to himself. *"I'm a bloody ghost. I cannot touch, and I cannot be touched."* His heart sank and he found a bench.

As he sat slumped like a tramp, Aiden watched the world rush past him. Everyone seemed to be in a hurry all of a sudden. Mums hastily pulled rain covers over push chairs to protect their precious cargo, old ladies put up their see through brollies and businessmen protected their pristine hair-dos with newspapers and briefcases. Their footsteps were splashing in the inevitable puddles, soaking socks and hems, leaving streaks of grime on neatly pressed suit trousers. Aiden smiled at it the scene. How many times had he been one of the unprepared masses for the autumn weather of London? How many times had his own head been covered by a newspaper and his own suit trousers needing to be cleaned after dashing for the tube or the bus? He missed that now, and he missed the feeling of the rain on his head. It seemed funny that it is quite often the trivial things you miss most, like a cup of proper English tea when in a foreign country.

Reflecting now on the warning Samael had given him, Aiden started to formulate his decision.

He desperately wanted to be with Naomi, watching over her for the rest of her days. He had promised her that he would never leave her and that was a promise he felt he could not break. The thought of leaving her alone at all never crossed his mind. He missed her terribly, despite being in the same room as her. But, he felt deaf and mute all the time around her, or anyone for that matter; the only person that could hear him was himself, inside his own head. He had so much to say, and now he had so little time in which to say it. Three days, and the Principium would come for him, and if he did not go with them, then they would allow this Charon character to find him and take him to Hell. He had to find a way to speak to Naomi.

He decided that he could not leave Naomi alone. An eternity with her was of course worth every year of it. But to leave Naomi alone, to fall in love with another man and be loved by him? No. No way. Aiden was the only man for her, the angel had told him so, for crying out loud. He couldn't let another man touch her. She was his. They were as good as married before he died. He even had his best man organised. He was going to propose at Christmas. The ring was well hidden in the toe of one his old pairs of trainers. Not very romantic, admittedly, but Aiden knew that was one place Naomi was never going to look.

However, if this was going to happen, he would have to find a way to stay away from Charon for the next sixty or so years. He would fight the ferryman, and claw his way out of hell to be with her if he had to.

Love does this sort of thing to a man, Aiden supposed. A man can be so in love with one woman that there is nothing any body or any thing can do to keep them apart.

Aiden started talking to himself. "It may have been my destiny to die so she could become the person she was born to be, but she will not do it alone. I'll keep watch over her. Bugger the Principium, and bugger the Ferryman too. I'm going to take back my destiny and make it my own."

30th October

Great Aunty Esther had seen a lot and the shelves in her room in the nursing home were a collection of the family history. Pictures of her lost brothers and sisters stood in dusty little picture frames on the shelves and her husband that died too young gazed down at her from above the bed.

She had never married again. She couldn't bare to love another after him. After he had gone, she dedicated her life to baking cakes and presiding over the family as the gentle, but slightly infirm matriarch. Slowly though she had deteriorated and it was Aunty Esther herself that decided to move into care, not wanting to be a burden on the family. Now, it was only Naomi who made regular visits. Esther didn't seem too worried. Her mind had started to stray and she revisited her memories and people through her photographs and treasured albums.

Naomi loved Aunt Esther very much, and made time to go and see her every couple of weeks at the home where she stayed with a sweet, but all-be-it slightly eccentric collection of other old dears. She quite enjoyed going to see her. She enjoyed making Aunty Esther a cup of tea or two and listening to her stories. She also secretly enjoyed the flirtatious comments she received from the old boys there too. They always had a twinkle in their eye when they saw her as well as a good old fashioned chat-up line or two. Having seen some of their photos, had they been fifty years younger, she would have gladly accepted a date with some of them.

They mostly sat in winged arm chairs with plastic upholstery that squeaked when they moved. These poor old dears had to have the furniture protected from any accidents they might have. They couldn't help it. They couldn't help that they had lost a lot of control of their faculties and functions, and smelt vaguely of urine and colostomy bags. Never-the-less though, her visits were always pleasant. It gave her a chance to escape from her hectic life and sit with her Aunty Esther and learn something of how life and love used to be 'back in the day'. It always brought a smile to her face to listen to the innocence of nineteen forties and fifties loving.

Walking into the home through the automatic doors, Naomi was overcome as always by the smell. It was too much cleaning fluid mixed in with the unmistakable aroma of old age. It didn't take long to get over it, it was just one of those things. Perhaps her sense of smell was numbed by the acid in the air.

Waving to the nurse on the reception desk, she walked through the living room and was greeted by the residents as she went. She stopped to pick up a tissue one of them had dropped on the way passed, handed it back to the old lady, patted her on the hand and smiled sweetly to her.

Down the hall, she passed a gentleman struggling on his frame. She knew Albert from when Aunty Esther came to the home a few years ago. He looked dreadfully frail now and Naomi helped him along to the living room and into 'his' chair. She feared he didn't have long left and gently squeezed his shoulder as she said that she had to go and see Esther. His crumpled old face drew itself unsteadily into a smile, a hand shaking it's way up to hers on his shoulder and patted it softly, thanking her for her kindness. Poor old chap.

Down the hall and looking into Aunty Esther's room, Naomi saw her sitting as she always did, looking out the window towards the hills in the distance, humming to herself an unrecognisable tune. The old lady seemed very happy for someone close to ninety years of age. She could still get herself around though. Nothing was going to get her down.

The sun was streaming through the window down onto her knees, allowing her to leave the blanket off her legs for a while, the natural warmth gently baking her old legs through her pop-socks and long skirt. Naomi stood against the door frame for a moment and watched her, happy in her own little world and a lifetime of memories to think back on.

"Hello, Naomi." Said Aunty Esther without looking. "Come in and sit down."

"How did you know it was me, Aunty Esther" Naomi replied with wide smile.

"Your smell, deary. Your smell. You don't smell like bleach and wee like everyone else here!" Aunty Esther chuckled to herself as Naomi came into the room and helped her out of her chair.

"I can do it, lovey, I can do it."

"Come on Aunty, let me help you" Naomi took the old lady's arm and helped her into her 'reception chair' as she called it: The one she sat in when she had guests. It had a clear path to the kettle and to the worn oval coffee table in front of the two chairs around it.

"Leave it. I can do it. Let me put the kettle on. Sit down, there's a good girl." Aunty Esther had a stoop and looked like she was constantly bending over to duck beneath low beams in an old house.

"Can I help . . .?"

"No, Naomi. Stop fussing, I'll do it. What brings you here today. I wasn't expecting you."

"Oh, well...I need to tell you something, Aunty."

"It can't be good news if you're stumbling over your words. Come on, out with it."

"It's Aiden, Aunty. I'm sorry I've not been to see you before now. You remember Aiden, don't you?"

"Yes, of course I do." She snapped "I may be old, but I'm not stupid. What about him? He's just come in, can't he tell me himself?"

Stunned, Naomi's heart began to race as she looked around her in the small room. There was no-one there with them. They were perfectly alone.

"No Aunty, he's not. He can't be. He . . ." Her voice trailed off as she reached into her handbag for a tissue and looked to the ceiling, apparently searching for strength to hold herself together.

"Have you two split up?" Aunty Esther filled the uncomfortable gap.

Naomi coughed back her need to break down. "Something like that, Aunty, yes. He died three weeks ago. His funeral was last week. I'm so sorry I couldn't get here any sooner."

Aunty Esther's fingers slipped on the glaze of the china cups and sent one suddenly skidding along the worktop. She stood perfectly still. The natural shake in her hands now gone. She looked at the cupboard door in front of her. "Really, dear? Maybe I'm so used to seeing you both together that my old mind is seeing things. Yes, that's it. My old mind is playing tricks on me. I'm very sorry to hear that. He was a lovely man. A real keeper."

"I know aunty. He was."

"Time to move on now, though, eh? Don't waste time moping about it. Pick yourself up, brush yourself down and get on with it! You're too young to be bowed down." Aunty Esther's matter-of-factness was interestingly refreshing. Here was an old lady who had seen her fair share of lost friends and funerals and had every right to be so blunt. These aged folk were made of much tougher stuff than most people many years their junior.

The tea now made, Aunty Esther carefully brought the tray over to the little table, spilling a few drops of milk from the small jug and nearly losing the teapot as her slippered foot caught the edge of the table. Naomi reached up and helped guide the tray down, but still giving the aged aunt a feeling of doing it herself. "Shall I be mother?" Naomi said with a smile as Aunty Esther sat down in her chair, leaning back slightly with her hands in her lap.

"Yes please, dear. You're very kind."

The two ladies sat in silence for a moment as Naomi made the tea, added two spoons of sugar for Aunty Esther, and none for herself. "What happened with Aiden then, Naomi? What happened to the poor boy?"

"He was out with some friends and he collapsed and died of an aneurysm. He was gone in seconds, apparently. The paramedics declared him dead right there. There was nothing anyone could have done." Naomi was surprised at how straight to the point she sounded. This was the first time she had really spoken about it to anyone, preferring to keep everything to herself, but now she felt a bit more ready to talk.

Aunty Esther looked shocked. "The poor, poor boy. So young as well. How old was he?"

"Thirty four."

"Such a shame, and such a nice man too. Very handsome, I thought." Aunty Esther looked at Naomi with a sparkle in her eye. *'The old girl always had a naughty side to her'*, Naomi thought. *'Perhaps that's why she's still so sprightly; an active imagination and a lust for life.'*

"And how are you getting on, dear?" Aunty Esther's tone was certainly serious. She adored her eldest niece. Naomi was the only one who bothered to come to see her and spend time talking to her, keep her up to date on family business. She was a very caring girl, a real catch for Aiden. Such a pity he had to leave her like that.

"I'm OK, thank you Aunty. Aiden's funeral was as nice as it could be. There were lots of people there. I had no idea how many people liked him enough to want to come. It was very touching. I thought I . . ." Her voice quietened again as she was about to mention what she thought she had seen, and then changed the subject. "The wake was very nice." She sounded dreamy, lost for a moment. "Lots of people came to that too, but mostly closer friends and family...I'm looking forward to getting on with my life now though. My good friend Jane came round on the evening of the wake and gave me a bit of a talking to. She said that I have to move on and let Aiden live in my heart and to never forget him."

"People are very different to those my age, you know, dear. When I was your age, if you lost your husband, that was it, you never married again. One love, that's all we allowed ourselves. When I lost your Uncle Joseph, I swore there would never be another man for me. I don't expect you to do the same, though, dear. You are too young and pretty to not allow someone else to love you. You deserve it, my girl. Look at you, you are a picture." Aunty Esther smiled again and the twinkle in her eye returned once more.

Naomi's phone rang out as she blushed at Aunty Esther's praise. She took it out of her handbag and looked at the message. She quickly put it back, so not to interrupt the conversation any longer. "Sorry, Aunty. Thank you."

"Seems like you already have an admirer." Aunty Esther was very intuitive and could tell when anyone was hiding something. She smiled a cheeky smile that Naomi instantly recognised as one of all-knowing and it wasn't trying to hide anything from her. She already knew.

"Just a friend, Aunty." She avoided eye contact, instead looking at the picture of Uncle Joseph on the wall above the bed.

"Tell me more, Naomi. There's more about Aiden isn't there? You can't tell me you're not keeping something from me."

"Well, at the funeral, I think, but I don't know for sure... and then when I got home. . ." She was struggling to find the right words to explain what she had seen. *'It shouldn't be this difficult, just tell it like it is!'* she thought to herself.

"You saw him, didn't you?" Aunty Esther's voice dropped to a near whisper, as if about to tell a secret. "And you don't believe me that's he's here now, do you?"

Naomi went cold. This was the second time Aunty Esther had mentioned him being there, but she couldn't see anything. "Yes, I thought I had seen him. I thought I saw him at the funeral and again when I got home. But it couldn't have been him, Aunty. He's dead, and there's no coming back from that. And no, I don't believe he's here now. I can't see him, or feel him."

"Hmm, Naomi you are so blind to your heart aren't you? When your Uncle Joseph died, I was just as distraught as you, but do you know something?" Naomi shook her head and Aunty Esther leaned forward and touched her knee. "There's a very thin veil between us and them, you know. The dead are only a heartbreak away and sometimes they are right by our sides. It only takes enough longing and desire of the heart to see through that veil for a moment or two, and then they appear, standing there in front of us, looking just as we remember them."

"I can't believe that, Aunty. Once you're gone, you are gone."

"Don't be so certain dear girl. When Joseph died, I missed him terribly, as I am sure you do, Aiden. I could see Joseph any time I wanted to for a short while after he died, and I didn't even have to close my eyes and dream. He was right there with me. That is, until he went with the Principium Angeli." She looked regretful now, missing her late husband.

"The principi what?" said Naomi, confused and not really wanting to continue the conversation, but was now very interested in what the old lady had to say.

"The Principium Angeli. They are the ones who come and take the souls of the dead to wherever they have to go to. Heaven, I suppose. They came and took Joseph. They said that it was time to go and with a wave goodbye, he went with them one day. Just after lunch it was, just as I was about to have a nap. Another cup of tea, dear?"

Naomi's head was spinning. "Please. But what is the Principium Angeli? Where do they come from? Who are they?"

"Like I said, dear, they take the souls away. Cleaning up the realm between here and wherever they all end up. They are angels. There are nine of them in all I think. Everyone has heard of the head honcho, Gabriel. He's the one who does most of the talking, he's the most powerful I think. There's also Michael, Uriel, Raphael and Samael. I forget the others, but everyone knows Sataniel. He's not with them anymore. He went a long time ago."

"How do you know all this, Aunty Esther? You're scaring me."

"Uncle Joseph used to talk to me in my sleep. We would share dreams together. It was nice for a few weeks after he died. It gave me a chance to say goodbye properly. We used to go anywhere we wanted and do anything we wanted to in my dreams for that short time. It was so lovely, and that is where he lives now. In my dreams." Aunty Esther started to look up to the photograph of her handsome Joseph above her bed. She sniffed and turned back to Naomi. "There's no need to be scared, my dear. It will come to us all, eventually."

Naomi couldn't quite find the words to reply with. Instead, she sat uncomfortably still with her tea in one hand and the other stroking the arm of the chair. She looked anywhere but at Aunty Esther who was again gazing at Joseph's picture in silence. Memories rushed through her head until she turned back and looked Naomi in the eye with a comforting gaze. "We will all meet the Principium when they come for us. Did I ever tell you I met them once, briefly."

Staggered, Naomi coughed, slopping tea in her china cup. "No, Aunty, you didn't. What happened?" She felt like she was entertaining a child who had come home from school with a tall tale to tell. She couldn't believe a word of it. God, Angels, the afterlife.? What a load of rubbish. As far as she was concerned, when you are gone, you are gone.

"Do you remember when I had my heart attack about 10 years ago?" Aunty Esther waited for an answer, seemingly keen to tell Naomi all about it.

"Yes, Aunty, I do. Didn't you nearly die?"

"Nearly? I did die that day. Not at home though, but when they got me to the hospital." Aunty Esther was almost excited to be telling her story.

Naomi started to become interested "Oh. I didn't know that."

"Well, after the ambulance got me to the hospital, the doctors and nurses did some things to me. I don't know what, but I seem to remember I had a drip in my arm and a mask over my face to help me breathe properly. There were a few of them around me, and I remember seeing them and hearing them talk about me like I wasn't there. But I was you know."

Naomi nodded and drank more of her tea knowing precisely what was coming next even though she had never heard the story before.

Aunty Esther continued. "I began to feel very sleepy and very light. The doctors and nurses started to move around me. Quickly this time, and I could hear a single high pitched tone in my ears. Then I think I must have fallen asleep and began to have a most bizarre dream." She sat as upright as she could in her chair and was now leaning forwards, beckoning Naomi to come closer as if she was about to divulge an incredible secret.

"It was then dear, that I died. The doctors told me afterwards. But it is what I saw whilst I was dead that I've never told anyone before."

Naomi put down her tea, completely intrigued by the old lady's tale. She leaned forwards too, taking hold of Aunty Esther's outstretched hand.

"Go on, Aunty. What happened in your dream?"

"Well," she purred "I don't think it was a dream as such, but I felt myself being gently pulled upwards. There was no resistance like my body was coming with me, but it was my soul leaving my body and moving upwards in the room. I could turn and see everyone doing things to me, but I couldn't feel anything at all, only peace."

Naomi raised her eyebrows at what she was hearing. It sounded completely plausible, but something inside her made her dismiss this experience as nothing but nonsense.

"Now, the next thing I remember was the ceiling of the room becoming very bright and I went to it. Inside the light, I could see nine figures standing there in front of me, blindingly bright and they had their arms out stretched, welcoming me. Like this." She pulled her hand away from Naomi's and copied the gesture. "I went to them and the leader spoke to me. He said *'You are The Lord's child, Esther, and he is ready for us to take you to him.'* I was all confused and asked them who they were. The leader told me his name was Gabriel and he was one of the Principium Angeli and that they are the angels that meet the souls of the newly deceased." She paused. "They are the guides from this life to the next, Naomi"

Naomi was so stunned, she wasn't sure when she had last taken a breath. Her eyes were quite wide at the conviction with which Aunty Esther was telling her story. It seemed so far fetched that she thought it could never be true. But there was something about it, and coming from this aged aunt that she looked up to, that said the story had to be true.

"What happened next, Aunty?"

"Other than the nine figures in front of me, I couldn't see anything else at all. I didn't feel hot or cold, elated nor frightened. I was wearing the clothes I had on before going to hospital and everything around me was blank. It didn't seem to have a colour, it was just blank. I can't explain it very well." She wet her lips with a sip of tea. "I asked who they all were, and all they said was their names. No second names, and they only said the one word each, except for Gabriel. He said, *'Esther, dear child. Now does not have to be your time. You can return to your body and live out your days until your time truly comes, or you can choose to come with us now and your time of life will be over.'*"

So engrossed with the story now, as tall as it may be, Naomi had blocked out all other sounds from her ears apart from Aunty Esther's voice. It was much quieter and lower than normal. Perhaps she didn't want anyone else to hear what she was saying. After all, this story was far beyond what you would expect to hear from a little old lady in a nursing home. Stories of nineteen fifties dance halls and staying out till ten o'clock, maybe. But a near death experience?

"Just then, Naomi, my Joseph walked up to me and took me by the hand." Aunty Esther's eyes began to well with tears and she reached up her sleeve for a tissue.

Naomi shuffled her chair forwards and she placed her hands on Aunty Esther's knees, squeezing them gently. "You don't have to go on, Aunty. It's alright."

"Oh, it's not painful, dear. It's the most precious memory I have. Not everyone can say they hugged their husband or wife years after they died, can they?"

"No, I suppose not, Aunty."

"Well, when I was holding Joseph he told me that I had to come back and finish my life and that I would be with him again soon enough. There was no rush, he wasn't getting any older! He looked so happy and younger than when he died. He told me that I had to come back for the family. He said you all needed me and will do for many years to come. Like now I suppose. You've come to me and I hope I've helped you."

Naomi smiled reassuringly at Aunty Esther. "Yes, Aunty Esther, I guess you have in a funny sort of way." Quite how she had helped, Naomi wasn't sure.

"So you see, I had to come back. I had a job to do. I didn't know it was the Principium Angeli that had taken Joseph that day during my map. I didn't make the connection until I had met them for myself. And now I am telling you, preparing you for when it is your turn to meet them. But you may not be lucky enough to come back for a second bite of the cherry. It depends if you still have a purpose for being here at all."

"But what about Aiden, Aunty? Is he really here?" Naomi had ignored the last part of the story with an involuntary shiver and was now more concerned about the presence of Aiden around her.

"I don't know for certain, dear girl. I thought I saw him, but clearly, as he is not here to see, I couldn't have. As I said, it must have been my old mind playing tricks on me. What does your heart say?" Aunty Esther looked uncomfortable as Naomi reclined in her seat, sighing deeply.

"Honestly, Aunty Esther, I have no idea. I thought I saw him at the funeral. No! I know I saw him at the funeral and thought I saw him at home that night. But does my heart say he's here? I have no idea what to think at the moment." Naomi was sounding frustrated.

"Well, dear. Has he tried to contact you? Perhaps in a dream or when you are alone at home?"

"No, I don't think so."

"I have Naomi, just not through your dreams, I haven't known how to." Aiden said, sitting on the bed beneath the photograph of Uncle Joseph. Coming here had been a very good idea; He had been given the key what he hoped would be the way he could actually speak to Naomi. All he had to do was get inside her head.

"Joseph used to come to me in my dreams. We could go anywhere and do anything then. My dreams became our world together. Tonight, as you go to sleep, be aware that if Aiden is with you, he may try to contact you. Now, it's nearly my lunchtime and I'm sure you've got better things to be doing than sitting talking to a batty old thing like me. I hope I'll see you again soon, Naomi. It's always a pleasure to see you."

Naomi felt as though she had been dismissed from her aunt's presence. "Oh, Okay, Aunty Esther. I'll pop by again in a couple of weeks." She sounded slightly put out, but polite none-the-less.

-|-

Escorting Aunty Esther to the dining room and sitting her down in her place at the table, Naomi then made her way back down the corridor towards the reception, rummaging in her bag for her phone. She needed to reply to the message she had received. On seeing the nurse Lucy, she stopped.

"Lucy? Really sorry to bother you. Do you have a moment?"

The young nurse stopped too, and her London accent sounded concerned. "Yes, of course. What's the matter?"

"It's Aunty Esther. Is everything alright with her? She's not been saying anything, err, odd has she?" Naomi wasn't sure how to put what she wanted to say.

"Nah, she's been really chirpy recently, and I've not heard say anything strange. Has she said anything we need to keep an ear out for?"

"Not really, I suppose. So she's not said anything about my Uncle Joseph, her late husband?"

"Oh him!" Lucy perked up and Naomi raised her eyebrows, wondering what on earth she was going to hear next. "Yeah, Esther talks about him all the time. What they got up to in their younger days. Joseph sounds like a real fun man."

Naomi was relieved. "That's good then. Yes, she loved him very much. She's not mentioned anything about seeing him recently, then?"

"Nah. She's as good as gold, is Esther. Lovely lady. Is there anything else?"

"No, thank you, Lucy. Bye for now."

"Bye, Naomi. See you in a couple of weeks."

As Lucy walked off, Naomi's eyes followed her into the dining room. There was Aunty Esther, sitting at the table with the others like it was some old people's tea party. She smiled to herself, pleased that the aged matriarch of her family still had some marbles left in the bag.

-|-

Sitting in her car, she pulled her phone out of her bag and read the message again. *'Hey, Naomi. Long time no see. When can we get together?'* She considered her answer carefully. Could she really rekindle her fling with him so soon after Aiden had gone? What they had together was nothing but a single evening together, snatched at a time when her and Aiden were arguing and he was feeling lonely. She replied honestly, but leaving the final answer open. *'I don't know.'* She typed slowly. *'It's not really a good idea, is it? We'll see. X'*

She felt bad that she couldn't give a definitive answer, and at the same time felt even worse because she could be interfering with someone elses happiness. It was all well and good having feelings for him, but could she? dare she start a relationship with him now? She wasn't sure, and as she drove off, she tried to justify to herself that it really was alright to start seeing him. She would take it slowly at first, and then get into it properly. But then she would doubt her decision and change her mind. She really didn't know what she wanted.

By the time she got home, a reply to her message had arrived. She sat down in the living room and looked at her phone again. *'It's been such a long time. You've got nothing to worry about now, have you? I can book us a table for dinner somewhere if you want to get away from the flat. I want you.'*

Banging the phone down on the table in frustration, Naomi got up and went to the bathroom. "How dare he send me a message like that? The cheek of it! He knows damn well that Aiden hasn't long been gone, and now he sends me demands like that." she filled the flat with a loud voice, as if talking to this guy in a different room. The sound made the flat feel less empty.

Although the message had offended her, deep down inside, she found it a little arousing. She could feel the tingle of the promise of sex with him well up inside her. It felt good, and he was right; she didn't have anything to worry about any more. But, she still did not feel like it was the right thing to do. But what did she have to lose?

Back in the living room, she picked up the phone again, and turned it absentmindedly around in her hands, deciding on how to reply. She pursed her lips and looked down at the smeared black screen. *'Hi. No. Not yet. It's too soon after Aiden. I can't do it at the moment. I'll let you know when, if I feel ready to see you.'* There, done. She pressed send after a short pause. Yes, she felt sure she had done the right thing. It was too soon after Aiden. He was only cremated some twelve days ago, after all.

All Aiden's things were still in the flat, and it really didn't seem right to be seeing someone else so soon after the funeral. But at the same time, it did feel right, even it was to have someone feeling close to her; body to body, skin to skin. Mouth to mouth. She thought the feelings must be a rebound reaction for certain, but she would resist them. Looking up to the living room door, she began to think that if she were to move on, she ought to begin to move out some of Aiden's things, but that would be a job for another day.

31st October

Halloween was always one of Naomi's favourite nights. She and Aiden always made an effort to go out for the evening dressed up as a spicy devil or a rotting zombie to one of the local pubs putting on a disco and cheap blood red cocktails. They would always book the following day off work too, just in case of a raging hangover. No such luck this year though. Naomi was sitting alone at her usual spot in the kitchen overlooking the street, and through the drizzle streaked window, she watched the parade of Halloween costumes marching up the road to the Royal Oak pub. Undoubtedly, that is where Aiden would have taken her tonight, if he was there of course.

A gaggle of scantily clad witches passed on the other side of the road to the flat. They were cackling as they tried to keep stay balanced on their ridiculously high heels. Once of them was hanging onto the arm of a wizard who was trying to hold her up. They must have had some drinks earlier in the evening as it wasn't even nine o'clock yet and this group were pretty messed up already.

Naomi thought that a couple of the witches should never have gone out dressed like that. It's all very well going out looking sexy as a witch, but like that? No. If you are going to dress sexy, then a size sixteen costume with a size twenty four body shoe-horned into it was never going to work, was it? She laughed to herself and then chastised her own damning catty sarcasm.

Bored and envious of the witches heading out for a fun time at the pub disco, Naomi retired to the living room with a glass of wine, a cushion to hide behind and the horror movie on Channel Four. She wasn't sure if she should be watching a movie like that, on a night like this given what she had been through recently. *'It's only a movie.'* she told herself and settled into the corner of the sofa and watched the same predictable story line of most horror movies.

She had seen the movie before and quickly her thoughts moved on to Aiden and what their future together may have held for them. Daydreaming of a family, a home in country and all the romantic things people do when they are in love, she found that a cold streak had formed on her cheek of a tear drying. She didn't even realise she was softly crying. The tears were just coming out. No heavy sobbing or anger or frustration, just a gentle remembrance of what was and what might have been.

Naomi found it comforting to be thinking about it, cleansing. She felt it was like she was moving on in her heart. There was nothing she could do to bring Aiden back and she was accepting that fact. She had been over it a hundred times before, getting angry at the thoughts, but now she found that she was calm, feeling bitter-sweet with the memories. The feelings and thoughts were being placed in their own box and kept someone safe and secure in her heart; Aiden's box of memories.

By keeping them tucked away, but easily accessible, Naomi figured that this was how she would be able to move on. She would have an emotional spring clean and then wake tomorrow with a clearer mind.

Plus, she had a coffee date planned with David in a couple of days time. He was sure to ask for more than just that coffee though. It was in his nature. He wouldn't be satisfied with just that. This was just the precursor for him to test the water. He had always fancied her, she could tell. Men were so easy to read. Well, she figured she would see how it went and wait to see what he said.

She couldn't go headlong into a new relationship though. It would be disrespectful to Aiden. No, if anything were to happen, it would have to be slow to start with.

The movie finished just as the witches made their way back down the street. It was after eleven now, closer to midnight actually, Naomi noted from the DVD player. Time for bed. The movie was as rubbish as it was the first three times she had seen it, but she had had a positive evening, though packaging up her thoughts and feelings for Aiden.

-|-

Aiden looked down on Naomi sleeping soundly. Her breathing was shallow and her eyes moved behind their lids. She was dreaming of the day on holiday where her favourite photograph was taken, the one on her bedside table. It was the last thing she had looked at before switching off the light and rolling over, hugging a pillow tightly. It was copy of this photo that she had given in at the chapel on the day of her funeral.

-|-

Baking sun shone down on Naomi's naked back as she lay on a sandy red towel on the beach on the island. There was not a single cloud in the sky as she watched Aiden walk up the sand from the sea, his lean body dripping with salty water. Romantically, she thought he looked like James Bond; all buff, tanned and strong. She smiled to herself and returned her eyes to the paperback she was thumbing through.

A warm breeze flicked up some sand onto Naomi's towel and with a huff, she brushed it off just as Aiden reached her and accidentally added to it with his footsteps. She growled playfully as she brushed harder. Aiden grabbed his from the ground and began to rub himself down before slumping down on the sun bed next to Naomi's. He placed his hands behind his head, biceps twitching as they warmed in the sun. He closed his eyes and took a deep breath. "That was a good swim." he said, sounding happy with himself for what Naomi could only consider to be a quick dip rather than a proper swim.

"Was it?" Naomi replied, not looking up from her book. "I'm pleased."

Aiden was content. "Hmm."

She turned her head and looked at his profile over the top of her sunglasses. He liked it when she did this. He thought it made her look like a naughty, sexy teacher. He missed it this time though, his eyes were closed and comfortable. Naomi admired his profile. She loved him with all her heart and soul. For such a strong character, she never thought she could love someone with so much passion. He had arrived in her life at a wedding not too long ago. It only took one dance and a conversation for him to completely entrance her. To her, he was now irreplaceable.

That evening, they dressed for dinner after making love in the shower. Their naked skin glowing with the aftermath of orgasm and a dowsing of hot water. It wasn't a very big shower, but big enough for a their encounter.

The white shirt Aiden had put on seemed to gleam in the light of the hotel bedroom compared to the deepening tan of his body. The shirt was cut and fitted in all the right places and made him look to her like her own Adonis. She loved looking at him, his body and the way he moved. Everything about him seemed perfect.

Lying on the bed, Aiden watched as Naomi finished drying her hair with what was possibly the worst hairdryer in the world. It seemed to take an age to dry, but it was a pleasure to watch her make herself look even more beautiful. She sat naked in front on the mirror and he could see her back and her front from where he was lying. 'The best of both worlds.' He thought.

Finally, her hair was done, hanging loosely over her shoulders. She stood up and went to the wardrobe. Reaching in, she pulled out two dresses. Turning to Aiden, holding one in front of her, she said "Well, which one?".

"Umm, don't know' he said, 'let's see the other one."

As quick as a flash and a twitch of her hips, Naomi switched the dresses, giving Aiden a tantalising glimpse of her body between them. "Errr, the other one again..." he teased. Again, the dresses quickly changed places giving Aiden another sneaky glimpse. God she was sexy. He considered not bothering going down for dinner, and just lying in bed all night draping themselves over each other.

"The other one." he said firmly, sniffing.

Hanging the blue dress back in the wardrobe, Naomi pulled the pink one over her head, and shaking herself and the dress into position, she adjusted her breasts into the cups and put on some strappy sandals. The fact that Naomi never wore underwear in the evenings on holiday would regularly drive Aiden crazy with desire. It was their little secret, and walking down the street, Naomi would egg him on by telling him how the breeze up her dress was keeping her cool.

After dinner and sitting at the poolside bar, they had both had too much to drink, and were laughing like a couple of teenagers when a photographer approached them and snapped their picture.

Aiden had put his arm around Naomi's shoulders and she was holding her wine glass between the fingers of both hands. Their faces were rosy with booze and after-sun lotion. They looked happy, and they were; The happiest either of them had ever been.

They didn't need any other company, they were enough for each other at the moment, and besides, they were too wrapped up in each other's eyes for anyone to get a look-in anyway. Other couples and families in the hotel would look at them having fun and reflect on their own relationships. Maybe they were as happy as them once upon a time. Not now though, and more than one couple were envious.

The photographer told them they could pick the picture up in the morning from his desk in the foyer and pay for it then.

After dancing in the club for most of the night, Naomi and Aiden retired to bed, very drunk indeed, but Aiden had other ideas rather than sleep.

Noisily creeping along the corridor to their room in the kind of sneaky way only drunk people can, Aiden pinned Naomi up against the door with her hands above her head. He kissed her hard. She tasted of wine, he of beer. It was passionate and messy; their tongues not always on target.

Grabbing both her wrists with one hand now, Aiden reached for the key to open the door. It swung open with a bang, bashed into the wall and they both fell through the gap with Aiden surprisingly agile in saving Naomi from hitting the floor. The door closed quietly, isolating them from the outside world. They were alone again.

Naomi hauled herself up off the floor, opened the balcony door and stepped outside. Aiden crawled onto the bed.

-|-

Naomi's sleeping body had began to move a little as if doing a little dance to some music in her head. She was humming quietly.

Aiden looked at her adoringly. He put his face close to hers to see if she was saying anything he could understand. He could smell her breath, it minty was and fresh and smelled vaguely sweet as he moved his face closer to hers. Without realising it, the end of his nose had started to penetrate Naomi's cheek.

'I wonder if this is how Naomi's Uncle Joseph made contact with Esther.' he thought. He moved closer still until he could feel her cheek on his and then, and without taking a second thought, he slowly pushed his face all way into Naomi's head, leaving a thin layer of sweat-like condensation on her skin where he had entered. He could see everything in her dream. Had he really entered her subconscious mind, just by looking inside her head with his? 'Now this could be interesting.' he thought.

Unaware of the visitor in her head, Naomi continued dreaming, reliving the night the photo was taken.

-|-

Feeling the breeze coming from the balcony, Aiden looked up and saw Naomi leaning on the rail, the wind blowing her short dress up at the back, revealing her firm, rounded buttocks, and just a glimpse of what lay between.

Standing up like a man possessed with lust, he walked outside behind her and put his hands on her hips. She felt good, roomy and the most sensuous thing any man could touch. With one hand, he began to undo the zip on the back of the dress, and with the other, he reached under the dress to the inside of her thigh. He felt her leg twitch as he moved the hand on the zip and the hand on her leg up. She said nothing but a quiet, appreciative moan. She shivered at the touch of his finger tips as they ran the zip down her back. The expectation was making her insides churn.

Tilting her pelvis back, Aiden's fingers began to feel how welcoming she had become during the evening. The smooth skin of her folds, allowing his fingers to explore them.

Naomi's dress fell off her shoulders and hung off Aiden's arm. She turned, forcing his exploring fingers to move away and the dress fell to the floor, the hems twitching in the breeze round her ankles like a hunted animal's limbs twitching as it's life slips away.

Facing him now, Naomi touched a finger to his lips, keeping them from coming near hers. Aiden stared deeply into her eyes and then began to follow her fingers down to his shirt-front. She undid each button carefully, and then let a fingertip cruise over his skin until it found the next button, and then the next. Aiden noticed her erect nipples and wanted to touch them, kiss them, but his movement was slapped away with a firm but playful "Nooo..." So he stood there and allowed her to undress him.

Using a finger to bring his chin up from his chest and the amazing view of her breasts, his eyes met hers again. Skillfully and unnoticed, her hands moved to his trousers. They expertly undid his belt, button and zip and then his trousers dropped to the floor with the metallic clunk of the belt buckle, slightly muffled by the dress that was already on the floor. Now, with the palm of one hand, she slid it over the front of his tight boxer shorts and with the other, she ran a fingernail down his chest and into the top of the boxers. He took a sharp intake of breath as Naomi's skin made contact, too scared to let it go, the excitement building. It felt slightly cooler than his own skin. It was then joined by the other hand, and between them, they swiftly dispatched the underwear to the floor to join the rest.

-|-

Enjoying sharing the dream with Naomi, Aiden also discovered that he could feel her emotions too. He could feel everything she could and hear her thoughts too. Could he really be inside her mind like this? Good old Aunty Esther, giving him the idea of how to communicate. If it was good enough for her and Uncle Joseph, it should be good enough for Naomi and him.

Her dream was so real, and he could feel himself as aroused by the dream as she seemed to be. He could stand at the edge of the dream and look into like it was on television. Or, he could walk around it just like he could in the living room of the flat or the funeral. He was observing the dream from inside the mind of the dreamer.

'Now this is very interesting indeed.' Aiden thought as he watched himself and Naomi making love on the balcony of a hotel room like the world would end tomorrow. He felt a lot like a peeping-tom observing a couple's most intimate moments through a window, which was ridiculous as he was one of the people he was watching. More to the point, he was inside someone else's head, which is where no-one should ever be apart from the person who usually resides there.

As the dream continued, Aiden stood silently and watched the couple on the balcony move inside to the bed and continue their lovemaking there. He didn't want to try to interact with her like this. It didn't feel right. There couldn't be two Aiden's in the dream with her. That would be too strange.

Reviewing the situation, Aiden decided that now was the moment to try and contact Naomi. His permitted time would run out tomorrow. This was the last time he could contact her and then that would be it if he chose to go with the Principium.

Her sleeping body lay still now , her face still damp with the contact of Aiden's presence. Her subconscious had begun to register that it was not alone and was searching for the source of interruption.

The dream ended abruptly. The hotel room vanished, the couple on the bed disappeared and left nothing but the black swirling of the inside of her eyelids at that heavy, semi-conscious relaxed state just before sleep sets in. Her body was so calm she couldn't feel the position of her limbs but was now very aware that she was not alone and that her face was wet. She began to wake up as her pulse quickened and adrenaline started to pump around her veins, the sense of being watched growing all the time.

Feeling the change in her, Aiden quickly took the opportunity to say something. He hoped Aunty Esther was right and that he could communicate like this. After all, it had worked for her and Uncle Jospeh. *"Naomi"* he whispered.

Her mind sprang into life at the sound in her head. *"Naomi, it's me, Aiden."*

The voice was so real and alive that it startled her awake. She scrambled up the bed and sat huddled against the head board like she had seen a huge spider on the duvet. She tried to get away from the sound. It sounded like Aiden was actually in the room with her, lying next to her, but there was no-one there. Her breathing was rapid.

She felt cold, her whole body had goose bumps and the right side of her face felt wet. She licked her lips. What she tasted was not the salty taste of sweat, but water. Strange. She quickly wiped it away and looked around the room, trying to find where the voice had come from. Her eyes looked panicked as they darted round the room from the dresser to the window and to the bedside table.

She noticed that in her scrambling she had knocked over the picture on the bedside table and a coffee cup had emptied itself onto the floor.

Aiden, who had been forced out of her head as she moved up the bed stood and looked on at the confused Naomi. What had gone wrong? She must have heard him. He tried again. Gingerly, he approached with the intent of properly talking to her from inside her head..

They were face to face again as Naomi started to calm down with her hand on her chest feeling her heart banging on her rib cage. Her hair was a damp, matted mess. She slumped back against the headboard.

As before, Aiden slowly started to push his face against hers, bringing their minds closer together. Naomi began to feel a light film of water begin to spread across her face, very slowly, gently. Aiden didn't want to startle her so he crept in slowly.

Naomi froze as she realised something was touching her face. It felt cold and clammy and made her skin prickle all over her body and her heart bang loudly in her ears. Gripped by a sudden and incredible fear, Naomi let the condensation spread over her face. She wanted to get up and run, but there was nothing she could see to get up and run from. She felt paralysed, frozen to the spot, confused and breathing heavily. Adrenaline was shooting round her body, making her feel light headed.

The condensation reached both her ears before Aiden decided to say anything. He had entered her mind again as carefully as he entered her sometimes where they were making love, but this penetration was somehow much more intimate than that. This was entering somewhere where no-one had ever been before.

"Hello, Naomi."

The voice inside her head sounded again like Aiden was very close to her. It was so clear, crisp, and unmistakably him.

Naomi let out a scream and scrambled towards the foot of the bed, getting the covers caught around her knees. She thudded onto the floor, landing on her shoulders, legs still tangled up. Kicking furiously to release them in sheer terror, she rolled onto her knees and freed herself. Blindly, in the orange tinged dark of the bedroom, she half staggered, half ran to the bedroom door with arms out in front of her, flung it open and made for the kitchen.

Fumbling her fingers quickly down the wall to find the light switch, she clung onto the back of the nearest chair, nearly tipping it over as she leaned most of her weight onto it. She could barely stand; Her knees were weak, shaking though a mixture of terror, confusion and panic. Her hands and arms too, felt like they would give way at any moment. The fluorescent light was flickering on and off, trying to get started. She panted hard as she tried to catch her breath and looked back into the empty hallway, terrified of what, or who might come round the corner at any moment.

She put her hand to her heaving chest again in an effort to control her breathing and her heart felt like it could have burst through her chest at any second.

"It can't be him. It can't be! Aunty Esther couldn't have been right. Joseph couldn't have been talking to her. It must have been a dream. This must have been a dream too." Shaking her head, she tried to convince herself.

The glowing green clock on the microwave said three seventeen.

Aiden stood at the kitchen door looking very worried. Evidently he had scared Naomi senseless with his attempt to speak to her, but that was the only way he had found so far in which to successfully communicate. All he had achieved was to frighten the poor woman half to death.

Naomi looked exhausted. Breathing heavily and looking very worried, she appeared incredibly vulnerable standing there in the kitchen, naked legs trembling and hair all messy. He wasn't sure if her shivers were from being cold, scared or a combination of both.

Aiden took a single step into the kitchen to try again for a third time, and as he did so, the kitchen light finally flickered into life and Naomi, who was still looking through the door saw him approaching her. With a piercing shriek and almost a jump backwards, she fell over the chair onto the table and heavily onto the floor, her eyes all the time on Aiden who kept moving closer, mouthing some words to her. He looked as frightened as she was, but she was not wanting to stay in that kitchen one moment longer. Crawling on her hands and knees around the table, as if trying to hide from him, she made her escape back through the kitchen door, slamming it closed behind her

She sat in the dark hallway, leaning up against wall opposite the kitchen door and sobbed loudly.

"Aiden? Is that you?" she whispered as her shoulders racked themselves up and down and tears ran over her cheeks. "Aiden? Is that you?" she shouted at the kitchen door, shaking her head. She didn't know what to do now.

Invisible again, Aiden was now through the door and kneeling on the carpet in front of her, looking straight into her face, but too scared to try to speak to her again. She looked so tired, rung out from everything that had happened to her. He couldn't possibly put her through something like this again. Not yet anyway.

"Yes, it is." He said, knowing that she couldn't hear him any longer, but just hearing his own voice made him feel somehow better. *"I'm sorry, darling. So sorry."*

"Why Aiden? Why? Why? Why?" her head resting on the wall now, she looked up towards the blackness of the ceiling.

"I don't know, Naomi. I really don't know."

After several minutes of sitting in silence, her eyes having returned to being fixed on the kitchen door, Naomi cautiously made her way back to the bedroom, looking around her all the time to check to see if there was anyone watching her, she reached round the door and grabbed her dressing gown. She quickly put it on, and feeling more secure now and sure there was no-one with her, she went to the living room and sat curled up on the sofa after turning on every light in the room as well as the television. The bright lights and the extra noise made her feel safer. She set the volume on the television higher then normal, so if the voice she heard came back, it might be drowned out by the drivel she started watching.

Everything that had just happened was spinning round her head. She felt invaded, and sat on the sofa protecting herself with legs tucked up beneath her and arms folded, neck wrapped up with the thick dressing gown. The voice was so real, and so Aiden. She must have been dreaming. Must have. But then she had heard it for a second time, and then saw him in the kitchen after it woke her first of all. She did see him, didn't she? There's something not right with that. Not right at all. She must have been dreaming, or could she just be so tired that when she woke, the dream lingered on and brought Aiden to the kitchen door, somehow mixing her dream with reality.

She reached for the phone.

-|-

David had spent the evening with work colleagues at their favourite pub and returned home around midnight. He was more drunk than he hoped or even needed to be. He had a whiskey nightcap in one hand and the television remote in the other. He had idly flicked from channel to channel trying to find something of interest to take his mind off the month's events. He had presided over the funeral of his best friend and he thought he had developed some feelings for Naomi that he really shouldn't have done.

With his head, swimming leisurely at the bottom of the glass, his thoughts were not getting any clearer and there was nothing on telly he could focus his attention on.

Switching it off and sitting only by the glow of his reading light, he dozed gently in and out of an alcohol induced sleep. It was comfortable there, slouched in the chair with his glass spot-lit by the reading lamp. At least he couldn't loose the glass in the darkness of the rest of the room.

His tie was undone and his shirt was now all crumpled across his belly and chest. He looked a mess, a little tramp-like, or like the gambler who had lost at the casino. He didn't feel like he was drowning his sorrows though, he wasn't that sort of guy. He was just numbing them for a while, just enough to help him sleep.

After snoring himself awake he dragged himself out of his chair, drained his glass and after pulling a sour face on the sharpness of the liquor, made his way to the bathroom, grabbing hold of the back of the chair to steady himself. He wasn't drunk, just a little tired and unsteady. That's what he told himself anyway.

Standing in front of the bathroom mirror with his shoulders rounded, he looked hunched as he yawned heavily and scratched the day's growth on his chin. He turned on the tap, watching the water spiral down the plug until he felt comfortable he could wash his face without scalding himself or freezing himself awake.

He looked more ungainly than elegant when he undressed. He wobbled on one leg, then the other removing his trousers and gave up on being vertical entirely for his socks. He dumped his suit over the back of the chair and collapsed into bed, dragging the sheets untidily over himself.

He didn't stir at first as the telephone started ringing, it just formed part of his dream. Eventually the incessant repetitive nature of the ring pierced the dream and he reluctantly returned to a vague sense of consciousness.

He half-heartedly picked up the phone, if only to stop the persistent ringing from disturbing him any longer. "Hello?"

"David?" Naomi's voice on the other end of the line sounded concerned.

"Hi Naomi, what's up? You OK?" David rubbed his head and rolled onto his back. *'Not now, Naomi.'* he thought. *'Can't it wait until the morning?'*

"David, can you talk for a minute? I'm really scared." Naomi's voice was breaking into tears.

He sounded as sincere as he could but was having problems focusing his attention on being awake and staying awake rather than listening. "Yeah, sure. What's happened?"

"Well, after I got home from the funeral, Jane came round with a bottle and we had a chat about things."

"Go on."

Naomi paused for a moment. She was thinking that what she was about to say was going to sound absurd to David. "Well, I thought I saw Aiden at the crematorium standing in front of me," David sat up "and a few minutes ago whilst I was asleep I was dreaming about our holiday last year when I heard his voice talking to me. It was like he was really there, David.

"It woke me up, and when I did, I heard it again. I clearly heard him say 'Hello, Naomi, it's me, Aiden'. I was so scared I ran out of the bedroom. My face was wet. I ran to the kitchen to calm down and I saw him there too. The only thing I could think to do was call you. So sorry if I woke you. Do you think I was dreaming the whole thing?"

"God, Naomi." David didn't sound convinced. His tone was more 'you mean you rang me to tell me that' rather than 'that's terrible, are you OK.' "Are you really sure you weren't dreaming? We cremated Aiden two weeks ago. And it's Halloween. Is he there now?"

The phone went quiet. David could only hear some light breathing from Naomi.

"Shit. Sorry, Naomi. I didn't mean to . . ."

"No, he's not. Don't worry about it then." Naomi slapped her phone down, cutting the line. Unimpressed, she had very clearly heard by the tone of his voice that he wasn't concerned for her.

Silence.

"Hello? Naomi? Dammit." David looked at his own phone like it had cut off the call. He really didn't mean to sound quite so dismissive. He lay still for a moment, cursed and called Naomi back. There was no answer. It rang and rang as it had done earlier and then clicked onto the voicemail. He left a message.

1st November

David returned to consciousness like a truck through a shop front. His head felt like it had caved in. He was dehydrated and his mouth felt like a wasteland.

"Shit, Naomi!" He dimly remembered talking to her last night. What time was it?

Picking up his phone he looked through the log. Naomi had called at twenty five past three. What had she wanted? He couldn't quite put a finger on it. Twenty five past three?

Carefully getting out of bed, allowing his thickened blood time to crawl its way up to his brain, he scratched, yawned and shuffled to the bathroom. He was very much a caveman in the mornings. Even more-so today.

Examining his face in the mirror with bloodshot eyes, he played with his memory of last night. Slowly he remembered a conversation with Naomi.

"Damn it." He said, knowing he had to call her back, right now.

He was glad he taken today off. Going to work like this would have been very unprofessional, not to mention uncomfortable.

Cringing with his eyes tightly closed against the reception he may receive from Naomi, he listened to the tinny tone of her phone ringing. This was one of those calls you would prefer to leave a message rather than speaking to the person directly, such was your embarrassment.

Naomi decided to answer the call despite her better judgement. David was not in her good books this morning and her voice made it sound like it too. "Hello David."

"Morning Naomi!" overly cheerful considering his mood, David held a hand to his banging forehead.

"What do you want, David?"

"I just called to say sorry for last night. I'd been out at a Halloween party and I was . . ."

"Drunk?"

"Yeah. I was really drowsy when you rang. So sorry. You want to talk about it now?"

"Not really. I was really scared and you were the only person I felt I could ring to help me. You let me down, David."

Cringing all the more now, David sank into his bed, hitting the covers as he slid down.

"Sorry."

"What did you go as, to the party?" Naomi found herself forgiving David. How could she be so weak? She was terrified last night and David had just brushed her off, and now she was going to let him get away with it.

"Nothing special. Just a ghost, and a bad one at that. A sheet with holes in."

"Would have been helpful last night when I saw Aiden in the flat." Naomi stuck the knife in. He wasn't going to get away with it that easily.

"What? You think you saw Aiden? Where?"

"I told you last night, David. Don't you remember?" twist the knife.

Grappling for memories of the conversation he had to admit he didn't remember all of what was said. His silence gave him away. He banged the sheets again.

"You have no idea do you, David?" twist the other way.

Naomi found herself smiling at the sound of him struggling with his memory.

"No. Sorry. Look, Naomi," he prepared himself for his defence. "I'm sorry, I really am, but do you know what? I went out last night and wasn't in a fit state to talk to anyone after I got home, and certainly not being woken at three in the morning. You can't be annoyed at me for going out, can you?"

Naomi was now on her back foot. He was right. How dare he be right! But he was right. She didn't have any control over him, they weren't together so he wouldn't come home to her. Aiden was hers though, and he *had* come home, on Halloween of all days, which he shouldn't have. He was dead for crying out loud. "David, I'm sorry. I was scared, that's all. I need some company at the moment. I think I've been on my own for too long in this flat." She looked round at all of her and Aiden's things. They looked lonely too. They hadn't been dusted or touched for weeks now. In fact, the whole flat needed a going over.

David's voice was now calming to Naomi's ears, reassuring her. "Are you OK though? Do you want me to come round? I've got today off."

"I'm OK. Don't come round today. I'll be fine. It was bad night."

"Are we still OK to meet on Saturday?"

"Yeah, sure."

David breathed a sigh of relief. She couldn't be that annoyed with him. "OK. Bye then."

"Bye." She surveyed the flat with a determined look, a frown almost spread across her brow.

-|-

"Aiden. It is time." The unfamiliar voice was demanding, yet soft and comforting.

Aiden was enjoying watching Naomi. She was buzzing around the flat like a woman on a mission cleaning and tidying. After she ended the call to David, she had resolved to clean and tidy the flat, to get things straight again. She wanted her home back, and it not to be a shrine to what she once upon a time had.

The voice was accompanied by whom Aiden could only assume to be one of the Principium Angeli. This angel was not Samael though. This one was different. A new face and much more serene and ethereal than Samael.

The date landed with a thump in the front of his mind. Today was the first of November. His deadline to deliver his message and leave Naomi. He looked nervously at the angel who was holding out his hand, fingers fanned and slightly bent, offering it to him to take hold of, like a father would do for his child.

Aiden looked at Naomi, concerned for her and then back to the angel. "I can't go. It can't be time. I need more." Aiden's will sank deeply to the pit of his stomach. He wasn't ready to go yet, he hadn't managed to speak to Naomi yet. All he had achieved was to frighten the life out of her rather than comfort her and tell her that he loves her. She was too scared to listen to him, so he felt he had to keep trying. Now was not the time to go.

Slowly approaching Aiden like a policeman does an armed suspect, Aiden moved to evade the angel. "We had an agreement, Aiden. It is time to go. You must come with me now."

"But I need to talk to Naomi."

"Your time is ended, Aiden. Gabriel desires you continue your journey now. You must come with me."

"Gabriel? Sure, whatever. But who are you?"

"My name, Aiden, although unimportant, is Uriel. It is time to meet your destiny." The angel moved closer, within an arms length.

"But Samael told me that my destiny was to die."

"That is part of your destiny, Aiden. You don't just die when you lose your life. Your death is complete only when your journey ends, when it is impossible for you to cross the veil."

Aiden looked confused, trying to work out what Uriel was saying. "So, I'm not completely dead?"

Reaching out quickly, Aiden didn't have a chance to move away and Uriel took hold of him.

"You will be soon."

-|-

The steps up to the entrance of St Paul's Cathedral were cold and damp as Aiden tried to cling on to them to prevent him being taken inside. He was begging Uriel to leave him to speak to Naomi, to give him one more chance, but the angel was not listening to him. All he was interested in doing was completing his errand for Gabriel. The use of force was frowned upon by the Principium, but in certain cases, like this one, force was the last option available.

Aiden had not known how he had arrived at the cathedral so quickly. Seemingly two seconds ago he was enjoying watching Naomi tidy the flat and now he was fighting with the angel who wanted to take him away. He felt like he was being dragged away from everything that he loved and cherished and this angel simply didn't care.

Visitors to the cathedral stood on the steps, taking photographs of each other in front of the towering pillars and clock face. The dirty white facade provided an imposing background for their snaps. How many of them actually visited the cathedral for the purpose of worship, Aiden didn't care to know. He was invisible to them, and he wondered what they would think if they could see this angel of God dragging him so forcefully up the steps.

Inside the nave, Aiden was easily dragged along the aisle. There was nothing for him to hold on to.

The living were taking photographs inside too, all trying to get as much of the great dome captured as possible. They were everywhere, nosing at the windows and marveling at the grand scale of the building. Like ants, they scoured the interior for all the interesting angles. Not one of them could see the light shining straight down from the dome onto the marble floor below, and they were all unaware of the solitary angelic figure standing on the brass circle laid into the centre. He stood gleaming brightly, long white hair glistening in the purity of the light from above.

Aiden was nearly there now. Time was nearly up, and the closer he was dragged, the more he could feel it. The emptiness of his destiny becoming more and more apparent.

The figure in the light could only be Gabriel. Uriel had

suggested that he would be there to meet them to send Aiden on his way. Where? The light was frightening, as was Gabriel. There was something very final about everything going on. The light was so bright that the rest of the cathedral seemed to be blanketed in darkness. There were some living people sitting in the seats looking towards the altar. Not many, and most of those were sitting with their heads bowed in prayer.

Hauling the reluctant Aiden into the light, Uriel dropped him to his knees in front of Gabriel. It seemed appropriate for him to be kneeling now. Gabriel's presence felt incredibly powerful.

Aiden felt broken, but not defeated. He must be allowed one final chance to ask for more time to speak with Naomi.

Uriel stood back towards the edge of the light, hands together in front of him. "My Lord. Aiden Williamson."

Gabriel regarded Aiden with pity as he looked up to see the impossibly tall angel standing with his hands by his sides. Aiden had to squint to see him properly as the light was almost blinding. He felt calm in this presence though, loved and cared for. He looked round and found that he could no longer see any of the cathedral other than the top of the dome high above him. The religious paintings had all become very relevant, and the painted columns in the dome itself looked like an entrance to a garden. Statues stood beneath the dome like gatekeepers.

"Uriel. Thank you." Gabriel was calm and spoke slowly and concisely, ensuring he was understood. "Aiden, welcome. You know why you are here?" Aiden nodded "It is your time to leave now."

"Yes, I know that is why I'm here, but I can't go yet. I still have to speak to Naomi."

Gabriel held his hands out, welcoming Aiden. "We gave you your chance, Aiden. And now it is time to go. Come, stand with me, and I will take you."

"No. It's not fair that I can't speak to her. I must be given more time."

Gabriel frowned at being challenged "You *must* be given more time, Aiden? Do you think that everyone gets to go back? We felt for you, Aiden, and we gave you time deliver your message."

Aiden began to cry, leaning forward on his hands on the cold marble floor, hanging his head down between his arms. "I know you gave me a chance. But I didn't know how to talk to her."

"But you did talk to Naomi though, didn't you?" Gabriel was matter-of-fact, smug almost.

"Yes, but all it did was scare her half to death. I have to tell her so she hears me without being frightened of me."

"Maybe she accepts that you are dead now, Aiden and that she wants to move on without you. You must give her that chance."

Aiden was shaking his head. "No, you don't understand why I have to tell her." He looked up at Gabriel, pleading to be listened to.

"Why do you feel you have to tell her, Aiden?"

"Because I don't think I told her that I loved her enough when I was alive. I just want to tell her one more time."

Gabriel reached down and touched the top of Aiden's head. He knelt on one knee in front of the broken spirit, blessing him, wishing him peace. "Aiden, it is time to go now. You will find that your destiny is to be with Naomi when it is her time to come here too."

Aiden didn't want to give up although he was losing his will Gabriel's calm serenity. "I know, Samael told be, but it is not good enough. I can't wait that long, and she will love someone else before she loves me again."

"She will love again, Aiden. That is what has to happen in order for her to become who she is meant to be."

High above Gabriel, a column of amazingly bright and warm light formed from the the top of the dome of the cathedral and began to swirl around like a hurricane. Slowly, the column extended all the way down to the brass in the centre of the marble circle. A feeling of eternity flooded over Aiden at the sight of this light. It was comforting, strangely comforting and he began to feel overjoyed, but the desire to remain with Naomi overpowered the surging desire to walk straight into the light and happiness that Gabriel promised. He stood up in awe of the light, but instead moved backwards towards to Uriel.

"No! I cannot leave her. Not without saying goodbye. Now is not my time, it can't be, it won't be." He turned to run, but Uriel stopped him.

"Don't make us give you to the Ferryman, Aiden." Uriel firmly took hold of his shoulders but spoke softly.

"You know what the conditions were Aiden. We will have to give you to Charon if you do not come with us now." Gabriel approached. "Come now, and you will forever be with Naomi, no matter who she loves in her life. Refuse, and you will never see her again, Charon will take you."

Aiden was swimming with emotion. He couldn't bare the thought of his beloved Naomi with another man, with anyone in fact. He wanted her to live alone and in mourning for him, like Aunty Esther had done for Joseph. He felt that his loss of Naomi was so much greater than that promised in hell, that a journey with Charon would be a walk in the park compared to the loss he felt in his heart; no burning in hell, nor second death could come close. Any pain doled out by Charon or the Devil himself would be a gentle caress until he could be with Naomi again.

Likewise, the desolation he felt without Naomi by his side could not be comforted by the long wait in Heaven for her to join him. He had to stay with her. He wasn't ready to go. He never would be ready unless she came with him.

"I can't go. I just can't."

"We have no choice, Aiden." The column of light from the dome vanished, as if switched off, leaving just the three of them standing in the circle, Uriel still holding Aiden by the shoulders and Gabriel shaking his head in disappointment.

"I don't like to have to do this, Aiden. Your destiny is now changed, as is Naomi's. She will now find a place with someone else, and you will cross the river Styx with Charon. And you will never return."

"Who? Who will she be with?" Aiden was becoming angry at what he considered to be an injustice.

"That is yet to be decided." Gabriel was sincere with his words, looking right into Aiden's tearful eyes. "Charon?" he called out. "Come and fetch your passenger. He's ready to go."

-|-

Charon, The Ferryman stepped out from the shadows of the south transept. He was tall, very thin with narrow shoulders and hips. His head looked as if it were too big for his body and his skin, what could be seen at least, was tight and dirty. The entire figure looked like he had been dried, his bones barely covered and the tendons and ancient muscles clearly moving beneath the meager covering of epidermis.

Tied up at the neck with a long piece of cord was a hooded leather cloak of different coloured hides, eight in all that Aiden could see. They were patch-worked together with crosses of black leather and the entire garment went from hood right down to the floor to form a small macabre train.

Covering his legs was more of this mysterious looking hide. It couldn't be normal leather. It was neither black, nor tan but more pinky in tone. Fleshy and very dirty. His feet were bare and the skin was as taught as the rest of it seemed to be.

Across his body, a decayed sackcloth shirt did its best to hide the ribs on painful show beneath it.

Peering through the shadow cast by the hood, Aiden could make out a dried-up face and deep yellow eyes, black in the centre. He had a lifeless mouth, turned up at the corners, grinning. Aiden took a step back as the emaciated Ferryman stepped forward to collect him.

In his right hand he carried an oil lamp. Rusted and wet with weed it glowed dimly, the glass smeary with river grease. In his left, he held a twisted, gnarled pole at least two and a half metres long. The bottom had a fork cut into it, like a snake's tongue. The top was formed like a shepherd's crook, looped over for the easy grabbing of sheep's necks. At uneven intervals down the pole were two branches poking out in different directions: handles to help him push his ferry across the river.

"Is this one for me, Gabriel?" Charon's voice was deep and hoarse, throaty and it sent a chill down Aiden like nails down a blackboard. Charon spoke slowly, deliberately. Confidently.

"Yes, Charon. Take him." Gabriel was dismissive, not caring for the company of either of them any longer.

"Has he got his fare? I can't take him without his fare."

"You will take him, fare or not, Charon. We have no

welcome waiting for him here."

The closer Charon came, the more Aiden could see of him and the more detail he could make out. There was a stagnant dampness about him that made Aiden shiver. Slightly hunched and sinister looking, Aiden was fearful.

Charon's cloak was lighter than leather, thinner and torn in places. It flapped slightly behind him as he walked. The flesh tones on the cloak and the trousers were more human than bovine. Human! Aiden was alarmed at what he saw. This haggard beast of a ferryman was clothed in human skin. His eyes widening with every step closer Charon came.

Aiden could clearly see where the flesh had been cleaved off several bodies and their hides laid out to dry and then stitched badly together to form the monstrous cloak.

However many hundreds of years of use Charon's cloak had had, the skins were darkened with filth and toughened with age. Aiden noticed that some of the panels had been changed as they looked newer than others. Aiden shivered again at the thought.

"Come. Now." Charon demanded and Aiden caught a sniff of his breath. Like a river at low tide, it tanged of weed and decomposing fish. The skin on the face beneath was shrunken, pulled tight across the skull. The lips had all but vanished and all he could see of the nose was the bridge. All the soft tissue had vanished. And the eyes, mouldy yellow with a green tinge stared at him from the dark hollows of the sockets. The skin there too, had retreated and dried, leaving the eyes without lids.

Aiden turned to the Principium, protesting. "You can't mean this. I still have my message to deliver."

The angels both looked at him as one. They had pity on their faces and their hands were held in prayer for him. As ethereal and powerful as they were, Aiden felt as though they had deserted him. He felt more alone now than ever. He couldn't go with Charon, just couldn't. Gabriel spoke, having the last word. "You agreed, Aiden, and now you must go. You were given your chance. You let it pass."

Speechless, Aiden looked at Charon who was reaching out to grab hold of his arm to lead him away. He stepped back to avoid it, then another and another until he was sprinting as fast as he could down the nave of the cathedral to the doors and the streets of London where he felt he might be safe.

Echoing round the arches, he heard Charon's dried out footsteps quickening after him. They gained on him quickly, and with a glance over his shoulder, he saw the crook of Charon's pole reaching forwards to grab him. Before he could turn back for the doors, the crook was round his neck and he found himself crashing to the floor and looking up the ornately decorated ceiling.

Smiling at the dazed Aiden, Charon leaned over him and flicked a lock across the opening of the crook. Aiden was trapped, the twisted and damp wood felt rough and sticky round his throat as he tried to struggle free. "On your feet." Charon picked up the pole by the two handles and guided Aiden roughly upright. "Time to go. You have a date to keep in hell."

-|-

For more than a mile, Aiden struggled to get free, the crook digging into him each time he tried to escape. Charon had kept a good grip on the pole, expertly guiding him through the streets, passed the living and the souls of those left wondering this world without a place to go to yet. Aiden had called out to them, but the terror in their eyes and their movements away from him ensured him that Charon was not one to mess with.

Like a dog on a catchers pole, no matter what Aiden tried to shake himself loose of the crook round his neck failed to make any difference at all. He tried clinging to trees and lampposts, but Charon was too strong and clever with the pole to allow that to succeed.

The closer they got to the Tower of London, the darker the sky became and heavier with clouds. A mist came up and the temperature dropped. The dead souls Aiden had been calling to had all but disappeared until they left the main road of Lower Thames Street and entered the cobbled part by the Tower. Then there seemed to be hundreds, no, thousands of them all lined up against the railings. Some sitting, some standing, but all were drawn, beaten, haggard looking creatures shackled to the fence. They flinched and turned their eyes away from Charon as he approached with Aiden, tired and scratched from the long dragging. There was a low moan in the air of sorrow and longing.

Observing the scene closer, Aiden noticed that despite these hundreds of people tied to the fences and the benches surrounding him and all the way down to Tower Bridge, there were the living walking amongst them, standing inside them, leaning over fence and taking snaps of the tower and the bridge. This 'halfway' world really was part of the real world. The two were truly separated by a thin veil. A veil of disbelief or not understanding. They were almost identical and inextricably interwoven. To step through the thin veil shouldn't be too difficult, should it?

Living people meandered around in the November air, going about their business, doing the things tourists do; A photograph with Tower Bridge in the background, looking along the river, sitting on benches and reading maps. They had no idea they were having fun in the queue for Charon's ferry.

The stench in the air made Aiden gag the closer to the bridge they got. The older and more haggard the prisoners seemed to become, rotting within themselves, waiting for their passage across the river. They were more slumped now, arms above their heads, hands shackled to the railings, shoulders dislocating. They watched Charon tugging at the still fighting Aiden along the boardwalk to the ferry, their eyes full of horror at the sight and fear that they may be called to join the stranger on the journey. A light rain started to fall on this side of the veil. On the living side, the day was bright and not unreasonably warm for the first day of November.

Pushing Aiden down into his punt-like vessel and releasing him from the crook, Charon unshackled several of the men closest to the jetty and herded them down towards Aiden. They could hardly walk. One fell into the river. He struggled for air, too weak to swim until Charon swished his pole into the grey brown water and fished the man out and flicked him onto the jetty. "Get on board."

The vessel was roughly constructed out of misshapen planks of wood, covered in sticky pitch and along the gunnel were blackened, worn thigh bones, arms and ribs that formed a rail for the passengers to hold. They were tied down by the same cord that kept Charon's cloak round his neck. Undoubtedly the sinews of many a poor soul whose misfortune it was to be carried across the river.

With no seats, the passengers had to stand and the rails were below waist height, making balance difficult. More joined Aiden and the first man in the ferry, standing ankle deep in septic dark green sludgy water. The smell was horrific. Aiden looked up to the river railing and watched the living enjoying a day out at the Tower of London. They were unaware that just a heart attack or stroke away, the misery of death lay just the other side of the fragile thing called life that they were all taking for granted.

"Where are we?" Aiden said to the first man.

Hanging his head down so Charon couldn't see his mouth move, the man spoke quietly, "Shh! The ferry across the River Styx. We're being taken to Hell. We'll never get back."

Aiden thought the man was delusional. "But this is the River Thames."

The man had a London sounding voice. It was loose and dropped most of the 't's. "On that side of the veil, yeah. This side? No. On the other side of the river is Hades, Hell. Once there, you're lost forever."

"Oh. How long have you been waiting for passage?"

"A hundred years. I had no fare to pay the ferryman, see. If you don't have your fare, you wait for a century before he'll take you. You stay up there." He flicked his head up towards to the happy tourists snapping pictures. "You stay there, chained to the fence until he's ready for you. Those at the front have been here longest."

Aiden looked along the wall and back passed the Tower of London. As far as he could see there were people like this poor fellow standing, leaning and sitting waiting for their turn. Each one shackled by one hand or both to the railing. He gulped.

"I guess you had your fare, then? You came straight here." The man said, sounding jealous.

"No. Not at all, The Principium sent me straight here."

"The Principium? You were sent by the Principium? My, we have been a naughty boy, haven't we?" he chuckled. "Getting on the ferry without a fare? How come they sent you here? Why are you going down with us, and not up with them?" He looked up at no-one in-particular and raised his eyes skyward.

"I broke a promise, that's all. There has to be a way back."

"You broke a promise to the Principium? That makes my murdering someone look like child's play. You mark me, you never break a promise to the Principium. It's like breaking a promise to God himself."

"Yeah, I kind of see that now."

"And there ain't no way back either." The man was deathly serious now. "You're proper done for now."

The rickety ferry was full and was rocking heavily as Charon stepped aboard. The fearful talking stopped and the passengers looked round at the misty water as Charon pushed off the bank and slowly moved his pole forward to propel the vessel across the river.

The murky, dirty water had a deep red and green tinge to it as if something were bleeding into a stagnant pond. Floating around in it, like driftwood were the bodies and souls of those lost at sea. Their faces stuck in the terrified expression of drowning. Most looked like they were gulping for air but instead were taking in lungfuls of water. Many were in uniform, dead sailors from two world wars, a lot of civilians, both young and old.

"Don't look at them." The man said very quietly. "They've not had a chance to be judged yet. They are just resting there for the time being, until the Principium or Charon get to them. They are pretty much forgotten."

Aiden's exclamation was not appropriate for this journey. "Jesus."

"Ha" the man said loudly and then quickly quietened himself. "Not worth mentioning him. He don't care about us no more. We're in his hands now." He shot a glance to the Ferryman.

Charon was pushing the punt forwards and Aiden looked over his shoulder towards the destination. It was like the Thames had trebled or quadrupled in width, if not more. There was a huge sense of foreboding flooding over him now, that this really was the end for him. An eternity without Naomi was looming on the horizon that was glowing red, flickering like a city in the blitz seen from a distance.

As the punt reached halfway across the river, the water started to thicken. It waved like an oil slick and slid down the sides of the vessel rather than running off easily. Charon was pushing hard on the bottom to keep the momentum. The slick was the colour of scabs; a bit brown, a bit red and flowed like cooling lava. It was lumpy now with the bodies of marine tragedy, a soup of death. Stinking and wretched.

Tower Bridge began to look ancient. The towers were crumbling and weed was growing up the brickwork as blackened ivy grew down towards the waterline. The mist was thickening and Aiden couldn't see either bank. He was lost and disoriented.

Charon continued in silence and the passengers stood huddled together, wondering what would be waiting for them on the other side of the river. They looked like Holocaust victims waiting for something unknown to happen to them, the mistrust in their hosts terrifying them.

Aiden was plotting. He had to find a way back across the river.

-|-

The glowing on the destination bank of the river Styx was clearly ablaze, and clearly London. There were thousands of people there, all burning too, running around in the agony that was promised to Aiden by Samael. This looked just as he had imagined Hell to be like.

Breathing was difficult, the smoke and acrid smell of flesh clogged up the lungs of the damned as they ran, walked, crawled here and there, no sign of knowing where to go.

Charon pushed through the passengers as the vessel beached and listed to the left, sending them off balance. Charon though jumped into the pitch-like water and hauled on a sodden rope to steady his craft from toppling right over.

There was a sense of irony in his voice as he spoke in his dark and raspy tones. "Welcome. Welcome to eternity. Go where you please, but there will be no returning across the river."

The man and Aaron were the first to disembark. They

loitered on the beach for a while talking about what they were going to do whilst the others made there way into the blazing city, resigned to their fate. As they climbed the steps, they burst into flames, immediately beginning to scream in agony as the flames licked their skin and their eternal punishment began.

"Duncan, my name is Duncan. Nice to meet you." The first man sounded very happy despite the agony that lay just a few feet above them on the street.

"Aiden. Are you mad?"

"We can't stay here for eternity. We've got to get up there with the others before the tide comes in."

"Not likely, I'm not going up there to burn with them. I'd rather stay here."

Duncan had pulled his middle aged but broken frame up and made his way across to the landing steps. "You'll drown if you stay there and join the rest of the bodies. If you want to get back across, you're gonna have to suffer for a while."

"Burning?"

"I don't see any ice around, do you?"

Aiden thought about it as Charon approached and snapped him round the neck again with his pole. Choking as he was swung up on to the dock, he could feel the temperature of his body rise quickly. The crook was released and left Aaron lying on the roasting stone. Memories of his cremation came flooding back to him and the agony he had endured then. He wasn't sure if he could go through it all again, and as for an eternity of it? He would rather drown in the slimy river Styx and let his soul be completely destroyed than suffer for that long without Naomi.

Duncan had already started to burn. His clothes had flicks of flame to them and his hair was singeing. Nothing about him was burning away though, there were just the flames and the associated pain. His face was grimacing with it as he knelt beside Aiden to assist him, his hands hovering above the doubled over body lying on its side.

Unable to let a howl out of his body, Aiden just lay still, hugging his knees, winded by the resurgence of the pain of his cremation. Duncan leaned over him, trying to comfort him. His teeth were gritted with his own pain. "Don't scream, Aiden.

Keep it in, or your voice will be lost."

Aiden nodded as the flames grew hotter and covered more of his body, licking his face now, he threw his head back, scraping his ear and cheek on the ground.

Duncan was growling in his own flames now. He looked around and surveyed the horrific blitz-like scene. Buildings were burning, partially collapsed into the streets but not collapsing any further, no working vehicles, no lights (the flames were enough) and the sky was glowing orange. It was apocalyptic. The people wandered aimlessly around, they had no purpose, they were just burning. Most of them mute from screaming, but not ever dying from their burns. All were despairing of their predicament, all wanting to leave. All wanted to get through the veil.

Aiden was numbing his mind to the pain. He had gone through it recently and was becoming accustomed to the feeling. It just took a little getting used to again. Slowly, he managed to sit himself up and looked around. "So this is Hell is it?"

Duncan smiled a flaming smile. "I guess it is. So, what are we gonna do?"

"Can you see that, Duncan?"

"What?"

Aiden was looking down along the river. Some of the buildings had crumbled into the road, blocking it. People were climbing over the masonry, but behind it, rather, in the shadows, he could see the same building as it would have been on that side of the river Thames. Looking to his left, he saw Tower Bridge, decayed and falling down, but in the shadows he could see how it looked this morning. Concentrating harder and getting to his feet, he walked toward the road.

"Hang on a minute, Duncan, let me figure this out." His walk was pained, like an old man's would be. The flames licking hard on him now as they took hold. He looked intently at something, but nothing at the same time.

"What? What is it you can see?"

"I can see what is on the other side of the veil. Not very clearly, but I can see the buildings on the north bank of the Thames, and some boats going by. But, I can also see the people. The living people! They are right here with us. Not exactly with us, but on their side of the veil. We're not that far away after all, and they have no clue we are walking with them."

"What, just like on the other side of the river?"

Aiden smiled and the flames on his face licked his teeth. "Yeah, just like that. Can't you see them? Concentrate"

"I can't see anything, mate. You must be pretty special to see that. The veil is supposed to be really thick on this side of the Styx."

The more Aiden concentrated, the clearer the picture before him became, but all he could see were still mostly shadows. He could see the living walking around from place to place, going into and out of the buildings. He could even make out some vehicles.

When he was alive, Aiden had no idea (why would he?) that the entrances to the afterlife were so obvious and that hell was quite literally a boat ride across the Thames. The real world was so close, almost within reach, but it was only shadows he could see now. The veil was surely too thick to try to get through. He looked at Duncan, then down to the jetty where they had arrived and then across the river, back through the mist, passed the rotting bridge and through the murk to where he had promised Naomi he would be with her again.

Duncan looked concerned. "What's the matter, Aiden? You looked troubled."

"Nothing. I'm thinking."

3rd November

David had been like a cat on a hot tin roof all day in anticipation of his coffee that afternoon with Naomi. He was excited and nervous at the same time. He loved the feeling and it made him feel like he was a teenager again, having struck it lucky with his crush and she had finally agreed to let him take her out. He felt blessed.

There was nothing on the television that could keep his attention for more than ten minutes. The washing-up was done, his laundry too had been put away. Not ironed, but put away none-the-less. A bachelor through and through, David had even cleaned the bathroom of a sort. Anything to help the time go faster until two thirty when he planned to leave to meet Naomi.

It was now one forty five and time to get ready.

David showered and shaved, ensuring it was a particularly close cut. He wanted to look his absolute best for Naomi. He didn't want to blow this first impression.

First impression? Don't be ridiculous he had thought to himself. She had known him for years, the first impression was long gone. Naomi had seen him at his best and his worst; looked after him when heartbroken, shared his joys and everything else. Except his bed. No, not now. Don't think about that. There'll be no rushing this time.

With his hair wet, and towel loosely round his waist, he stood in front of the mirror looking at himself. He wasn't in bad shape, he supposed. A little more spread round the middle than he had been when he first met Naomi, but not bad. He turned sideways and sucked in his tummy, puffed out his chest and pushed his shoulders back.

Slumping back down his usual figure, he laughed at himself. "What the hell am I doing? So adolescent!" Giving himself a cheeky grin in the mirror and sarcastic wink, he whipped the towel from round his waist and began to dry his hair.

-|-

Naomi was taking it easy. She had suppressed her nerves about meeting David and had a productive day so far. She had been shopping and that always made her feel good. And now she was reclining in the bath, listening to some music, a cup of coffee on the side.

She was thinking about what she was going to say to David if the prospect of a relationship was to arise in their conversation. It was bound to, so it would be to her advantage to have something prepared so she didn't seem awkward.

Deep, deep inside her, she felt bad about going to see David, but so long as she concentrated on their being friends at the moment, she would be just fine. She didn't want to disrespect Aiden at all and she certainly didn't want to gain herself a bad name for hooking up with someone so soon after dispatching her boyfriend. But, she also thought that she had had her forty days of mourning, and besides, she felt like she was ready to get on with her life.

After all, she was only thirty five and she was not prepared to carry on for much longer in the misery she had allowed her self to dwell in. It really was dull and she wasn't used to it.

-|-

Rummaging through his wardrobe, David had found a selection of shirts to wear. One of them had to suit the only pair of clean jeans he had left to wear.

The jeans he had chosen were a deep blue pair of boot cut Levi's. They hung loosely off his hips as he pulled each of the shirts up to his chin to check which one would work best. Whichever one he chose also had to look good un-tucked. He didn't like tucking shirts in anymore. They accentuated the slight bulge over his belt, his muffin-top. It wasn't big, but was large enough for him to be uncomfortably conscious of it.

Throwing each of the shirts onto the bed as he checked them against himself in the mirror, he decided to settle on the one shirt that went with everything. The white one. Predictable? Sure, but he was comfortable in it and he felt he had to feel comfortable if he was to engage in conversation without worrying about his appearance. *So juvenile*, he thought.

Fingers in gel, neatly applied to his hair, spreading it round until he was happy with it, a spray of deodorant and a pair of leather shoes, David was ready to leave.

With a gleeful smile, he grabbed his jacket off the back of the door and closed it behind him.

This afternoon was going to be interesting. If he played his cards right, and slowly, he could end up with the girl he had admired for so long.

-|-

Damn! Quarter to two! Hardly enough time to get ready and walk across the park to the coffee shop.

Quickly towel drying herself and throwing on the nearest knickers and bra, Naomi also found a pair of skinny jeans, flat shoes and a nice fitted top to put on. Low cut, but not too low. Not for what may turn out to be a first date, anyway.

Without time to do anything too pretty with her hair, Naomi had to settle for a quick blow dry. It looked nice hanging loose. It always had done. Her school friends hated her for it, and her social girlfriends were envious too. They would complement her on it, but secretly they wanted hair like hers.

Earrings in, pendant round her neck (but not one Aiden had bought her. Mistake? Yes. Change pendant. She didn't want to make it look to David that she was so soon over Aiden.) make-up, lipstick. Done.

Two fifteen by her watch. Just enough time to get to the coffee shop only a few minutes late.

One last thing. She pulled on a long woollen coat with

large lapels and heavy collar. She did it up, but left the matching scarf behind. It wasn't quite cold enough for that. It would be a bit overkill to wear it.

Handbag over shoulder and a glance back round the bedroom and living room, Naomi closed the front door behind her.

With a large, deep breath she stepped out into the street, ready to meet David.

-|-

Even the sky seemed to be on fire as Aiden and Duncan explored the city, the heavy clouds glowed in changing shades of orange as if they themselves were ignited by the towering flames below. Occasionally, there would be a burning shaft of lightning coming down into the city, followed shortly by the harrowing cries of those caught in the impact. Then the sound would then lead to the erupting moans of disabled souls coming round.

Nothing could kill anyone here. That was their punishment; They would constantly die and be reborn with their souls intact, an eternity of death and dying, with all the agonies thrown in for good measure.

There was anarchy in the streets of this God forgotten London. The spirits of some of the damned doing anything they could to prevent further pain and misery. They hid where they could, in the burning buildings, in the gutters and sewers and in plain site, sitting quietly, consumed in their own flames and despair. These 'Lesser Souls' were outnumbered though, by the truly evil 'Greater Souls' who would hunt them down in packs and exact their earth-borne anger and hatred upon them. They were the ones who ensured the continuing misery.

Should a Lesser Soul be caught, they were put through disgusting trials. They were hung, drawn and quartered, beheaded and torn apart, or any number of other grisly attacks.

Aiden had seen a pack of demons attacking one individual Lesser Soul not long after he and Duncan had arrived. They had chased this poor, measly looking thing along the streets and cornered him against a pile of rubble. They were laughing like hyenas and baying for his blood, and the twisted look of terror on their victims face, and the tears, and the begging made just made them more mad. They broke his legs with sticks, repeatedly hitting them until the bones were pointing in different directions. Then they had stoned him, taking care not to hit his head, ensuring the greatest possible pain. Eventually, the Lesser Soul just lay still, body broken and bleeding and the pack of sickening demons moved on to their next victim. Slowly, the body began to reform and the Lesser Soul came round. He looked even more despairing than before. And this was the job of the demon; to drive every ounce of hope out of them.

Duncan and Aiden approached carefully, keeping a look out for the demons.

The lesser soul scrambled backwards up the rubble, trying to get away from the two strangers. It was hot beneath his fingers, and he left skin where he touched, pulling it off in patches. He didn't seem to care. He was too used to it. "Keep away from me, I've just been had. Not again, not now, no!"

Aiden looked at the man, concerned. Duncan made his way up the rubble to get closer, to reassure him they meant no harm. "It's alright, we're not going to hurt you." He held out his hand. "Are you OK?"

The man looked at them both. His deranged mind not understanding that they were trying to help. "You won't escape them. They'll get you again and again." He stumbled to his feet. "They'll take you to pieces until there is nothing left. And then they'll come back for more."

Aiden glanced around as he made his way up the pile to Duncan. "Who are 'they'?" he said.

The man described how the pack were the souls who had become demons. They were promoted by the Devil himself for being the essence of evil. They hunted indiscriminately and plagued everyone without warning. Each time, the demons attacked a soul, the victim would become whole again, rebuilding itself, ready to be hunted, found and killed again. An eternity of victimisation.

-|-

Agostino's Cafe was a popular place for thirty-somethings late on Saturday afternoons. They would often meet there for a coffee and a bite to eat before moving on to big and more alcohol oriented establishments, and today would be no exception.

David stood at the bottom of the steps leading up from the street to the front door. There was barely room inside for another person waiting to order. A large group of friends were noisily filling the entrance and servery area. He hoped they would be ordering take-aways or at the very least he and Naomi would be able to sit away from them when, if, she arrived.

He had regretted putting the lighter of his jackets on this afternoon. Although the day itself was not cold, the wind had a bite of early winter about it. He pulled it round himself and fished in his back pocket for his phone. Two thirty five. She's only five minutes late. *'Another five minutes, and I'll give her a call.'* he thought. *'But then she'll only be ten minutes late. It might seem desperate if I call her after only ten minutes being late.'* He looked up and down the street for Naomi, not sure from which direction she would come. He looked back into the cafe and found that the queue had reduced to the last few of the friends. Quieter now, David assumed they had gone out the back to the longer tables so the friends could all sit round together, leaving the front of the shop available for couples.

"Hello, David." Said Naomi from behind him, her hair blowing in front of her face. She swiped it away quickly before her could turn around. It was a tousled mess now, but not unattractive.

David's heart leapt into his throat with joy and a sudden tension. "Hi, Naomi." He said as he turned around to see her.

Now he felt awkward too. Does he hug her, or go in for a kiss on the cheek too? He chose the hug, but Naomi had chosen the other option. The resulting confusion of half-hug, half-peck on the cheek made them both blush. David was thrown completely and he stammered the invitation for her to lead into the cafe.

Inside Agostino's was a collection of chairs and tables, mainly set for two people and there were landscape pictures on the walls of rolling Italian fields and village scenes. The varnish on the wooden floor had been worn away to expose the bare timber and their footsteps echoed hollow but reassuringly solid on the boards.

The short, stout man that was Mr Agostino prepared them both their coffees with his usual jolly Mediterranean style. He sounded like he was singing whenever he spoke. His English was good, but with a heavy Italian lilt to it. He chatted to David and Naomi whilst he went through what seemed like a lot of bother for only two coffees. He delivered them as they took their seats at the window. He looked tired. Neither David nor Naomi had ever known Mr Agostino take a day off and the cafe always opened early and closed late.

For a few moments, David stared out of the window, trying to find something to say. Everything he had planned in his head to say had vanished and he was now struggling. The first impression he wanted to make rapidly dissolved in his mind.

Naomi sipped at her coffee, flinching at the heat. She too was worrying about what to say, but more about what David was going to say. She shuffled her feet and awkwardly looked around.

"What a lovely afternoon?" David nearly sank under the table as he spoke. Of all the things to talk about, he had to mention the weather, the typical English fall back position for an awkward silence.

"Yes, it is. The wind is chilly though, don't you think?" At least Naomi had asked a question, something that he could respond to.

The conversation continued for the next hour around pointless small talk, a further two cups of coffee and a pastry. David could not find the right place to bring up the topic of 'them' and vanished into silences every once in a while, trying to get the words out.

Naomi had a suspicion that he was going to ask her out, but she let him waffle on about inane things. Perhaps it was bad taste, but she quite enjoyed watching him feel more and more out of his depth as he spoke. If he was going to ask her about what she thought he was, then she already had an answer in store for him, so there would be no harm done, she supposed.

Yet another awkward silence fell between them and Naomi was feeling that she needed to work the conversation now. David was increasingly uncomfortable and his fiddling with the sugar sachets and spoon was getting annoying. She reached over to his hand and took the items away from him, the way a mother does from a fidgety child: Gently and without making a fuss over it. "David?"

"Yes?" he said, the relief evident in his voice.

"How have you been since the funeral? Honestly." She looked intently at him, over the top of her third mug of coffee.

"Fine. Fine, I guess. I've had a few moments, you know. Upset myself reminiscing and stuff." Naomi nodded at him, understanding. "But we all have to move on, don't we? How have you been?"

He was very glad that she had brought this up, and not him. He didn't feel it would have been appropriate for him to do so, given what he was planning on saying, when he could eventually summon up the courage to do so. A lot now rested on what Naomi said in response. He swallowed and picked up his own mug of coffee, his caffeine fuelled heart banging loudly.

"I've been OK too. I've cleaned up the flat, sorted out most of Aiden's stuff and feel I am letting him go. It won't be quick, but at least I am on the right road, don't you think?" Naomi had given David the cue he was clearly looking for. This was his chance.

On the outside, she was coming across as being confident with herself, which is what she wanted everyone to see. On the inside though, the thought of going on without Aiden was still raw and it bit her sometimes when she least expected it. She had to get over the feelings she was having of betraying him if she started seeing David. It was, after all, only natural that she would want to find someone new.

'Here goes.' David thought, taking a deep breath. "About that, Naomi. I was wondering." He winced at the words as he let them go.

"What, David? What were you wondering?"

'Just take a deep breath and let it out, David. Come on!' He egged himself on as he looked at Naomi. She was sitting back in her chair, relaxed and looking into her mug, fingernail tapping the rim. Was she frustrated? "I was wondering if you would mind if I were to invite you out for dinner."

Pouncing on the chance to tease him again, Naomi looked at him and pursed her lips. "I don't know the answer to that David, you haven't asked me." She felt cruel to have said that, but if he was going to ask her out for dinner, he should ask her properly, and not with a thinly disguised question-cum-statement.

David's coffee had turned into butterflies in his stomach and they were banging to be let out. He fingers started to tremble and a light sweat appeared on his brow. This was it.

"Naomi." Cough "I know that you've gone through a lot recently. I've shared that experience with you. So, to cheer ourselves up a bit, or a lot, would you like to join me for dinner one evening? Just you, me and a bottle of wine."

There, he had done it. It was out there. He sat back in his chair and looked out of the window, waiting for her answer. He would be crushed if she said no.

"David, that is very sweet of you."

'Here it comes. No.' David though to himself, pulling a finger across his lips.

Now Naomi had actually heard his invitation, she too began to quake with nerves. She was flattered, touched and a little shocked too. She had known that David was going to ask her out, he was so easy to read, but she also felt that she shouldn't be going out with him at all, or anyone for that matter. Not now. Not yet.

"I'd like that very much." The words escaped her before she could control them, but she felt comfortable with them.

David's relief was obvious, he let out a breath as if he had been holding it for minutes. Perhaps he had been holding it in anticipation of Naomi's answer.

"That's great." He smiled broadly at hearing her words. "I'm really pleased. Thank you."

Naomi blushed. It had been what seemed like a long time since she was asked out on a date, and she didn't want him to get too keen. "Thank you, David. But don't start getting your hopes up too soon though, will you?"

"No, no, of course not. I'll be on my best behaviour." David had always had a naughty side, and he gave Naomi a deep look that made her feel like he was looking right into her soul. She found she liked it, she liked it a lot and found it rather arousing. He had never looked at her like that before, and there was a passion within the look that she had never imagined could have come from him. He had always seemed quite flat before now.

Naomi found herself blushing again and inwardly kicked herself for it. "I know you will David."

"Of course! What days are good for you?"

Naomi had a fit of conscience, panic almost. She found she felt that all that she was doing by accepting David was betraying Aiden's memory. She wanted to go out with him, just not yet. But she had said yes now, and that would have to be good enough for the moment. "Do you mind if we don't fix a date for our, er, date just yet? I'll let you know when I feel ready for it. It's all a bit soon, don't you think? I will let you know, I promise. I need to do some thinking first."

David's heart deflated with disappointment and Naomi noticed his eyes turn downward. What had, for a few seconds been elation had now turned darker.

"Don't look like that, David, please."

His tone was dejected. "Like what?"

"All grumpy!" Naomi tried to laugh it off, but David's uncomfortable silence spoke volumes. "I said yes, didn't I?"

"Yeah. But then you blew me out."

"No I didn't, David. I just suddenly realised that it might be a bit soon and that I would have to think more about things. We will go out for dinner, David. I promised. Just perhaps not as soon as you would like to. Please, be patient." She now felt incredibly awkward and stood to leave, blubbering an apology at the same time.

"Don't go, Naomi. It's fine, honestly. No problem." Standing too, David sounded feeble, almost begging her to stay.

"I'll give you a call David, when I'm ready. We'll talk about it then. Bye for now." She walked round the table and gave him a peck on the cheek.

Naomi's reassuring smile didn't work, and David simply returned the gesture with an empty nod of the head and a heavy slump back down in his chair. He watched through the window as Naomi walked across the road and down the alleyway to the park the other side of the buildings opposite.

6th November

"I think he's gone now, Aunty. I saw him one more time since I last visited you. It scared me so much, I didn't know what to think."

Aunty Esther looked at Naomi over the top of her glasses and tea cup before putting it down. She looked concerned. "Did he not say goodbye to you?"

"No, there was nothing, just him saying Hello and his name. I was so scared I ran from him."

"Were you not comforted by his voice, my dear?"

"No! It came from nowhere, I could feel something inside my head and my face was wet. I freaked out completely. Was that wrong?"

"Wrong? Of course it was wrong! He was trying to speak to you, and you pushed him away. How do you think that made him feel? Rejected? Unwanted?" she paused, her old, wise eyes peering accusingly at her eldest niece. "Unloved?"

Immediately Aunty Esther uttered the words, Naomi regretted what she had done. Aiden must have been feeling very alone, and of course she loved him. How could she have been so stupid not to have let him in? It was her own strong will and denial of the possibility of an afterlife that made her run. She was scared, plain and simple.

Aunty Esther reached over and topped Naomi's tea up. "If he has gone, Naomi my girl, then his time was up. He had to go. There was nothing he could do about it, I'm sure. You'll have to wait now, like me. I won't be long now. I'll be with Joseph again soon enough."

"You mustn't talk like that Aunty. You've got years left in you yet." Naomi frowned.

"And you have many more years left to wait than me. You will love again, and if you are destined to be with Aiden, then you will be. But never, ever forget that he tried to contact you. He loved you, anyone could see that, and his sense of loss would have been every bit as painful as yours. Remember, he lost far more than you did. He lost everyone, and every thing he ever had. You only lost him."

"You're not making me feel any better, Aunty."

"I feel sorry for you, Naomi. No I don't, I pity you." There was a venom in Aunty Esther's voice that Naomi was not familiar with. She didn't like it at all. "You had the opportunity to speak to him again, and you pushed him away. How am I supposed to make you feel?"

"I don't know, Aunty, a little better perhaps. A bit more supportive, I suppose. I didn't mean to react the way I did. I was dreaming about us on holiday, and then, all of a sudden I felt like my head was invaded and I heard his voice. I couldn't see anyone or anything around me and I panicked. He invaded me and I just defended myself."

Aunty Esther was getting cross with her Great Niece. She put her tea cup heavily down on the saucer and scornfully looked at the young woman before her.

"That's where you were wrong then! You would never have had to defend yourself against Aiden! He worshipped the very ground you walk on, the air you breathe. He tried to come back from death to talk to, and you and you bloody well pushed him away."

Naomi reached into her handbag, fumbling for a tissue. This reality check had upset her. Esther had made her doubt if she ever loved Aiden at all. Perhaps he had just made her feel good for the last five years. And now, when he left her so suddenly, she had felt betrayed and in return shunned his advance. She was confused now. She wasn't used to having her own feelings brought into question. She had always been so sure of herself.

Aunty Esther, with so many more years wisdom on her side just sat and looked at Naomi's face as she tried to keep herself composed. The matriarch was teaching the baby a stern lesson.

Naomi stood up. "I think I'd better go now, Aunty. Thank you for the tea."

"I think you had. I'm disappointed in you, Naomi." Aunty Esther stood too, and turned her back to her niece and made her way to the window, shaking her head.

Looking like a lost sheep, Naomi glanced around the room, uncomfortably waiting for Aunty Esther to say something, but the old lady kept her peace. "Bye then, Aunty. See you in a couple of weeks."

Aunty Esther didn't make a sound not move. She just took a deep breath, clearly visible to Naomi, and let it go again.

Waiting for a few more seconds for a reaction but seeing none, Naomi turned and left the room, closing the door quietly behind her.

-|-

Naomi sat in the car and thought back to that first dance with Aiden. Had it all been a lie since those moments she held so dear in her heart? Had she just been swept up by his handsome good looks and charm? Had she ever really loved him?

The memory was so pure in her mind. He had asked her to dance, and she had accepted. Was it just lust for all the years they were together? They were kind and caring towards each other and tender and loving. But did she love him after all? Aunty Esther had confused her now, made her deeply question her emotions and actions.

She was glad that she hadn't mentioned her afternoon with David, that would have been the nail in the coffin, so to speak. Now though, she was beginning to regret agreeing to go out to dinner with him.

Although they hadn't set a date yet, the thought that she could have hurt Aiden so much when he tried to contact her made her feel that she should put the date off for a while. A few weeks maybe, just so she could get her mind straightened out. Maybe for longer.

Wiping her eyes on the back of her hand, Naomi started the engine and switched on the wipers. As she pulled away, she noticed Aunty Esther standing at one of the windows of the home. She held her hand up to wave. Her face was drawn into a small, sympathetic smile. Naomi stopped the car opposite and looked hard at the old woman in the window. Raising her own hand, she half-heartedly waved back and drove slowly away.

At a set of traffic lights, she plugged the headset into her phone and dialled David's number.

-|-

"Good afternoon, David speaking. How can I help." He sounded official today, it was Tuesday and he was at work.

"Hi David, it's Naomi."

"Oh, hi. One moment and I'll go outside." His tone mellowed and his voice seemed to smile as much as he did on hearing Naomi.

Naomi waited and the lights changed. She drove off whilst David was putting on his suit jacket and leaving the office.

"Yeah, hi, Naomi. Really sorry about that. I'm at the office. What's up?" He stood beneath a tree, the thinning canopy of leaves providing little shelter from the cold rain. He huddled against the trunk under the largest of the branches, phone to his ear and he shivered in the chill.

Half concentrating on driving and trying to find the right words so not to offend David, Naomi paused.

"Sorry, David. I'm driving. It's about Saturday." Whoops. That hadn't come out right.

David was worried now. She must have changed her mind. Why else would she be ringing about it?

"I had a really lovely time with you, and thank you so much again for the dinner invitation."

Here it comes. He thought he could hear the words. *I don't think it is a good idea.*

"I really enjoyed it, thank you for coming, it was good to see you." He sounded cheerful enough, but inside he was only delaying what he thought was inevitable. He could also barely hide the quiver in his voice from the cold.

"I don't know when you were thinking of our dinner out, but..."

David interrupted. "Well, I wasn't thinking of immediately." He clutched at straws "Perhaps in a couple of weeks? Three?" he hoped that by delaying it, she may change her mind. He had convinced himself that she was going to call off the date.

"That's just what I was thinking, David. Thank you. I went to see my Aunty Esther earlier and she gave me a bit of a talking to. So I think I need to do some more thinking and soul searching. I'm sorry."

"Don't worry, Naomi. It's fine, honestly." David lied. He felt let down, but at least he wasn't totally brushed off. Yet.

He guessed he would have to be patient. If he wanted her, she would have to be ready to accept him for who he was, rather than a replacement for Aiden. They had agreed to take it slowly, and whilst Naomi was still thinking about Aiden, then he would have to be happy to take a back seat to those thoughts and be there for her if she needed him, as a friend.

"Are you sure?" Naomi was concerned. She loved David dearly as a friend and hated to be another female to let him down or hurt him.

"Of course I'm sure." He lied again, and Naomi heard the disappointment in his voice. He hadn't disguised it very well. "No problem. Let me know when you're up for it and we'll sort it then. Just give me a ring if you need anything. I'll help you however I can, Naomi, you know that."

"I know, David. Thank you. Just a little more time. Aunty Esther gave me some things to think about, that's all."

"What things?" David was curious as to what the aged aunt could have told her to make her 'think about things'.

"Doesn't matter now, David. I'll tell you over dinner. I'm driving at the moment. I've got to go. Bye for now." She hung up quickly without giving David a chance to talk again.

David heard the line go dead and looked at his phone. "Bye, then." He said to it. He sniffed and dashed back into his office. If he had to wait for her, he had to wait for her. *'What's a few months over the last few years?'* he thought to himself. Just knowing that he was at least in with a chance gave him some hope.

8th November

Two evenings had passed since Naomi had called David after seeing Aunty Esther. What had she given her a talking to about? Aiden, he supposed and moving on so quickly.

He had analysed the conversation they had had over and over again. He was sure he did everything right. He had left the ball firmly in her court about giving him a ring about their dinner date, and he had done his best to not sound too disappointed by the result.

He should be disappointed, and she should know it too. If he hadn't have shown his disappointment, then she might have thought he wasn't that interested in her after all, which of course was not the case.

David didn't think that Naomi was moving on too quickly. She had responded to an honest request for her company and they had agreed to take things slowly whilst she got over the worst of losing Aiden. Nothing wrong with that, surely.

Work had been a write-off for the rest of Tuesday and most of Wednesday. His mind was too preoccupied with thoughts of Naomi. Despite his efforts to look busy, his lack of productivity had not gone unnoticed either. He had been caught looking at Naomi's social media pages. She hadn't posted anything for weeks. There were at least pictures to look at.

Every second thought was one for her. He had beaten himself up over this silly teenage crush getting too deep far too soon. There was a glimmer of an opportunity though and he didn't want to miss it.

Such was this crush that he thought he was falling in love with her, even though he had known her for years and not felt anything other than the fondness of a good longterm friend until now. He had always had a bit of a crush on her, but this was going way beyond what he had felt before.

The feelings cupped his heart and lifted it gently every time he thought of her. The mention of her name in conversation or even in his mobile phone contacts list brought a little grin to his face.

Sleep hadn't come as easily as before either. He had spent the last two nights deep in thought and daydreams about what might be between them one day. He had planned their lives together in his mind, ensuring the happiest possible outcome as every good teenager would do.

Eventually drifting off anywhere between three and four in the morning, he was getting up later for work and was late on both days, something that was very out of character for him.

He doodled whilst on the phone to customers, sketching capital 'N's on the corners of his notepad, much to the amusement of his colleagues.

They could tell he was falling love. He we behaving like they had never seen him before. Of course, he had had the odd girlfriend here and there, but he never ever behaved like this over any of them.

-|-

Naomi had always thought that she had a bigger soul than the one she was searching now. She was now playing with the thought that perhaps she had never loved Aiden at all. It hurt to think that she could possibly have been that shallow for the last five years of her life.

For certain, she had cried the tears of a widow at his funeral and had sunk herself into a depression she felt she was now beginning to leave behind. But had she really loved him?

After her dressing down by Aunty Esther, Naomi supposed that the older generation knew what love really was. One love for him and one love for her, and that was all they allowed themselves. Perhaps love back then was more righteous and was held rightfully in the reverence it deserved. Perhaps they knew what love was really like, the sense of loss at the end so profound that the thought of loving again could not enter their minds.

Aiden had been the love of her life, or so she thought. Now she wasn't so sure. She wanted to love again, and find someone to love her. But was that right?

She was a beautiful woman. Aiden had told her often enough. He *did* worship the ground she walked on, she could see that now, but why couldn't she see that before? It was playful to her and fun too. Had she thought of being with anyone else before now? Maybe, but nothing serious. A little fantasy here and there perhaps, and after an argument she may have thought about straying from the nest for some respite. She never did though.

How often had she told Aiden that she loved him? She couldn't remember.

As the rain began to stream down the windows, she remembered Aunty Esther standing in the window of one of the living rooms at the care home. She was just standing, looking at her.

She understood the old lady's disappointment now. The man that loved her had come back from the grave to talk to her, and she was too scared to bury her own fright and let him in that one last time. And now he had gone.

Aunty Esther had accepted the subconscious advances of Uncle Joseph and had shared more time together with him after he had gone, and she was so very happy that she had done so. She seemed to live off those memories now, those secret meetings with him in her dreams. The last possible escapes were taken to anywhere and everywhere they wanted to go.

All this romantic return from the grave stuff had all happened for Esther, but now would never happen for Naomi. And that was something she would have to live with if she did indeed love Aiden in the first place.

She just didn't know anymore.

-|-

No matter what she thought or how she felt, there was a lot of Aiden's clothes and things that she didn't need in the flat any longer and resolved to pack them up and take them to his parent's house at the weekend. She picked up the phone to call Jack and Anna about visiting them on Saturday with a car load of things.

Flicking through her list of contacts, Naomi thought that this would probably be the last time she would speak to Aiden's parents. They had been there for them both, to help them move into the flat, decorate it and help sort out some other problems they'd had since they moved in. She felt sad that this would be it for them now. She would take Aiden's things round on Saturday give Jack and Anna a hug and a kiss, perhaps a tear or two and then leave. That would be the end of the line; another chapter closed and another step closer to moving on without Aiden.

The voice-mail clicked on. Naomi waited for the beep at the end of the greeting, rapidly thinking of what to say without it sounding callous or cold.

BEEEEEEP

"Hi Jack and Anna," Naomi tried to sound happy, but not overly so. "It's Naomi. I hope you are both well. I've got some things of Aiden's I thought you might like..."

Jack picked up the phone, cutting Naomi short. "Hello, Naomi. Sorry about that, I was in the garden. Anna's out. How can I help?"

Naomi took a deep breath. She hadn't spoken to either of Aiden's parents since the funeral and was nervous of doing so. She felt it was silly really as she had known them for five years or more, but then, she hadn't had to phone them and tell the she would be bring back their dead son's odds and sods at the weekend before. Awkward. She avoided the main reason for calling for the moment, although all she wanted to do was get it out as quickly as possible. "Hi Jack. Good to talk to you. How are you both?"

"We're OK, thank you. Getting along. How about you?

We haven't heard from you." It was now Jack's turn to sound and feel awkward. He was acutely aware that neither of them had anything common, and now that Aiden was gone, there was even less.

"I'm not too bad, Jack, thank you." Naomi saw her opening to cut the conversation short before it became too uncomfortable. "I've got some boxes of Aiden's things. I thought you might like them back. I was going to bring them round on Saturday for you. If that's alright."

"That's fine, Naomi. Thank you. We were wondering if you would be kind enough to return some of his things. We didn't like to ring. It felt a bit, er, odd."

Naomi let out a nervous laugh of agreement. "Yes, Jack. I agree. I'm so sorry I've not been in touch sooner. It's been a bit difficult, you know?"

"Yes, we know, Naomi. Of course we know." Jack sounded as if he was telling Naomi off for her comment. Of course they knew how difficult it was! They had just lost their son and his girlfriend was now bringing back his stuff, or course they knew how difficult it was. Stupid girl. "We are going out about lunch time on Saturday. Do you think you will be round before then?"

"I should think so, Jack yes. In fact, I'll make sure I am. Thank you. See you Saturday."

Before Jack could sign off, Naomi had hung up the phone.

10th November

Naomi had suffered a very bad night. Hardly able to sleep with the thoughts running round her mind, she had spent most of it either in tears or staring out the window at the orange glow that silhouetted the suburban London skyline.

She had never thought so deeply about anything before in her life. Was she ready to move on without Aiden, and did she actually ever love him?

Answers were needed to these questions before she felt she could actually do anything useful with herself from this moment on. The questions had been there all along, but with the upset of Aiden leaving her so suddenly, the funeral and the mixture of emotions which ranged from hatred, anger, pain, betrayal, and. . .the questions had been pushed aside. They needed a sense of calm in Naomi's mind before they could be answered.

The problem was, they all wanted to be answered at the same time, providing Naomi with another avalanche of emotions to deal with. They had all raised their heads over the last couple of days, and it was all thanks to Aunty Esther giving her that telling off.

After filling two boxes of Aiden's affects and reminiscing

about each item as she packed them away, Naomi believed she had reached the answers she was looking for, and, for the moment at least, she was happy with them.

Firstly, despite being angry at him for leaving her without saying goodbye and leaving her feeling betrayed, used and alone she really had loved Aiden. It was painful to have to sift through everything she was feeling to find the bare root of her feelings for him. But when she had found the root, the realisation of how she felt was refreshing, comforting.

Secondly, she had decided that she now felt ready to move on. There was no bringing Aiden back, and if he had actually tried to contact her, he had gone now. It was ten days since his last visit and there had been no further sign of him in her dreams, thoughts and she had not seen him in the flat or anywhere else.

Her mind was made up. There was no sense in clinging on to the past. If Aiden wasn't coming back, then there was nothing left to hold on to. Definitely time to move on.

-|-

Jack and Anna's house was an unremarkable semi detached house with four bedrooms nestled on a mid nineteen eighties estate in the north of London. There was a bit of space for a couple of cars out the front where Jack had concreted over the garden to make some extra hard-standing space for a second car as Aiden was growing up. Naomi had parked in the space and, in Anna's eyes, who was standing in the window watching her would-be daughter-in-law's arrival, brought everything full circle.

Anna could see the boxes loaded into the back of the little car. There were only a handful of boxes full of bits and pieces plus some clothes in bags. She looked at the car and Naomi getting out of it, and then over to the mantelpiece where Aiden's ashes stood in their urn. Expressionless and numb, she opened the door for Naomi and the first of the boxes and bags.

"Hello, Anna." Naomi was so unsure of how to come across with her. Should she be all happy and la-di-da, all morose and depressed or somewhere in the middle? In fact, she was beginning to wonder if she should care at all. They weren't part of her life any more, and she was returning what she guessed was sort of rightfully theirs anyway. She put the box down on the step in front of the door and waited for a response from Anna. "I've ..."

Anna interrupted. "Hello, Naomi. Yes, I can see. Jack told me you were coming this morning. Won't you come in?"

This had stumped Naomi. She now had no idea what to say or do. She hoped Jack would arrive and rescue them both from each other. The two women who loved Aiden the most in the world, struggling to find anything of any interest to say to each other, or even start a conversation that they could have started so easily a couple of months ago.

"Naomi! How good to see you." Jack came round the corner from the side gate. "Anna, put the kettle on while Naomi and I will unload the car."

That was that then, Naomi supposed, decision made. She would be staying for a while.

-|-

Duncan was beginning to succumb to the misery of Hell. The constant pain from his burning skin and the breaking and repairing of his bones when he was captured and tortured by the demons were taking their toll. He had complained to Aiden that he just wanted to give up and let whatever was to happen to him, happen. He no longer had the strength to fight anything off.

Aiden too had been attacked several times in the last two weeks. He was subjected to several stonings, a hanging and once he was torn apart by the demon's own hands. Each time though, he was brought back together again, a bit more tired, and a bit more subdued. But these events could not completely batter the will out of him. Indeed, it had strengthened his resolve to escape. He kept it hidden though. He had noticed that those newer to hell were those more heavily subjected to the cruelty. Perhaps they provided more sport for the demons; They put up more of a fight than those who had been there a while.

By keeping very subdued and in the shadows, Aiden had discovered that they weren't picked on as much. Duncan was thankful for this advice, and they spent most of the time as far from the centre of the city as possible.

The two of them had trawled the streets for places to hide, and to talk about the possibility of escape. On the roads, and in the buildings, there were too many people to talk openly about their thoughts and ideas. They crammed the rooms in the shops and houses and virtually filled the streets in places. Each one was aimlessly wondering, searching for something they would never find. Their mind's were beaten and their bodies battered. Even if they could escape they had neither the will nor the strength. The demons had them right where they were told to keep them: On the edge of a second death. They had to be content with their lot; burning slowly, walking on broken feet, using mutilated hands.

There had to be a way back. Perhaps back over the river by Tower Bridge, or even through the veil itself. Aiden could just about see through it, after all. Surely it was possible. Duncan didn't think so. There must be people here more angry than Aiden and no-one he had heard of an escape yet.

The view from the top of The Shard, where they both now sat was orange, black and red desolation, like the world was melting beneath them. All the buildings as far as they could see were on fire and collapsing. There were no trees, no grass, no flowers. The flames licked high into the sky, and even though Duncan and Aiden were sitting over three hundred metres above the city, they could still feel the raging heat from below.

Aiden found the scene strangely beautiful. It was like the city was a reflection of how he felt inside. It raged out of control and seemingly, the only sense came from the demons within. Oddly comforting.

From far below them, they could hear the agonising shrieks of the Lesser Souls being captured and beaten. It was harrowing of course, but by now, Aiden and Duncan had grown accustomed to it. Not entirely though; part of the torment of being here was that you had all your senses and feelings as if you were alive, and they were constantly being worn down, more and more, but were never quite destroyed, because if they were destroyed completely, then you would no longer feel the misery and despair that this place dished out so professionally.

"What do you think of that idea, Duncan?" Aiden looked at his new friend's profile. It was sullen and depressed.

"I don't think you'll get through the veil, Aiden. It's just too bloody hard. There is something about you though that tells me you might make it back, but not through the veil."

"I'll need your help though."

"What have I got to lose?" Duncan's tone was resigned. It had only taken the demons two weeks to get to him, and now it seemed, he was theirs.

"Not as much as me, Duncan. Will you help?" Aiden stood up and made his way back to the roof door.

"I'll do my best, Aiden."

"Come on then. Let's get going."

-|-

Tired now, but with a fresh and clear mind, Naomi sat at her spot in the kitchen and looked out of the window. Her smile felt like the first proper smile she had achieved in a long time. It made her feel good as she watched the Saturday shoppers bustling around outside. The sun came in and out between the clouds and the chilly breeze made the pedestrians pull their coats up tightly. Winter was most certainly on the way.

With David in mind again, Naomi thought she ought to give him a ring to organise dinner. He had been very good since they met and not hounded her. He had also not made and contact at all since she called him after her cross words with Aunty Esther. She appreciated the time to be alone to gather her thoughts and now was the time to take the second step in moving on.

Heart fluttering, Naomi dialled David's number and waited, tapping the table with her fingernails.

"Hi Naomi! How are you?"

"I'm great, thanks. Yeah. Really good." She didn't have to convince herself anymore. She really did feel great, and the smile in her voice was very evident.

"Excellent, I'm so pleased to hear that, Naomi. Had any more thoughts on dinner?" David hadn't engaged his brain before speaking and cringed at his question. Too soon in the conversation? Probably. Oh well, it's out there now.

"As a matter of fact, David, I have. How about next

Saturday night?"

Taken back by Naomi coming straight out with the invitation, David stumbled over his words, not absolutely sure how to respond, other than positively. "Yeah, perfect. No problem. Great. What time? Where? Posh? Pub? You choose."

Naomi felt flattered by David's fumbling of words. He sounded genuinely surprised. "Anywhere you like, David. I'm not worried where we go, so long as it is a nice place." She grinned.

"OK! That's great. I'll come round at seven thirty?" David was grinning widely, and Naomi could hear just how wide his smile was. She grinned quietly to herself. He really was pleased to be taking her out for dinner, and if the truth were to be known, she was pleased to have been asked and to have accepted the invitation.

"That would be perfect, David. See you next week."

"Yeah, I'll look forward to it. Shall I text you in a day or two?"

"Of course you can, David. Any time you like."

It had been a long time since either of them had dated, and they both shared the same nervous apprehension about what would be expected of them, what to say, how to act and react. As they both ended the call, both of them were overcome with a lightness and absent mindedness that only comes with excitement and the promise of something great and new about to start. In short, they felt like they were both in the early twenties again, and they liked it. A lot.

-|-

Slumping down on the sofa with a cup of tea, Naomi looked around the living room. It was clean, bright and it looked new. It reflected how she felt, positive.

She had spent the afternoon cleaning and tidying. A spring clean in the winter never did anyone any harm she had thought to herself and although she was dusty and tired, she felt like she had been really good today. An 'up' day when so many recently had been down.

There had been moments, when clearing out some of Aiden's things that she thought she was being disrespectful to his memory, but some of the things just had to go. She had bagged-up most of his clothes to take to charity and had shed some tears when memories of him wearing the items came back to her. She had hugged them, smelled them and bagged them. She had kept telling herself it was time to move on and it kept her strong. Perhaps if she were much older, then it wouldn't have been so difficult. Her and Aiden would have had a life together, fulfilled their purpose of procreation, perhaps had a couple of grand children to spoil rotten, and then the only thing left to do would be to sleep, forever.

Jack and Anna had been very understanding earlier that day, and Naomi appreciated their honesty and openness. They had made the experience of dropping of Aiden's things a lot more bearable than she had expected.

The photograph of the two of them on holiday had now moved from the bedside table to the living room and the book shelf by the television.

Curled up on the sofa, feeling snug, Naomi picked up the phone and dialled Jane.

"Hi Jane! How are you?"

"Wow! Hey Naomi, I'm good thanks. You sound really well."

Naomi shuffled on the sofa, swapping ears and putting her tea down on the freshly cleaned table. "I'm moving on, Jane. I've spent the day cleaning and sorting through Aiden's things and took them round to his parent's house. It's been good for me. I feel ready to meet David for dinner next week."

The line went quiet. Jane was considering her answer. Naomi could hear her breathing. "David? Really? Are you really sure you should be meeting him? He was Aiden's best friend."

"Yes, Jane, I'm sure. He asked me a week ago. He's nice. I've always been fond of him."

"Bloody hell, Naomi. I know you're fond of him! But he was Aiden's best mate. Is that not a bit... I don't know... Sounds to me like you are on the rebound."

"Jane! Please, I am a grown woman. When I say I've always been fond of him, I mean I've actually quite fancied him. Not as much as Aiden, of course, but a bit, yeah. Who wouldn't? You do!"

"What? No I don't. OK, maybe a bit. He's handsome, and that's all. You are only meeting for dinner aren't you? Nothing more."

Naomi was enjoying the conversation. It made her feel like a teenager again. "No, Jane, nothing more. I'm not ready for that! Not yet, anyway. I want to talk to him about what we could possibly have together and let him know some stuff, that's all. No heavy petting." She chuckled girlishly and twirled her hair "It's just dinner. There's no need to mother me, Jane."

Jane sounded defensive, but took the comment as a joke. "I'm not mothering you, Naomi. Just looking out for you. That's what friends do. As long as it is just dinner, I'm happy with it. Just don't let him try anything. He's a bloke, they are all predators."

"I'll be fine, Jane. We're going out. He's only coming here to pick me up."

"It's the picking up of you I'm worried about, Naomi!" Jane burst out laughing.

Naomi smiled.

18th November

Naomi had spent almost the entire day getting herself ready for her evening out with David. Despite her excitement, the day had passed her by quite quickly.

David's day, on the other hand had gone slowly. He too was excited, but had also been incredibly nervous. He had been in Naomi's 'friend zone' for so long now, he felt certain that this would be his only chance to escape from it, or he would forever have lost his chance.

As promised, David had picked Naomi up from the flat promptly and they walked together the mile or so to the restaurant. Naomi sat opposite him and had felt completely relaxed all evening. Her conversation was light and bubbly whilst David's had been more serious and about them as a couple. He was gentle with his comments, but it had not escaped Naomi's attention that David was fishing for something a little more than just a boyfriend/girlfriend relationship. She didn't mind this conversation though, but it did feel like it was a bit too soon. Still, she was happy to amuse David to keep him happy, he was clearly still nervous, even into the third bottle of wine. If she had found the conversation too uncomfortable, she would have told him. She had supposed that it must have predominantly been the wine talking.

David watched Naomi closely and admired every little move she made. She was so graceful that David thought, through his intoxicated mind that each movement must have been rehearsed, they were so perfect. He had held her gaze for a couple of seconds longer than he was normally comfortable holding, and Naomi had responded favourably by not looking away too quickly. She returned his gaze and then bore down into him with the eyes that David was quickly falling for. Everything about them was, in his mind at least, perfect. The colour, the shape and how they blinked. Her eyes were simply beautiful eyes.

The longer he looked at them, the deeper his feelings for her became. He was falling very quickly in love with her. He had been slowly falling for years, but now she had him on his own, he had reached the summit of his desire for her, and if he were to just take a couple more steps forward, then the slope down the other side into love would be steep and very slippery.

-|-

Walking Naomi home from the bar, David made sure he held her close, his arm tightly round her waist to ensure she didn't fall over.

He had promised that he would walk her home, and that is exactly what he did. They stood outside the door to the flat. It was cold and Naomi could feel the warmth of his steaming breath on her face as he looked slightly down into her bleary, intoxicated eyes.

Naomi looked into David's eyes. They were a bit bleary too. She saw something in them that made her completely forget Aiden for that moment. She saw how genuine David really was and how he felt for her.

"Thank you for walking me home" Naomi said, as she clung onto the door handle for support. "You're great. Thank you."

Naomi reached into her handbag for her keys and managed to drop them on the pavement. She giggled as she bent over to pick them up, but David stopped her with a grab of the shoulder, stood her up and bent over to collect the keys himself.

"That's very sweet of you David. Thank you." She burped. They both laughed loudly as Naomi let them into the hallway.

"David, I think it is time you went home now, don't you?" Naomi was slurring quite badly. She was certain of her words, but not really certain she wanted David to go home. She wanted him near her, close to her, touching her, naked and without the memory of Aiden between them. She really quite fancied David at the moment, and he was there for the taking.

David felt the same. He wanted Naomi. He had done for years. But he was a gentleman and suggested that he walk home. Half and hour and he would be home. He was playing a game with her. Would she invite him in to stay, or let him walk home. He bet that because they had been lightly flirting all evening, that she would invite him in. And she did.

Naomi had changed her mind now. "David, you may as well stay here the night. I'll make up the spare bed for you." She wobbled and slurred a little.

"Are you sure it won't be a problem for you?" David smelled his chance to get into bed with her. The chance he had been waiting for was finally right in front of him.

"It's fine. No problem at all. Come on, let's have a night cap." She grabbed David by the wrist and led him up the stairs.

"It's very quiet in here. Don't you think? I'll put on some music." Naomi said as they walked into the living room.

Naomi hadn't played any music for more than two weeks and was not sure what would come on. She was also not certain what she wanted to happen next with David really should. She felt like she needed to be close to someone; closer than would normally be acceptable for two friends. She needed someone to be inside of her, loving her, keeping her tightly within his arms. It felt like a deep urge, her pelvis craving for the push of a man against it, inside her, making love with her. It all felt so wrong, but right at the same time.

The music played. She drew David close, letting her inner desires take over. She hadn't the strength any more to fight the urge to kiss him. David opened his mouth to say something, but she broke the words off with a finger placed firmly against his lips before he could say anything.

"Shut up, David and hold me." Naomi ordered. And they stood, swaying slightly to the music; David held her awkwardly and Naomi leaned into his chest like he was an island and she was stranded there, hugging the sand, scratching it, and grateful she was washed ashore before she drowned.

David began to stroke Naomi's hair down her back and she felt her shoulders shuffle at his touch. He could smell her shampoo faintly beneath the aroma of wine. He used his fingertips and ran them down the back of her arms. "That tickles." Naomi whispered into his shirt buttons.

"Does it?" he whispered back. "Sorry."

"Don't stop. It's nice"

As the track finished, Naomi looked up, her arms and shoulders covered in tingling goosebumps, she turned David round and sat him in a chair. She left the room with a promise to be back soon. David heard the bathroom light turn on and the door close. He sat and waited, wondering what would happen next. She had said that he could sleep in the spare room. Perhaps she was collecting some sheets.

Still he waited. A few minutes later, he heard a door open and the light switch off. Then another light switched on, then nothing again. He craned his neck round to see if there was anything behind him, but he could see nothing or no-one there.

After another five minutes of sitting in silence, waiting for Naomi to return, David got up to look for her. As he had slept in the spare room before, he checked there first. The room was empty and dark, but with the light from the hallway, he could see that the bed was not made.

Down the hall, he saw Naomi's bedroom light on and the door slightly open. He opened it a crack and saw Naomi lying on the bed half dressed. It looked like she had been thrown there, but looking down to her feet, it was clear that she had fallen onto the bed trying to remove her jeans and given up.

-|-

Demons from across the city were gathering on Blackfriars Bridge. They stood around in groups, talking about what was to come, their bent and twisted forms turning this way and that, looking at where they would be going and laughing at what they would be doing. There were hundreds of them.

No-one south of the river had seen anything like this for a long time.

Aiden, Duncan and a group of others stood watching from the large crossroads of Blackfriars Road that lead to the bridge, Stamford Street and Southwark Street. All the masonry from the surrounding buildings lay in smoldering piles. The railway bridge had collapsed and the massive metal sections of it were lying molten and deformed across the road.

Trying to listen to what the demons were saying, Aiden moved closer, keeping as hidden as he could around the rubble of what used to be a riverside restaurant. The tables and chairs were scattered across the road. He couldn't get any closer without being seen.

He heard them discussing a rout of epic proportions. A huge gang attack on the Southwark part of London. They were to capture and torture as many as possible. "Bring as many of them to their knees as possible." He heard one demon shout. "Get yourselves ready." There was a loud cry, a baying for blood.

Aiden got back to the others as quickly as possible.

"We've got to go. You need to get away from Southwark as quickly as you can." Aaron panted. "They are coming, and they will not be light handed with anyone. There are hundreds of them. Go."

The group made off. Some made their way along Stamford Street towards Waterloo Bridge, whilst others headed back into Southwark to warn as many of the others as possible.

Through the flames and confusion of people trying to find the quickest way out of Southwark, the sound of the demons beginning their rampage came. It moved the smoke and the flames as demons moved quickly, like animals hunting in a wood. They seemed to come from nowhere, jumping out of windows and over piles of masonry, attacking anyone that wasn't one of them.

Hunting in pairs or threes, the demons picked on the slowest and the weakest of the Lesser Souls first, whilst others enjoyed chasing the fresher souls into corners, mercilessly beating them and setting them free again, only to be captured by another group nearby.

Most of the souls who were close to giving up just stood

and accepted their punishments, too weak and mentally battered to fight back. They were mown down with pipes smashing their skulls and cracking their limbs. The pitiful wretches just fell where they stood, slumping to the ground with their eyes rolling back in their heads, waiting to be beaten again by the next group. They would be in one piece again soon enough, and they knew it.

In the middle of all the destruction and carnage strode Charon, his human-hide cloak flapping behind him with each powerful swish of his pole. It sent anyone in front of him out of his way, crashing into the ground. He would hit others across the face with the shackles he carried in the other hand, lacerating bodies and faces.

He called to the demons to move faster and to get more. His orders were maniacal, purposeful and determined. He barked instructions to the groups as he came upon them, standing tall above their hunched and decrepit forms, egging them on to be even more cruel to this one than that one.

Aiden and Duncan were hiding in the crumbling ruins of a building along Tooley Street, opposite the entrance to Battle Bridge Lane. The remains of a great glass building lay shattered across the road. It cut them both as they hid, listening to the chaos. Duncan cut to his legs badly as he jumped over a pile of bricks and landed on a large pane of broken glass. It stuck out of his left leg. He grabbed hold of it and tried to pull it out, his shriek of pain temporarily drowning out the furor going on around them.

"Aiden, go! Leave me here. I'll hide, and I'll be OK."

Finding a rag nearby, and nearly being spotted by a pack of demons, Aiden tore out the large glass shard and dressed the wound as best he could. He didn't care about Duncan at all, but this unwitting friend was needed for Aiden's own plan to escape. "You're coming with me. I need you. Come on."

Half running, half hobbling, Duncan clung to Aiden as they hurried as quickly as they could down Battle Bridge Lane, passed English Grounds and down to the river.

Aiden had forgotten the stench of the bodies floating in the water. It stung his nose though as they got closer, making him gag. Duncan was getting weaker. "Come on, Duncan. Stick with me. We're nearly there."

Fresh bodies in the river from the demon's rout had joined those already bloated and decayed by the putrid water. They had turned the water browny red in colour, fresh blood added to septic scum that was already floating on the surface; hundreds of years of death at sea, all washed up long the banks on both sides. They had been warned that if they entered the river, their soul would be destroyed and will not be judged on the day of Armageddon. Such as it was for these poor souls, they were completely extinguished. No chance to have their sins forgiven.

Demons were close by as the pair reached the end of More London Place and the wreck of the building known as The Scoop. It lay, fallen over and smashed into millions of tiny piece of glass. They could only be a hundred metres from Tower Bridge now, and the jetty for Charon's Ferry across the river.

This had been Aiden's plan, to steal the ferry and return across the river on it. Simple, but surely effective given that they couldn't swim across.

Now the demons had picked up their scent. The trail of blood left mainly by Duncan's torn leg was a path for their thirst leading them like sharks to the meat. They could hear their running footsteps behind them and their cries as they continued to struggle their way to Tower Bridge.

Looming high above them, the decaying and ivy clad towers were a welcome sight as they clambered down the steps towards the ferry. It lay in the water, leaning over to one side, half out of the water.

"Can you stand, Duncan?" Aiden's voice was urgent, his eyes widening at the noise of the demons as it became louder and louder.

"Yeah, just about." He grimaced with the pain from his leg.

"Give me a hand to get it further out into the water."

The ferry was heavy on the fetid sand of the river bank. They pushed as hard as they could, and just as they were about to get their feet wet, the demons appeared at the top of the steps and charged down towards the thieves. Some were spattered with blood where they had struck their victims with pipes, wood or anything they could lay their hands on. Others were completely covered, their red figures glistening even deeper red in the glow of the surrounding burning. Behind them appeared Charon. "GET THEM!" he roared and all the demons jumped down to save the ferry and punish the thieves.

Aiden jumped in quickly just a Duncan made one last push to get the boat afloat. He clung to the bow, his legs dragging in the water behind him and the demons waded in after them.

"My legs, Aiden, my legs. I can't hold on any more." Duncan looked into Aiden's face, regretful of anything that he had done once alive and Aiden could see that this was Duncan's second death. The water was eating anything beneath the surface, the hands of the sea-dead reaching out for him, dragging him down to be with them. Duncan began to cry, realising that there was no hope at all.

Aiden stood and watched Duncan struggle to keep a grip on the bow of the ferry as it turned in the water. There was only room for one person on this escape, and Aiden had no intention of helping the murderer to survive.

Duncan's fingers were slipping on the slimy wood of the ferry. Aiden continued to watch the panic and pain rise in his eyes until the strength left his fingers and Duncan took the first mouth of the stagnant river. He floated in the water, seemingly having given up, quietly drowning. He couldn't say anything, his mouth was full. He struggled for a moment, and then sank with a thrash of his legs. His eyes never left Aiden's, and Aiden could see the betrayal he felt in them.

"Sorry, Duncan. There was never going to be space for you on this journey." Aiden sat heavily in the middle of the boat and looked towards bank where the demons were furiously shouting and calling for his blood. In front of them stood Charon. He stood still with his pole horizontal in both hands. He was shaking it with rage. Aiden watched him until the mist obscured his view of the bank and the glow of the city disappeared. He was drifting back from hell, he had escaped.

Charon's voice drifted through the mist "I'm going to hunt you down, Aiden. I will find you." The sound pierce every fibre of his soul. Aiden shivered and looked towards his destination. He had little doubt that Charon would be after him as soon as he got his ferry back.

-|-

Feeling that he couldn't leave her looking so undignified, David finished undressing Naomi himself. He felt awkward. He didn't feel like he was being very gentle with her. The jeans came off easily enough, leaving a black thong on show, teasing him. Standing by her head, Naomi's top proved a little more difficult to get her out of.

Handling her as carefully as he could, he pulled it up to her chest, pulled her arms above her head before yanking it over and almost off her arms. As it came over her face but with her arms still trapped inside, he leaned over her and kissed her gently on the lips. She sighed and he kissed her a little harder.

David was surprised when he felt her tongue flicking his lips. 'Oh God.' He said quietly to himself as little bolts of electricity shot though him.

Without warning, Naomi woke and with a twist of her body had released her arms from her top and was kneeling in front of David wearing nothing but the black thong and lacy black bra. She suddenly looked sober and more than a little playful. She laughed and walked on her knees over to him.

Grabbing his shirt collar she pulled his face to hers. With a sudden feeling of guilt, he mumbled something that could have been 'Naomi, this isn't right. It's too soon.' It didn't stop him kissing her back though, such was his weakness when confronted with a woman like her.

"I don't care, David. Not now. I have to do this. It will help me move on." How David could have stopped then was anyone's guess. His guilty feelings put to one side, he had decided that he was indeed helping his dear friend move on.

He started to unbutton his shirt whilst Naomi took care of the belt and trousers, their mouths struggling to keep together in the process. He grabbed her under the arms and lay her down on the bed when he had shuffled out of his shirt and kicked the trousers off. He lay on the bed beside her, admiring her skin by the light of the hallway.

"This is wrong, Naomi" he said, the guilt returning like a sledge hammer to his libido.

"No, it's not." She said grabbing his shoulder and pulling

him down to her again. The mixed touch of lace and skin on his chest was electrifying. "Make love to me, David."

David paused for a moment, taking his mouth away from hers with a wet smack. "Are you really sure, Naomi? This should not be happening at all. Not yet, at least." A hand rested on the top of her thong.

"Yes, David, just do it before I change my mind."

Feeling as lucky as any man would do when confronted by your drunk crush almost begging to be made love to, David moved down the bed and grabbed the thong that was pulled tight across her hips. As he began to pull them down, Naomi arched her back a little, just as the short trimmed hair of the mound between her legs became slowly visible. He slid the thong down her legs, making sure his fingers could feel as much of her skin as possible.

Taking down his own underwear, David surprised himself by how ready he was when he sprang up from beneath his boxer shorts. He was keen and eager to discover what it would finally feel like to be with this woman who had loved and lusted after for so long. He hoped she wouldn't be disappointed. Naomi had removed her bra for him already and now lay naked on the bed amongst the scruffy sheets.

He lay down next to her again with his hand running up her legs, pausing between them for a moment, feeling the hair between his fingers. He could feel tiny movements of her pelvis, encouraging his fingers to move down further. Tenderly he stroked before moving taking a gentle handful of breast.

Deftly moving on top of her, Naomi allowed him in and wriggled as he settled, the breath of anticipation escaping him as an immense relief. On his elbows, he stroked Naomi's hair away from her face and looked into her eyes. He could feel himself moving inside her, she felt so close around him, welcoming. Her skin against his, her feet tucked behind his knees and arms around his neck filled him with a sense of being wanted, but her comment about doing this to help her move on from Aiden stayed with him, spoiling the mood a little as he felt she didn't really want that to happen.

Their bodies were moving together like a shallow wave on a hot summer's day; moving steadily up and down, smoothly, almost lazily. Their mouths copied the motions of their hips, moving in and out, tongues exploring and lips feeling their way round faces and necks. Both of them could feel a storm on the horizon as the tide of their movements began to rise to the breakwater. Naomi's movements under him were so rhythmic, precise and constant that the point of no return was nearly upon him and David felt he was about to wreck himself. With a sudden lurch like a ship crashing onto rocks, David could not help but let himself go, and felt himself drowning in the waves of his elation and he became completely helpless for a moment. Naomi had joined him on the rocks and she too was struggling to keep herself afloat, gasping for air in the waves.

They lay on the bed as survivors of a wreck would do a beach. Their heads reeling with what had just happened, and now seemingly fully sober. The regret on David's face was clearly evident. He should never have done that, and Naomi acutely aware of what she had just let herself do was now getting out from beneath David and making for her dressing gown to protect what dignity she had left.

-|-

Aiden had seen everything from the bedroom door. Too shocked to do anything about it at first, he was content to let the rage grow inside him, letting the fire build and build, allowing the anger to engulf him completely. He stood trembling at the very thought of what he was about to do. His eyes had turned black with envy; Envious that they were alive and that he was dead. But more than that, he was jealous that David had just fucked his girlfriend. His oldest friend, his best friend, the man he would have chosen to be the best man at his wedding had just taken the woman he loves to bed, and fucked her right in front of him. He didn't care that he had stopped and checked with Naomi that it really was alright to carry on. He should have had more respect for him than that.

"I'm going to make you pay for this, David you bastard" Aiden said calmly to himself. *"And Naomi, oh my dear Naomi, you will pay for it too."*

Naomi returned from the bathroom wearing her dressing gown. She shivered as she walked through the door where Aiden was standing but paid no attention to it. The evening was cold anyway. Aiden moved to David's side of the bed.

Sitting on the bed next to David, she noticed that he had put his underwear back on and was laying on the bed with a hand on his forehead. "David? Are you OK?" Naomi said as pulled his hand away and held it loosely.

"We should never have done that, Naomi. Not so soon after Aiden."

"Too fucking right, David!" Aiden shouted, allowing the anger to overflow and he threw a fist into David's head, grabbing hold of his soul and twisting it tightly round his hand as if it were a rope. He didn't know how he was doing it, he was just following the actions he would have made if he were alive.

David convulsed in agony as Aiden pulled hard on his subconscious mind. Letting out a blood curdling cry as his back bend painfully too far backward, his arms hung helpless back from his shoulders. His face turned red with the effort of trying to bend his body forwards again, the veins in his neck bulging from the strain. Aiden let him go. David dropped to the bed, shocked and in pain.

"Oh, this is good" Aiden growled through gritted teeth, realising what he was capable of.

Naomi was stunned and dashed from the bed and was stood against the wall, pinned their from her own fear, unable to move. Aiden flickered in and out of view in front of her. She could see him move in fits and starts, visible one second, gone the next. His face was twisted and growling and at the same time gleeful. He looked like he was exacting revenge on David's body.

Not finished with David yet, Aiden reached into David's head again and took hold of him with both hands this time. *"You bastard, David, I'm going to tear your fucking soul to pieces."* He was spitting venomously at David and screwing his hands round in a ball.

"Aiden, NO!" Naomi screamed into the room, but seemingly at nobody other than David.

With a horrifying gurgle and pops from the joints in his body, David was forced to twist his into an impossible shape like his subconscious mind had lost the ability to control movement. His joints were over extending and the tendons and ligaments were stretching, causing David to nearly faint from the pain. He was panting to try to control it. His eyes were fixed on Naomi who could just stand watching, too terrified to move. David looked like he would snap and his eyes didn't know how to react, they went from tightly closed to wide open, to crying and back again. Aiden held him still, half rolled over on the bed, arms behind his back, his fingers nearly touching his toes. They were bent backwards and his feet and toes were pointing straight, like a ballerina.

Letting go for a moment, Aiden allowed David to recover his position. He lay panting on the bed when Aiden pushed his head in to David's. *"Hello. David."* He said menacingly. *"Guess who."*

"Aiden." David was trying to catch his breath and said name whilst breathing in.

"That's right, David. It's me. I'm not very happy with you. Leave Naomi alone, and I'll leave your soul intact."

"I can't do that, Aiden. You're dead, not me." David tried to sound defiant, but was in too much pain, and he wouldn't know how to stop him even if he wasn't.

"That may be so, David. But I can do THIS." Aiden twisted David's body round again, but further this time and all his fingers popped at once with the over extension and David could feel what seemed like the vertebra in his back begin rubbing together. *"And . . . there's nothing you can do about it"*

Through tightly gritted teeth, David began to scream again in the most excruciating agony.

"You were my best friend, David. And you do this to me?" Aiden dropped David and turned his rage to Naomi. *"Now it's her turn."*

David lay panting on the bed, unable to quickly straighten his twisted and stretched body as Aiden approached Naomi. All he could manage to say was a warning for Naomi to run, but she never got out of the front door, Aiden become more and more visible the more angry he became. Aunty Esther had warned her of this. She had said that the more angry and jealous a soul becomes, the more likely they are to break through the veil.

Aiden was upon Naomi like a wild cat landing on it's prey. He pushed his hands and arms into her body and took control of her, forcing her hard into the front door, banging her head against it. With his head thrust firmly into hers, he began to speak again. *"Naomi, how can you do this to me?"* she could hear him clearly; the upset and tears in his voice. It was the voice of someone who felt completely betrayed, and angry. *"You know I love you. How could you?"*

"You're hurting me, Aiden? If you really loved me you wouldn't hurt me, would you?" Naomi was trying to reason with him.

"No, no. Of course not..." Aiden staggered backwards out of Naomi's head, staring at his hands. What had he done? His rage had overtaken him and he had used his rage on her. The end must have come for him now. He felt he could never forgive himself for being so jealous. He shook his head and looked towards Naomi, not believing he could ever have hurt her.

Naomi, quickly recovering from her encounter watched Aiden retreat from her and flicker in and out of view again, his rage subsiding. The veil was taking him back to the other side. He looked at her, eyes pleading and mouthing some words she couldn't hear. "Go, Aiden. Go away. You don't belong here anymore." The tone of her voice was so pained, sad and longing him to go.

He flickered out of view one last time. His desperately sorry stream of apologies and begs for forgiveness were never heard.

-|-

David had managed to straighten his back and limbs and was lying face down on the bed, feeling the ache in what felt like every bone in his body reverberate through him. His breathing was shallow to avoid his ribs expanding too far.

Naomi climbed carefully onto the bed next to him, not sure where to touch him.

"Has he gone?" David's muffled voice came from the pillow. His face was embedded into it.

"Yes, David. He's gone. Are you alright?"

"I don't know. Everything hurts. Not sure if I can move much at the moment. I'm cold. Can you put a blanket over me, please?"

"Of course." From the wardrobe, Naomi took a clean fleece blanket, laid it over David and crawled underneath with him. She stroked the hair from his face and he looked at her out the corner of his right eye, the other one tucked out of sight by the pillow. She looked so drawn, scared and yet, she was caring for him. He gave her as much of a smile as he could and moved a hand onto her arm.

Naomi laid her head down on the pillows next to his and looked at him, still stroking his hair. "I'm so sorry, David."

"I've not known a jealous ex-boyfriend like that before." David's tone was sarcastic "That was some beating. I couldn't do anything to stop him. He was so strong." David tried not to laugh at his own joke, leaving Naomi to join him in seeing the humour in it. He failed and chuckled, but stopped quickly when the pain in her chest bit him hard. "Are you sure he's gone?"

"Yes, I'm pretty sure. I saw him disappear. He looked really upset. I think he hates me now, like I betrayed him with you. I don't think he'll come back now. We've hurt him too much." Naomi's voice was regretful. She had not ever wanted to hurt Aiden, but he was dead, and what was she supposed to do? Live alone forever?

"Good. I doubt I could go through that again. I'm here for you though, Naomi. If you'll have me, that is."

She smiled at him, leaned over and gave him a kiss on the cheek. "You're not much good to me at the moment, are you?" she looked beneath the blanket at his half naked, beaten body. He rolled his eyes at her. "I'm joking, and yes, I think you'll do fine."

"If it's alright with you, I think I might stay away from you for a few days. You know, just to make sure he's not coming back. I'll call you every day though." David made to get up, grimacing as his joints complained at the movement.

Naomi was whispering now, keeping her words private. "Stay, David, please. Just for tonight. I'll do you breakfast in the morning, then you can go."

"OK. Not sure if I can get up anyway! Thanks."

19th November

The streets of London were a lonely place for the dead. The busy living people seemed to rush everywhere, totally single-minded without sparing a thought to what may be so close but unseen - the world according to the dead. Aiden was sure that if some of them would just concentrate hard enough, and let their minds open to the possibility of the invisible becoming visible, then it would happen and someone might see him. Nothing like that had happened in the six days days since he lost control of his anger and attacked Naomi.

Sitting on the top of Primrose Hill, Aiden looked beyond the open space to scattered trees that were stripped naked by the winter frosts towards the city. He could see the skyline silhouetted in front of the bright blue sky of the morning. The frost on the grass around him were slowly burning off as the sun lazily rose. A few dog-walkers, all wrapped up against the bitter chill of the morning plodded round the footpaths, throwing balls and sticks for their over excited pets. Each one of them looked like smokers; their breath steaming in the frigid air like they were chain smoking cigarettes.

Aiden sat and looked regretfully towards the city, dreaming of what might have been. He was slumped on the bench, homeless and lost. And dead.

All his emotions has drained away, he was numb with the knowledge that he had hurt Naomi, something that he thought he was not capable of doing. He had kicked himself time and again since then for being so stupid and hot headed. How could he begin to contact her now, after what he had done? He would have to wait until he felt ready to go back there. He had time. He had an eternity of it, provided Charon didn't catch up with him in the meantime. Then he would have to wait to see if she had forgiven him for what he had done, and that would most likely take even longer.

One of the dog walkers sat on the other end of the bench to Aiden. She started talking to her dog, fussing it and rubbing it's ears. Then she threw a ball for it. It tore off down the hill after it, running so quickly that it over shot it and had to turn quickly to catch it before it bounced over it's head. Catching it, it dutifully trotted back up the hill to it's owner. "Daft dog!" she said. "Good boy. Off you go!" She threw the ball again, degloved her hand and pulled out her phone.

Aiden leaned over and looked at the screen. She was texting someone called Richard Green.

Morning sweetheart. Put the kettle on. I'll be home in 10. X

Pressing the 'Send' button, she stood and began to walk up the hill behind Aiden. "Come on Jake!" she called out behind her and the faithful dog cam charging up the hill towards her like she was going to leave him behind.

Aiden figured he would miss the chance of taking a dog for a walk and going home to Naomi's warm welcome who had made him a cup of coffee, or better still, be curled up in bed all cosy and waiting for him to jump back in with her.

-|-

"Aiden? I'm Camael, member of the Principium Angeli. Mind if I join you?"

Aiden looked up to see a stranger standing at the end of the bench. He was surprised to have someone talking to him. He had been alone for six days now and to be engaging in a conversation felt odd.

The Principium had been looking for Aiden ever since he had managed to escape from Charon. Camael was a shifty looking angel dressed in neutral tones of pastel grey. His long coat was hiding something Aiden couldn't quite see. He didn't have a chance to invite Camael to sit, he just did, crossed his legs and stared towards the early morning London skyline.

Aiden didn't say anything. He simply looked at Camael. There was something threatening about this angel. He kept his coat wrapped around him and arms folded.

The two of them sat on the bench for a couple of moments in silence, each thinking what to say. They looked like a pair of secret agents meeting for the first time, ready to impart their information, but they had to exchange code words before they could and neither was prepared to go first. They both sat defensively, arms and legs crossed, not looking at each other, but very aware of the presence of the other.

A chilly wind blew round them both. Aiden shivered both through nerves and the cold caress of the wind on his arms.

"Charon's looking for you." Camael said quietly, turning and leaning his head towards Aiden.

Aiden did not look back. He just stared towards the top of the London Eye he could see on the horizon. "I can't think he's very happy with me at the moment."

"That's putting it mildly, Aiden. You have a choice now. You can come with me now, and I will take you to him, or you can run and hide from him until he catches you." Aiden turned now and looked at the Camael. "He will catch you, Aiden. I promise. And then your time in hell will be worse than what you have already seen."

Aiden's tone was dispassionate, emotionless and uncaring. "Doesn't take kindly to escapees then? What can he possibly do to make me feel anymore desperate and alone?"

"That, I cannot tell you."

"How did you find me then, and Charon hasn't?"

Camael smiled a suspect smile, his grey eyes narrowing and he raised a finger to his nose. "I'm cleverer than him. You see, he is looking for around the area where Naomi lives. That is where he expects you to be. But I know what happened last week and that you fled, so I've been looking in places you might hide. Remember I am an angel and know a lot about you."

"I went back to the cathedral. There was no-one there. It was empty. What happens if I want to go with you back to Gabriel?"

"You cannot. It is not allowed. Your time to pass through the light has gone. I cannot rescue you, but I can give you an easier time with Charon if you come with me now. The choice must be yours though, I don't want to force you. None of the Principium want to force anyone to face their destiny. It will come to them one way or another."

"Uriel dragged me to the cathedral against my will."

"That is as maybe, but you were given the choice to enter the light though, weren't you? And you chose not to."

"Yeah, I guess." Aiden was feeling very sorry that he had not gone into the light when he had the chance. He felt that he now had a fight on his hands to stay here with Naomi to look after her. How could he fend off the Principium and Charon? They both wanted him away from this earth. They wanted him tucked up out of the sight and mind of the living; somewhere where he couldn't influence or contact them. He really had lost Naomi now, hadn't he? Yes, he feared he had. But the thought of going with Camael to Charon was almost as unbearable as seeing Naomi with David. He had to stay and do his best to keep away from them for as long as possible.

"Through your jealousy and anger, Aiden, you have been changing your destiny. You were promised by us that you would spend eternity with Naomi, that you were destined to be together. You have lost that chance now. But you can still share eternity if Naomi chooses to come to you when it is her turn to die. Do you think she will want to go to hell and spend eternity in misery with you?"

"No." Aiden was sinking fast. He couldn't spend an eternity without Naomi. He felt the familiar feelings of anger building within him again. He started breathing heavily, thinking only of himself and the misery he would be facing.

The pair looked at each other, the strengthening wind blowing wisps of hair across Camael's face. His wise but serious eyes boring into Aiden's. "If you think you can change Naomi's destiny to enable her to spend eternity with you, Aiden, then I am afraid you are not going to succeed."

Aiden began to think quickly. He had managed to speak to her, even if he did threaten her. He knew he could break through the veil and confront her. Perhaps if he could break her mentally, then he could change her destiny that way. He would pick away at her until she depended on him and his guidance. And then, he could make her want him. Yes, that's what he would do.

Aiden stood and went to walk away. "Camael, thank you. You have been very helpful."

Camael grabbed his arm and stood to face him properly. "Don't make me take you, Aiden. It will be easier for you to come with me now."

"You don't understand how much I love her and want to be with her, do you?"

"Yes, I do, and that is why you must come. Your love, or rather, obsession with her, will break her. This is not your place any more. For the love of God, Aiden, come with me! You will do more harm than good."

Camael's protest was not heard. Aiden had pulled his arm away and was walking off down the hill towards the city. He would have to lose himself if he were to stay safe. The Principium and Charon would both be looking for him now.

"Don't do this Aiden. We will find you, if Charon doesn't find you first." Camael called his final warning and then walked in the opposite direction, slowly vanishing into the wind.

Aiden heard the warning, but chose not to heed it. Under his breath he muttered his last will and testament. "I'll have to make sure I hide well from you then, won't I? Naomi *will* love me again, and we *will* spend eternity together, even if I have to drag her to hell myself. She will always be mine."

21st November

With growing anger at Aiden, Naomi had relived her dinner out with David and the events afterwards. How dare he think he can come along and almost break David in half and then threaten her like that? He's dead for crying out loud, and he should remember that. No way should he be permitted to interfere in her life. Exactly that, *her* life.

She felt she had to find a way to let Aiden know that he was no longer welcome and that he should go to wherever he needs to go. They will meet again soon enough. After all, a lifetime is nothing but a blip compared to an eternal death.

"Do you think I should try to contact Aiden, Jane?" They were sitting enjoying a glass of wine at The Royal Oak next to the open fire.

Jane nearly spat out her wine. Shocked, she wiped her mouth carefully and leaned forward so she could be heard with a quiet voice. "Are you serious? Keep your voice down, will you. You can't go and say things like that in front of everyone."

Naomi looked around. Being Wednesday, the pub wasn't very busy so there weren't many people in that could have heard her. And they all could have heard; she had had more than a couple of glasses and her voice was louder than normal

"Nobody heard, Jane. So, how can I do it? A seance? Ouija board? Or should I go to a medium?"

"Jesus, Naomi, you're serious aren't you?"

"Yes, I am. Deadly." She smirked at her poor taste, as did Jane.

Jane coughed and thought quickly. She had brushed with occult practises in the past and she had no real desire to revisit them. Some had been really good, and others had been so terrifying that she and the groups involved has vowed never to speak of the event again. But she had to give Naomi an answer.

"Let it go, Naomi. Don't go messing with things you don't understand or know how to control. Why do you want to try to contact him anyway? Have you seen him again?" Jane remembered her visit on the night of the funeral.

"Yes, and more besides that." She went on to tell Jane exactly what had happened three nights ago at the flat with David and what he had done to him and how he had threatened her. She neglected to mention that she had been caught by Aiden making love.

Jane was shocked and worried for her friend too. She was as confused as Naomi about how Aiden could have been so callous towards her. As a jealous late-boyfriend, she could understand, but as a loving long term partner, no. What would make him come back from the grave to do that?

"I can't believe he would do that to you."

"He did, and that is why I want to try to contact him and send him on his way. I want him gone and to leave me alone." Jane heard the anger in Naomi's voice.

Reluctantly, Jane offered a glimpse into her secret. "I've dabbled in this sort of thing before. It can be very dangerous if you don't know what you are doing. You understand that, don't you? You need to find someone who can help you properly."

"Can't you help? You just said you've dabbled before."

Jane recoiled at the suggestion, waving her hand in the air. "No way, Naomi. I love you lots, but if Aiden has actually physically attacked David and tried to control you, then this is right out of my league." Jane thought for a moment and held Naomi's gaze whilst she thought. She really want to have to go through this stuff again, but Naomi was her friend. "I know someone who may be willing to help though. Do you want me to call him for you?"

"Yes. Who is he?"

"He's an old friend. Darryl Cowling is his name. I used to do this kind of stuff with him. He was always very good and looked after us. If I can find him, I'll ask him for you."

"When did you last see him?

"Must be fifteen or twenty years ago now, I guess. I'll have to track him down. We had a big scare one night and some of the group never came back, it scared them so much." Jane's voice trailed off, she was sickened by the memory of what happened.

"What about him? What happened?"

"I'm not saying, Naomi. I swore to everyone that I would never talk about it to anyone, not even to those in the group. Needless to say it was horrendous. Darryl said he would never do the Ouija Board again. That was the last time I heard from him."

"Thank you so much, Jane, I really appreciate it. If you can find Darryl, I'd like to do it on Friday night, and I want you, Peter and David there with me. A united front of Aiden's friends, if you like, you know, to tell him where to go!"

"Oh, Naomi, I don't think that would be a good idea. What if...?"

Concerned, Naomi looked at Jane with raised eyebrows. "What if what, Jane?"

"Nothing, nothing. If I can find Darryl, I'll do my best to contact him for you. But I make no guarantees that'll he'll want to talk to me or even help you out. Peter will be there if we can arrange it and I can talk him into it."

"OK. Great. I think! I'll work on David. I think he'll be reluctant though."

-|-

Searching the internet for Darryl Cowling wasn't difficult. He had become quite well known in occultist circles for his apparent abilities for contacting spirits and his expert use of Ouija boards, not to mention other communication methods.

His blog was awash with posts about what he had been up to, paranormal investigations and the like. Jane was hopeful.

The page about Darryl himself showed a picture of a weathered man, clearly him but looking much older than when she had last seen him. His face was lined and looked very wise. There was no mention of the activities of the first group he formed for investigations into paranormal experience some twenty years ago. This was the group that Jane had been a member of and now she became doubtful he would remember her or even return her message.

Filling out the contact form on the page, Jane typed a note.

Hi Darryl,

You probably don't remember me, but some years ago, you formed a group in Hampstead looking into paranormal experiences and you guided us through some interesting seances and things like that. Anyway, the group disbanded in the summer of 1993 I think it was, and we all lost touch.

My name then was Jane Penrose and a friend of mine really needs some help with her late boyfriend. He won't leave her alone. He died at the beginning of October and has yet to cross over.

I know we agreed to go our separate ways, but there is no-one else I can think of who can help. Please Darryl, contact me, even if you can offer some advice. I am very scared for her.

Blessed be,

Jane.

SEND

There. She had done all she could for the moment.

She was scared for Naomi and hoped that Darryl would contact her sooner rather than later, but inside, she knew that the last experience they had had together was so terrifying that he would probably just delete her message as soon as he read it.

It was a cloudy night, and Jane looked at her reflection in the kitchen window whilst she filled a glass with water. She looked at herself closely and thought aboutr her brushes with the occult in the past.

She had always had success with a ouija board. Her old friends used to say that she was the key to it working, that she was a channel for the spirits to come through, until the last time she had taken part that is. The remembrance of that night came back to her now; the cold in the room, their breath steaming in the warm summer air and the shuddering of the table beneath the board.

Jane remembered the goosebumps on their skin, and the terror of not being allowed to leave the table by the vicious demonic thing they had contacted.

Occasionally she would dream of what happened. It would make her wake up in a cold sweat, screaming with the feeling of cold hands around her neck and invisible knees in her chest. Her eyes were searching for someone to help her, but her so-called friends retreated and watched her get choked by the demon they had set free. It was only Darryl who came to help. He said some words she had never heard before, perhaps in Latin and then the attack stopped with an incredible wind and further chill to them all, and a loud howling.

Eventually, the spirit left, leaving them all shaken and scared to the core. They vowed never to speak of it again, or ever do a board again in case it came back.

'D-Dink' a new email had arrived.

Jane looked slowly round to the breakfast bar with her laptop on. The email screen was open and at the top she could read, even from the sink, that the message was from Darryl.

Hardly wanting to open it to see his response, the fear from all those years ago crept up her spine.

The message subject simply said *'Call me. Now.'* Inside were no words other than *'Hi, Jane. Long time no see. Darryl'* and his mobile number.

She stared at the message feeling that she had already gone too far and began to fear the worse. She had to go through with it for Naomi's sake, and Aiden's she supposed.

Going through her coat pockets, she found her phone, sent a text to Naomi and then called Darryl.

23rd November

The sky darkened quickly as the clouds trundled in. They smothered the sunset with their heavy threat of rain and the feeling they were bringing with them something bad. Naomi watched from the living room window, a feeling in the pit of her stomach swelled up, making her feel sick. She was worried about the evening and what it would bring, and she worried even more about what it might take away.

Over the last few days, her feelings for David had grown. He had called every day as he had promised and was now, thankfully feeling better after his experience with Aiden. Their conversations had been long and only the first one mentioned Aiden by name.

Naomi confessed that she had no idea if Aiden had actually gone or if he was there in the flat watching and listening to her. As a result of this confusion, their conversations were cryptic, non-specific, and certainly not about them as a couple, just in case Aiden was there and turned nasty on her.

If Naomi was honest with herself, she was terrified of Aiden and what he was capable of. Tonight she may have to face that fear if this strange Darryl person turned up. Jane had said he would, but then she had backed that up with an 'I hope' statement.

Darryl had suggested that Jane arrive before him to run through what will happen and to set everything up for when he arrived. Naomi had been out to buy candles that morning as well as some furniture polish, for nothing more than making the table smoother with some wax. It was now cleaner than it had been since it was bought, probably.

When confirming that Darryl would be coming, Naomi had asked her why she had not been in touch with him for such a long time. Jane had instantly gone into a defensive mood and refused to answer the question, saying that it was long time ago and a lot of water had passed under the bridge.

When pushed for an answer and Jane had curtly said that Naomi 'would not understand' but 'might do after Friday night.'

Naomi hadn't liked that answer one little bit and it made her feel very uneasy. What had happened in her past to make Jane so jittery about it?

-|-

David looked pale as he knocked at the door, the clouds hanging heavily above, ready to open themselves all over him. He looked up at them as Naomi let him in. She kissed him and took his coat.

"No-one's here yet. You OK? Good to see you." She lead David up the stairs.

"You too. I'm fine, but really not looking forward to tonight." His hands twitched in the kitchen as she made him a drink. She sat down with him at the table.

"David, thank you for coming. This will be the only time we do this, I promise. It means so much to me that you are here."

David looked at her. He looked right into the backs of her eyes. "I'd do anything for you, Naomi. You know that." His voice was determined and nervous at the same time.

Naomi felt his gaze, and returned it with one of her own. "I know, David. Thank you." She leaned across their drinks and kissed him, properly this time. Her touch giving him reassurance and the shot of confidence he needed.

"What about this Darryl chap that's supposed to be coming?"

Just then, there was a knock at the door.

"One minute, that'll be Jane and Peter." Naomi left David alone in the kitchen.

David spoke under his breath and looked out of the window at the sky. It was starting to rain. "Whoever he is, I hope he knows what he is doing."

There was uncomfortable laughter from Peter as he came into the kitchen to see David. Naomi and Jane went straight to the living room.

"Hi David, how you doing?" said David, banging two bottles of wine on the table in front of him. "Think we might need some dutch courage if this Darryl guy is as good as Jane says he is."

David gulped. "Hmm. Maybe. I guess you heard what Aiden did to me last week."

"I did. Are you alright? Did that really happen?"

"Yes, it bloody well did. I'm still aching now, and I'm not looking forward to tonight."

"Don't blame you, mate." He went through the cupboards looking for some glasses. "Darryl has promised Jane that he'll look after everyone and not let it get out of control. He does it all the time apparently."

"Somehow your words don't fill me with much confidence, Peter." He chuckled, feeling awkward at his joke.

"It'll be alright, I'm sure. Darryl sounds like a decent bloke."

Jane and Naomi came into the kitchen. It was six o'clock. "Right," Jane was remarkably cheerful but underneath it, Peter could feel her tension. "We've got the candles in their sticks and chairs around the table. We just need some letters and numbers on squares of paper now. Who's going to do it for me? David?"

From her handbag, Jane produced a handful of small squares of paper and a marker pen. She pushed them across the table to David.

"Right, Peter. Pour the wine, we can't do this with closed minds. A couple of glasses of wine each should loosen us up a bit."

Peter obeyed "Right. Red or white anyone?"

-|-

The stranger, Darryl had not yet arrived. He had texted Jane to tell her he was running late and to start preparing the board for when he arrived. It was eight o'clock and he was already an hour behind.

With the candles lit, the room lights turned down and the chairs pulled around, Naomi, David, Peter and Jane each looked at the torn-up scraps of paper neatly arranged in a circle on the table. Each one had a hand written letter of the alphabet on it, plus the numbers from zero to nine.

In the centre was a small upturned glass medicine tumbler onto which each of them would place a finger. Around it were some more scraps of paper - One with a sun on, another with the moon, plus four more with 'Yes', 'No', 'Hello' and 'Goodbye' on.

The friends looked at each other out the tops of their eyes as their faces continued to peer at the table before them.

None of them had done a ouija board apart from Jane, and they were all apprehensive about 'playing' with one now.

"It all looks okay to me." Said Jane after a moment of silence. She took a large mouthful of wine. She really wasn't sure if this was a good idea.

"Does it?" said David. "I wouldn't know. This kind of thing freaks me out. I'm sure it will be OK. We're not starting Darryl gets here though, are we?"

"It'll be fine, David. Don't worry about it. I did this a lot as a teenager. It's fun, and if we get hold of Aiden, then. . ."

Naomi interrupted. "Then what, Jane?" She was beginning to feel very nervous now. She had heard of bad things happening when people did not treat a ouija board properly.

"I guess we ask him how he is, Naomi." Peter snorted, trying not to laugh.

"How the hell do you think he is, Peter? He's dead for

Christ's sake!" Naomi was now believing this to be a very bad idea. She glanced at David quickly and cautiously, remembering what had happened between them just last week. What if Aiden did 'come through' and make contact? What would he say, and what would he do? After the attack, David had stayed away from Naomi, restricting his communication to phone calls and text messages only. He returned her glance with one of his own, his heart in his mouth with nerves. He was banging so hard in his ears, he thought he may not be able to hear anything when they eventually get started.

Trying to calm the mood between the friends, Peter suggested that they would find out shortly hopefully, or rather, he hoped that their intoxicated attempts at contacting their dead friend failed and they could all have a good laugh about it.

"OK" said David with a cough. "What next."

Jane cleared her throat too, hoping for the best.

All four friends jumped at the loud banging on the door downstairs.

"That'll be Darryl." Said Jane and she went to let him in, patting her chest to calm her racing pulse.

"Scared the crap out of me, that did!" said Peter, standing up and going over to the curtains. "Crappy night out tonight."

From the bottom of the stairs they could hear the deep voice of Darryl coming in and greeting Jane like a long lost friend, which they were of course. They chatted a while, and then their voices quietened. Naomi couldn't quite make out what they were saying, but she clearly heard Jane mention 'Aiden' and 'dangerous'. She drank some more wine to soften her nerves some more.

Jane reentered the room and introduced Darryl to the group. He was tall, long haired with more than a few days growth on his wide chin. He looked friendly enough and his deep voice was reassuring.

Darryl was very interested to meet Naomi and David and asked them lots of questions about what had happened on the night of the attack, saying that he needed to know what he might be dealing with. He seemed confident that he could successfully manage Aiden if he got out of control and made an effort to attack again. Besides, he should have a guide with him.

Getting himself comfortable, Darryl said some words to himself and apparently blessed the table and the glass. Then he leaned forwards. "If anyone doesn't want to do this. Leave now. Not just the table, but the building." He waited. The four friends looked at one another and especially David. He sat still and looked at each of them in turn.

"I'm not going anywhere." He said defiantly.

Darryl continued. "Right. Good. We all place an index finger lightly on the glass, and no-one is allowed to remove it. You can swap it with the other hand but make sure you do not let go. This is very important. You can lose the spirit if it is not strong enough to communicate through less than five people. I'll ask the questions to start with. Got it?"

The friends nodded to each other. They weren't sure if the temperature in the room was dropping or it was just their imaginations. None of them mentioned it though, for fear of sounding silly, but they could all feel it.

Gingerly, they all stretched a finger forwards and placed it on the glass.

Darryl continued. "OK. Everyone comfy?" They all nodded or uh-huh'd their readiness.

"Is this the bit where you say 'Is there anybody there'?" David asked

"Yes, and try not to laugh. This is not a game." Jane swallowed hard, a sense of foreboding came over her making her regret being pushed into this.

"OK." Darryl coughed, clearing his throat "Here goes." He paused again. Both David and Peter had hung their heads down and were giggling silently, their shoulders giving the game away.

"For crying out loud, boys! Give it a rest. This is serious." Jane said quietly, as if already in the presence of the spirits and not wanting them to hear. They stopped as best they could. "Go on, Darryl. Sorry. Bloody amateurs." She laughed away her own nerves.

"Is there anybody there?" Darryl said confidently.

The glass remained still on the table. The candle flames burned straight up. Nothing else.

"And again." Jane said.

"Is there anybody there?"

Still nothing.

"Is there anybody there?" Darryl said again, a little louder this time.

"Oh, this is ridiculous. I need another glass of wine." Peter was losing patience. He didn't see the point of staring at an empty glass sitting on a table with shreds of paper on it and getting a sore shoulder in the process without some refreshment.

"Peter, don't . . ." But before Jane could finish the sentence, Pete had left the table and gone for another bottle of wine from the kitchen. Jane called after him "Bloody hell, Peter! You shouldn't do that."

Naomi and David agreed that there was no problem and that they too fancied another drop of wine. Jane felt deflated, but a little relieved.

After cussing at the situation in the kitchen, Peter returned, refilled all the glasses and took his place back at the table. "OK," he said. "Let's go."

All the fingers returned to the glass and the group composed themselves again.

Looking round at the faces of her friends, and feeling that she was the only one who could actually make the board work, Jane said "Do you want me to start?" They all nodded their approval.

"OK." Said Darryl.

"Is there anybody there?" Jane's voice was serious.

"Is there . . ." The glass began to move slowly. It tipped slightly as it caught on the grain of the table. It stuttered it's way to the piece of paper with 'YES' printed on it in marker pen.

"Shit." Said David quietly.

"Oh my." Peter followed

"Is it Aiden?" whispered Naomi.

"Unlikely. It's not normally who you are looking for first of all. It is usually a passing spirit who might act as a guide for you." Darryl said.

David shivered. "Is it getting colder in here, guys?"

"Shh." The joint voices quietened him.

"What is your name?" asked Jane confidently.

The glass began to move again, unsteadily, tripping over itself on the way to the letter 'D'.

"Not so hard on the glass, it's struggling." Jane's instructions came with experience. The lighter the touch, the quicker the message.

'I'. Then it moved back to the middle of the circle and out again.

'Y'. Back to the centre and once more out to 'I' before coming to a slow rest in the centre once more.

"Di Yi?" said Naomi. Doesn't sound like a name to me.

"It doesn't have to be an English spirit. Remember, they don't have borders any more." Jane replied with a grin across the top of the glass.

"Sounds Asian to me." David was beginning to calm down now. His heart was no longer in his mouth. This could be fun.

"Hello, Di Yi. Thank you for talking to us. Will you be our guide and help us find our friend?"

The glass moved once more to the 'YES' piece of paper.

"Thank you." Said Jane. "We are looking for an Aiden Williamson. He died in October. Will you find him now for us?"

Once more, the glass moved to 'YES'.

-|-

Aiden had discovered that his perfect hiding place from Charon and the Principium was on the top of Primrose Hill. From there he could see all around him. He was alone all the time and he enjoyed the solitude. It allowed him to think and build up his frustrations to new heights.

Looking down the hill, he spotted a man jogging up towards him.

"You're needed at Naomi's flat. Come with me, now." said the stranger.

Aiden looked surprised and quickly looked round to see if

anyone else was with him. They were alone on the hill, in the rain.

The old man looked Chinese and was smiling broadly at him. He looked kind, his wrinkled face friendly and warm. He was hunched and had to look up to Aiden who was frowning at him.

"I'm a spirit guide. My name is Di Yi. I can help you to communicate with your friends. They are asking for you. I'll show you."

"What? How can I communicate with them? How did you find me?" said Aiden.

"I'm dead too. If you know how, you can go anywhere you want to and find anyone you want, if they are still here of course." Said Di Yi placing a reassuring hand between Aiden shoulders. "They are using a Ouija board and have asked me to find you and take you to them. Come now, please."

Aiden was genuinely shocked and he felt the anger fade from within him. "But why? I am surprised they want to talk to me."

"The curiosity of the living for the unknown and unseen is relentless. But, they give up when they get bored, tired or too drunk. Always the way. Come now." Di Yi was almost dragging him down the hill.

"How do you know?"

"I have been doing this a long time."

"How long?"

"Emperor of China I once was, during the Shang dynasty. Father was Tai Ding. I reigned for thirty seven years." He sounded proud "I've been a guide for the dead since the Principium Angeli gave me permission in ten seventy six BC. A long time."

Aiden contemplated the idea of three thousand years. It was indeed a very long time, but not as long as eternity, and that was his goal - to spend eternity with Naomi.

-|-

DI Yi and Aiden had arrived at the flat. They stood in the living room behind the friends and Darryl. Aiden was elated at the thought of being able to communicate properly now. He said nothing, too engrossed in watching what was going on in front of him.

There was Naomi, looking gorgeous, but nervous. Jane looked more comfortable than Peter, but only just, and there was David looking dreadfully scared. *'Good'* thought Aiden.

"Here we go" said Di Yi. He moved to behind David so Aiden could see. *"Watch. Listen and learn."* He smiled and raised his arms. *"I need to build up some strength. I will take it from the atmosphere in the room."*

Naomi's nerves were on the edge of fraying. She was terrified at the thought of talking to Aiden again after what he had done to David and her.

"It is getting colder in here isn't it?" said David

"I, I think it is." Goose bumps were pointing the little hairs on Naomi's arms upright. She shuddered as she looked at the others. Their arms too were lumpy. David looked across at Naomi, fearing what would happen if Aiden did actually make contact.

Feeling the energy build around them, Di Yi was confident now that Aiden could take the conversation over when his turn came. *"He is here."* He said to the table.

The glass stuttered again and began to move. It spelt out **H E I S H E R E** and returned to the centre of the table.

"Oh god." Peter was very unsure now of the decision to have a go at this. The dead should be left to rest, not come back for a chat.

Jane took a deep, wavering breath. "Aiden? Are you with us?"

"Just push your energy down towards the glass and speak well." Advised Di Yi. Aiden tried to push the energy down to the table as instructed.

"Yes." His voice was strong.

The glass moved a little beneath the nervous fingers. "Lighter on the glass, everyone. He may be weak." Darryl announced.

"May be weak?" said Aiden to Di Yi. *"I'll show them!"*

"Easy, my boy. Don't try to scare them. They are your friends."

"He isn't." Said Aiden pointing to David, allowing the first flickers of his rage to resurface.

"Do not try to scare them. You do not have the knowledge on how to control yourself."

"Is that you Aiden?" Jane's voice was comforting, encouraging, like she was talking to a child.

"Yes." Aiden was pushing the energy hard down towards the glass. The friends jumped in shock as the glass shot across the table.

YES

"Uh oh. Hello, Aiden. You alright?" said David. He could feel the energy in him drain away as if someone was drawing it from him.

"Do not answer him, Aiden." Said Di Yi. *"Later, yes. Now. No. Answer questions only from this one."* He was pointing at Jane.

"But why?"

"You need to get used to this first. And you need to be less angry. I can see the anger in you, and this one can feel it." Di Yi was looking at David who was shivering and looking round the room for the source of his discomfort.

"Aiden, it's me, Jane. I'm here with Naomi, David and Peter, and this man is Darryl."

"I can see you." Said Aiden and he saw the glass begin to move slowly at first, but the more he focused on the message, the quicker it moved. It caught occasionally on the uneven surface, requiring extra effort but Aiden quickly got used to bringing the energy around.

The friends spelt out the message letter by letter. Jane was making notes with her free hand as the glass scraped along.

I C A N S E E Y O U

"Do you think he really can, Jane? Is he really here?" Naomi was sounding more worried.

"No reason why he can't see us." Jane was smiling at the thought that she had managed, again to contact someone. She felt confident. "Aiden, how are you?"

Aiden couldn't believe Jane had asked such a stupid question. It hurt for him to have to answer honestly, and it was not the answer he wanted to give.

DEAD

Feeling even colder now, the friends shivered at the same time as the answer was revealed. Darryl leaned over on the sofa and whispered in her ear. She nodded.

"Do you mind if we check to see if you are who you say you are?" Jane was still sounding kind and gentle.

NO

"Thank you. What is the name of the person sitting opposite me?"

Aiden took a deep breath and focused as much energy as he could down towards the glass and moved it away from Jane. It skidded bumpily across the table and landed between two letters directly in front of Naomi, the noise of the scraping on the wood sent spikes of nerves down their backs, like nails down a black board.

"Yes, that person."

Aiden was feeling very nervous now. He was so close to be talking to her. *"Naomi."* He said slowly, and the glass moved once more, smoothly this time towards the letters.

NAOMI

"That's it. Good." Di Yi said quietly. *"Keep it up."*

Naomi brought her hand up to her mouth, her eyes beginning to weep silently. "Hello, Aiden." She couldn't think of anything else to say. Her voice was choked.

"Aiden. Would you like to speak to her?" Jane asked.

YES

"Okay. Naomi. Off you go. Your turn."

Naomi looked at Jane across the table, very aware that the room was getting colder and colder with every passing moment. Aiden was drawing every single bit of energy he could. She paused, then whispered "How? What do I say?"

"Just ask him anything you want. He's here, but we can't see him, that's all." Darryl was encouraging.

"OK." She paused again, thinking what to say. "Apart from dead, how do you feel Aiden?"

The glass paused for a moment after moving a little. They

all watched for the answer with anticipation. Aiden had moved to between Jane and David and was leaning forward to touch the glass himself, as if to move it with them, to become part of the group again. A sheen of condensation formed slowly on the outside of the glass where he touched it.

LONELY

"Of all the questions to ask, Naomi. How do you think he feels?" Peter spat, hoping that they had not annoyed Aiden. "Wait, it's moving again."

"Shut up Peter." Naomi threw a glance at him for his petulance.

ENOUGHPETER

"I miss you Aiden, and we all love you." Naomi was openly weeping now forgetting how much she despised him at the moment. But she loved him too, and she believed that she could be falling for David too. She was confused and struggled to keep her dignity in place in front of her friends.

MISSYOUTOO

Aiden was beginning to feel the anger build inside of him again, the frustration of being so close, yet so far away had bugged him a lot recently. The more his temper built, the colder the room became. He could feel it too now. Condensation was appearing on more than just the glass now. The wine goblets were starting to fog over, and the friends were starting to shiver.

Di Yi was becoming nervous of the changes in the room and in Aiden's strength. *"Calm down."* He said urgently. *"You are taking too much energy from here. You'll break the veil. Stop it. NOW!"*

"Did you say I would break the veil, Di Yi?" he wanted to know more before he ran out of energy to channel that of the room.

"You do not know enough to break the veil. You will be destroyed if you do. Your soul will cease to exist if you break it and don't know how to repair it."

"Is there anything else you would like to say, Aiden? We're all here." Jane broke into the conversation to keep Aiden there in case he moved off during the silence.

The Veil

Y E S there was a pause.

D A V I D L E A V E H E R A L O N E

"What does that mean?" Peter was curious. Naomi threw another glance at David, very worried that something was going to happen again.

"Shit." David's voice was wobbling and he was breathing heavily.

"Well, David? Naomi?" Jane was curious. She remembered her evening with Naomi after Aiden's funeral and the conversation about dinner and the attack. What else was there?

David gulped, reached over and touched Naomi's knee. "Naomi and I are getting together. We've been there for each other for all these years now, and a lot recently as you know. And I think she's just great." She smiled a big smile at David.

"What the hell was that? I thought it was a one night stand." Aiden said to Di Yi, surprise outweighing the anger that wanted to break free and reap some kind of havoc on the group. *"I told him I would tear his soul to pieces."*

"You must not make contact like that, Aiden. It could kill him."

"Really?" Aiden smiled, feeling the energy build inside of him. We was feeling invincible now. If he got rid of David, then Naomi would have to remain his, and especially as he now knew how to control people. *"I rather like the sound of that."*

"Please, do not try to break the veil. The Principium will come for you. You won't be able to get away from them."

"They've tried that already. I refused to go with them."

"Maybe, but they will come and they will succeed in taking you."

Jane looked at Peter's scornful expression. "Peter? Are you OK?"

"Just fine, thanks. No problem. I had no idea about this at all." His eyes did not leave David's. Snapping away and trying to bring the mood round he said "Lets get this finished with, shall we?" with a big false smile that was evident to everyone.

Aiden could feel more energy in the room to bring in to himself. He felt strong and powerful. He sensed Peter was exuding the new energy. He breathed the energy in deeply and the room temperature dropped further.

"I don't like this. I don't like this at all." David looked at his wine glass "I am so cold. There's ice on my fucking glass! I'm leaving." He was starting to panic.

As the air chilled further, Aiden sucked every ounce of energy into himself he could.

"No David. You can't leave now. I don't know what will happen." the worry in Darryl's voice was obvious. "You have to stay. He's getting stronger. We mustn't make him angry."

"Jesus, Jane, look at your breath. Stop this now. This is too much." Peter was sounding worried too as Jane's breath began to condense in the air above the table. Every breath they exhaled hung in the air like a fog. It

"Yes," said David. "Let's let Aiden go. We should never have done this at all. Sorry mate." He stood to leave, but Jane grabbed him and pulled him downward before he could let go of the freezing cold tumbler on the table.

N O Y O U W I L L S T A Y The glass began to move slowly in a circle around the inside edge of the letters, the sound making them all cringe with the scraping noise. It carried on relentlessly getting faster and faster, the volume getting louder with each rotation.

"Aiden STOP! NOW!" Di Yi grabbed him. Aiden lost concentration and the glass stopped instantly and directly opposite Naomi again.

"Leave me alone, Di Yi. I can handle this."

"No, you cannot, you are taking on too much. Can't you feel the veil between us and them is weakening?"

"I'm just great, Di Yi. Leave it to me. I won't break the veil. I promise. I might wear it thin though, but I won't break it. I have messages for Naomi and David, then I'll be done. I promise." Aiden lied. He had more planned than that. He grinned and began to focus the energy again.

"Shit, we've pissed him off." Said David.

"Aiden's okay. I'm sure he is." Naomi sounded sure, wanting to carry on talking to him.

"I think he's gone. It's getting warmer in here now." Peter breathed a sigh of relief.

The glass shuddered and began to move again, scraping

itself across the table one more time.

"What's he saying now, Jane?" Naomi was curious.

OLD

"I'm not sure. That says 'old'." Jane checked her note.

Playing with them now, Aiden paused, waiting for a response. He wanted this to be very memorable. Especially for David.

"Old what, mate?" David tried to sound cheerful but was deeply nervous about what may come next.

TRAINERS

"What does that mean?" said David

GETTHEMNOWPUTTHEMONTHETABLENAOMI

It took Aiden a little while to spell the message but as soon as Jane read it out, Naomi dashed to the bedroom and rummaged round in the bottom of the wardrobe for the old trainers Aiden had kept for doing odd jobs in. She was lucky that she had missed them when clearing Aiden's things out.

They were spattered with paint and flecks of wall filler, glue and other such DIY niceties. They looked at the battered footwear when Naomi put them on the table as instructed.

'Excellent', Aiden thought. '*This will piss David off!*'

The glass moved round them in a near perfect circle, getting faster and faster as Aiden moved the energy around him, and once more the temperature dropped, further this time, and all the friends started visibly shivering.

Playfully, Aiden stopped the glass next to the left shoe and tapped the toe with the glass, like a puppy nudging a ball to be thrown by its master.

"Looks like he wants that one, Naomi." Peter said with a hint of humour.

YES

Naomi picked it up and examined it. Blue paint, lavender paint, wallpaper paste, laces left tied and a somewhat stale odour.

"Anything inside it, Naomi?" Jane said.

"I don't know." Naomi fumbled her fingers inside and

down towards the toe. Her finger tips found something hard. She could not quite get a grip on it, so she banged the heel on the table. A small black box dropped out and came to rest against the upturned glass. The friends looked at it, none of them knowing what to say. David was fearing the worst. He knew what was inside. Peter and Jane knew too. Aiden had told them the week before her died.

Sitting, leaning forwards on her knees, Naomi stared at the box. It was on its side. It had a leatherette cushioned top with a gold border and more gold around the middle where the two halves of the box snapped shut.

"Well," said Jane "open it." She was excited for her friend although she was not ever expecting anything like this to come through a ouija board.

"I can't. I don't want to." Naomi looked at Jane across the box, the glass and the collection of fingers resting on it.

Aiden was kneeling now, between Jane and David looking intently at Naomi whose bottom lip was quivering. She knew what it was. It had to be what she thought it was. Aiden moved the glass behind the box and pushed it towards her, then returned it to the centre.

OPEN IT

Shaking, Naomi put the shoes on the floor and picked up the box. Her fingers were so cold and nervous they were shaking. The box flipped open with a quiet snap. Nestled in white satin was an exquisite single mazarin cut diamond mounted in a square platinum setting with the band tucked neatly into the box lining. She was breathless with the candlelight that sparkled through the stone. It was so pure and the metal so pristine. The whole thing was perfectly made. She could see a distorted reflection of herself in the contour of the band, her face looked warm in the orangey glow of the candles as she turned it round in her hands, examining it closely.

"It's beautiful, Naomi. Put it on." Jane said as excitedly as a bridesmaid. The glass began to move again.

PUT IT ON

"Thank you Aiden, it's beautiful." She was talking to the glass. She desperately wanted to put the ring on, but that would seem to seal something between her and Aiden and she could not allow that to happen. "I can't put it on. It wouldn't be right. I'm sorry."

Aiden felt a clawing anger beginning to scratch at the inside of his head. He held his fists tightly together and spoke again, but more forcefully this time. The glass moved quicker, more confidently. The anger giving it more speed.

PUTITON

"Aiden, please. I can't. You know I can't." Naomi pleaded into the air and for some reason, perhaps coincidence, she looked at the space between Jane and David, right into Aiden's eyes. He tensed up, sat up on his knees in anger and raised his arms towards the ceiling. *"Put the ring on Naomi. Just put it on! Please!"* he shouted at the top of his voice.

The glass sprang off the table and landed by the door. The friends jumped backwards in their seats, shocked at the violence of the movement. The table had a thin film of ice over it now and their breath sank to a hanging mist in the stillness of the air. Shivering, Peter fetched the glass and put it back on the table. Melted ice left two finger marks on it where he had picked it up. "Right, time to stop now, don't you think. This is now out of control." David was serious and he raised his voice. "That is enough!"

The glass moved again, but no-one was touching it. Aiden's anger had overflowed and he had begun drawing it from their fear. Ice was appearing on all the shiny surfaces now, including the ring in Naomi's hand. Picture frames were frosting over and the medicine glass was spinning around, and moving to random letters, pushing them off the table.

Di Yi was panicking. *"Don't, Aiden! Don't break the glass! It will tear the veil! You will bring the Principium here."*

Beneath her breath, Jane was muttering something.

Fear gripped them all as the glass began to vibrate uncontrollably as it dashed around the table. Too scared to run, the friends sat and watched, hypnotised by its movement. "Somebody grab it before it smashes." Jane said over the top of the scraping sound. "If it breaks, we're in trouble."

"Wait! No!" called Naomi. "He's spelling something out. 'L'."

"Grab the glass, now! It will break!" Darryl was beginning

to lose patience as his experience was running out.

"Leave it alone, David!" Naomi smacked his hand away from the table. "'O', 'V'"

Jane looked up on hearing what Naomi was spelling. They all knew what was coming next.

"'E'. Love! He said love." The letters sat untidily next to each other facing Naomi.

David quickly leaned forward and tried to grab them but his body was thrown backwards into the seat as Aiden reached into his head with his fist, took control of his muscles and forced him to sit down. *"Shut up, David. I'm not finished yet."* Aiden's voice was vicious, ready to punish David for even breathing Naomi's name. The glass continued to skate around the table. Naomi and Jane watched David twitch and struggle for no apparent reason. Aiden didn't let go of David's muscles, making them cramp in his neck. He felt strangled.

"David!" Peter stepped over the table to see if he was alright. David was choking. His throat was tightly closing in on itself. His neck looked thinner, like invisible hands were squeezing it inward. His eyes were bulging, face reddened. "Shit! Look at this! He's choking."

"Aiden, LET HIM GO! NOW!" demanded Darryl.

Aiden was sucking every last bit of energy he could out of the them, trying to break the glass, but he could not quite summon enough to shatter it.

"Vitae est nunc extincta, Et effugare ab hoc loco reditum, de quo egressus es, Spiritus ergo noster est fortius quam tuus, Ergo iam non estis suscipit mi. Vade ad spiritum deorum!" shouted Darryl at the top of his voice. "That is enough, Aiden."

On hearing the words, Aiden felt like someone was fighting back to suppress his anger. He tried not to let go of David, but the charm Darryl had called forced him to drop his grip on David who gasped for breath and sank into his chair rubbing his neck. The glass span on its rim for a moment, then toppled over, leaving a faint circular line in the frost on the table. The room was icily silent. The words had forced Aiden to let go

The room began to warm-up a little. The ice melted and left a smeary puddle of water on the table and it ran off the sides of the glass. "I think we'd better stop now. Don't you?" David croaked, trying to make a joke of it, but was obviously terrified. He sat up in the chair.

"Are you alright David?" the friends all looked very concerned.

"Yeah, I'm fine. Scared to death, but I'm fine, thanks." He rubbed his neck and coughed his throat back open

"Oh no." Said Peter. He was looking at the table and the remaining pieces of paper. They were all lined up facing Naomi. "That's not good." He whispered with his head cranked round to read the message.

L O V E
S T A Y
W I T H
U

Naomi read the message for herself. They must have missed it being written in the confusion. "Oh, Aiden, you can't stay." She looked around the room, tears welling in her eyes. "You shouldn't be hear any more. Please go to where you need to be. I have to move on now."

Aiden listened intently and dropped to his knees. He couldn't believe what he was hearing. She didn't want him any more.

"You cannot blame her, Aiden. You are one of us now." Di Yi put a comforting hand on his shoulder. *"You must let the living live. You'll meet her again soon enough, if that is your destiny."*

David was fed-up now and angry. "Aiden! Naomi is with me now. Leave us alone will you, and go and haunt someone else!" he looked around the room for someone to talk to.

"David, NO!" Darryl and Naomi tried to silence him, but it was too late. Aiden's anger tipped over the edge and a blankness shot across his mind of reason.

"SHE IS MINE!" Aiden stood up quickly, shouting at the top of his voice.

Jane and Naomi screamed as the ice immediately returned the table and it started to shake. Their breath began to fog the room again in the rapidly chilling air. Aiden was becoming more and more powerful.

His anger, combined with the fear of his friends brought the veil to tearing point. The glass was vibrating, making a high pitched ringing sound. And then it shattered, sending hundreds of tiny shards of glass into the air, pricking the faces of all present, except Naomi. The veil, so fragile between life and death had been torn open.

Aiden's rage was so strong that his desire to live outweighed his belief that he was dead.

DI Yi was terrified at the consequences. *"Aiden, what have you done? You must not pass through, you must stay here and close the hole!"* He tried to hold Aiden back.

Aiden was deaf with jealousy. He heard none of Di Yi's protests and threats of the Principium coming for him.

The hole was only visible to Aiden and Di Yi. It waved like net curtains in a breeze; transparent, gentle and silent. The invitation to walk through this window and finish what he had promised was too great. He stepped through.

Aiden now stood visible before them all, slightly hazy and blurred at the edges. Enraged at David and Naomi, Aiden felt what he had to do. He could not let David have her.

What colour was left on their skin in the cold drained from their faces, their pulses sped and their hair prickled. The vision of Aiden standing before them, so bold and vehemently angry sent the friends in different directions, terror leading them to different corners of the room, and David to the door. But Aiden got there before him, disappearing and then reappearing on the other side of the room. How he managed it, he didn't know. Didn't care. He was only interested in taking David's soul.

Darryl moved between Aiden and David and calmly put up his hand as if to stop an approaching car. "Vitae est nunc extincta, Et effugare ab hoc loco reditum, de quo egressus es, Spiritus ergo noster est fortius quam tuus, Ergo iam non estis suscipit mi. Vade ad spiritum deorum!"

"HA!" Aiden cried out and reached into Darryl's head, using his muscles to force him out of the way so he could face David. Darryl crumpled as he hit wall near the television. His experience was exhausted now, he no idea what to do to help now.

David went to wrestle Aiden to the ground but passed straight through him, Aiden's signature condensation and freezing chill of death leaving him shivering on the floor by the book case. He knocked some photograph albums to the floor as he landed.

"Aiden, NO!" Naomi screamed at him, tears streaming down her face, blurring her vision "Not again! No!" Jane and Peter stood back by the window, keeping away from the other three.

Aiden turned, his chest heaving with rage. *"I can never leave you, Naomi. I will always be with you, until you come and join me."*

David righted himself. "Leave us alone, Aiden. You don't belong here anymore." His punches, again passed straight through Aiden, sending him off balance again and crashing to the floor at Naomi's feet. She knelt beside him, trying to help him up. "Oh, Aiden, no! You can't do this!"

Reaching down into David's head, Aiden took control of his muscles again, and stood him up, right onto tip-toe and pointed his chin to the ceiling. David began to choke once more.

Peter and Jane, huddled by the window could see the figure of Aiden with his hands plunged into the back of David's head. They could see the blank look of anger on his face as he lifted the helpless David higher. He looked like a shark whose eye's had rolled back into it's head as it went in for the kill.

David looked like a hanging rag-doll ballerina en-pointe. His arms flailing to keep his balance as the tips of his toes slipped on the floor.

Naomi was panicking now, unable to make any decision on what to do to help. "LEAVE HIM ALONE, Aiden. I DON'T WANT YOU HERE ANY MORE!" her scream was high pitched and she shook her hair in front of her face as she did so in panic. She stood up and grabbed hold of David's waist, trying to pull him away from the hands in his head but it made him choke more. Aiden was not going to let go.

"I told you, David, that I would tear your soul apart, didn't I?" Aiden couldn't concentrate any longer. The power within him had consumed him. All he could focus on was finishing off the

struggling David. *"Time to say goodbye."* David coughed up a mouthful of spit. It trickled down his cheeks towards his ears as his head was bent so far backwards.

Naomi was sobbing hard. Begging Aiden to leave David alone. She kept saying his name over and over again into her matted hair that was hanging all over her face. From her knees, she looked up at him and Aiden stopped for a moment to look at her, keeping David on the points of his toes.

"I will look after you, Naomi. I'll love you, always."

"Aiden, you don't understand. How can you love me? You have gone. You left me. You died, remember? I want to be with David now."

"I have been told that my destiny was to die so you could become the person you were born to be, Naomi. No matter what had happened in my life, I would have met you because of those two." he pointed to Jane and Peter who cowered further away.

His voice was desperate now, sounding like it was begging to be alive again. *"We are meant to be together, Naomi, and we will be together again when you die. Your destiny is not with him."* he shook David *"It is with me."*

"Aiden, I'm sorry. I really am, but I cannot control my destiny. You have to let me live now. If we are meant to be together when I die, then so-be-it." She was speaking as calmly as she could, despite her insides crying out for him to finish dying and leave her and David alone, but Aiden's rage was growing again. His fingers began to wriggle in David's head, making his limbs twitch like a puppet.

"But I have to live a life first, don't I, Aiden? And that life has to be without you now." Naomi begged.

"I can't wait that long to be with you again Naomi. I'll stay with you, look after you. Protect you and love you. I promise." As Aiden spoke, David's body started to lose it's fight as his muscles were running out of air.

"You can't, Aiden, and I don't want you to. You don't belong here any more. David and I are together now. He's not your replacement. He's someone new, and I think we may love each other one day. If you love me, Aiden, you will let go of David and leave us alone."

The tide of anger inside Aiden broke free of its defences and he let it all out on David's soul.

The oxygen starved body began to flail around like a hanged man on a noose before his neck breaks, legs kicking out to find something to stand on, the muscles in his neck tensing to hold back the strangulation, his face turning red. *"I can't allow that to happen, Naomi. I love you too much. That's why I've come back. There is only me."*

"Go to hell, Aiden." David managed to gurgle out the words, his eyes bloodshot and terrified, his body crying out for more air.

"I have come back from hell to stop you loving her, David." Aiden spat back. He smiled and stepped into David's body to wear him like a living suit and be completely in control.

-|-

The Principium Angeli were meeting within the circle beneath the Dome of St. Paul's Cathedral. Each member was standing one one of the tips of marble points that formed the giant star that signified the gateway to eternity above.

The nave was in darkness and the only visible light was streaming through the very top of the dome, illuminating the circle as each member took a turn to speak.

Di Yi appeared at the end of the nave. He was intimidated by the brightness and holiness of the light he had to enter. Not since his own death had he had to face the light. So bright and welcoming, but at the same time, so powerful that the mere presence of it was overpowering.

The Principium were powerful. They were the Archangels. The messengers and work-doers of God. They had the power to completely destroy a spirit so he entered neither Heaven nor hell. This second death meant there would be no judgement on the day of Armageddon if they were too displeased. It would be the complete annihilation of his soul.

They had to be told about Aiden and his actions though, for the safety of Naomi and the others. They had to be told that Aiden had torn the veil and was not returning or even able to repair it.

The angels were in discussion about Aiden's escape from Hades and evasion of Charon.

"How could this have happened, Gabriel?" said Raphael "We have to repair what is done before this becomes out of control."

Uriel interrupted "We cannot allow him to continue. I will go and return him here, or to Charon, whichever is your choosing."

"I agree we have to find him and prevent him from trying to make contact with Naomi again. She has seen enough, and Michael, you have to protect her. His jealousy is making him evil and that in turn will change her destiny."

"As you wish." Michael bowed his head with his hands held in a prayer-like clasp by his waist.

Di Yi began to run toward the group, his old face dropping with worry about the reaction they would have to his news.

The Principium all turned as one to look at him as he approached. The gaze of all of the once stopped him dead.

"Di Yi, what a surprise. We weren't expecting you." Gabriel's voice was calm.

"It's Aiden, my Lords. He's broken through the veil."

-|-

David's body stood, unmoving in the room by the table. His head hung heavily forwards, stretching his neck, arms hanging loosely by his sides and he was barely breathing. He looked like a chastised child, standing listening to a telling off from his parents. He looked sorry. And sorry he was now that Aiden was inside him, doing his best to fulfil his own prophecy.

"I told you David, that would tear your soul apart, didn't I. I hope you enjoy it."

"No, Aiden, I will not let you do this to me and Naomi." David could hear the voice inside his head and could talk to Aiden purely by thinking alone.

"Really, I'm sure you'll enjoy trying."

Aiden was fighting for possession of David's soul, trying to envelope it completely and take control of his body's function, but David fought back hard. He had to leave his physical body unattended, fall asleep almost so he could focus on keeping Aiden away.

The body slumped heavily to the floor, David's knees buckled without warning and his back bent the wrong way. He looked like all the life in him had been instantaneously removed, like a soldier shot in the back on a battlefield. But the scrap for control was still going on the inside.

"Is he alright, Darryl?" Jane was worried. Her hands were shaking, aware that David was in big trouble, if not dead.

Darryl was lost, not knowing what to think. "I don't know, Jane."

The friends gathered round David's crumpled body, talking to him, trying to rouse him, tapping his hands and supporting his head. He was hardly breathing, but his pulse felt fast, pushed onward by the adrenaline of the fight inside. Naomi looked at Jane, the panic in her eyes obvious by their redness and by how wide they were. Peter and Darryl began to haul him up onto the sofa to make him more comfortable.

"Give me a hand." He said as he took hold of David beneath his arms.

Jane and Naomi grabbed a leg each and between them, they managed to unceremoniously half drag, half carry David onto the sofa. He lay, unmoving, head lolled over to one side. Unconscious.

"What the hell are we going to do." Lost for anything else she could do for him, Jane sat herself in an armchair and put her chin in her hands with her fingers covering her mouth, the worry evident on her face.

Peter made a suggestion. "Maybe we should call and ambulance."

Before anyone could answer, David's eyes flicked open. He looked dazed, almost drunk. He struggled to sit up, his limbs unsteady with the effort. He licked his lips and looked around at his friends.

Naomi was so relieved, she blubbed some tears into his shoulder as she hugged him. "David! Thank God." He returned the hug, enjoying feeling the softness of her hair on his face. He smiled. "Oh, David, are you OK?" Naomi looked him in the eyes.

"Hello Naomi, it's me." Aiden's voice sounded through his friend's mouth. Naomi pushed David back and took three steps rearward, shivering all the way, hair standing up on end all over her body. Unconsciously, she wiped her arms and body, as if brushing insects off her top. Jane and Peter moved away also, Jane holding Peter's arm for support, his hand grabbing hers in return. Darryl just stood there, out of his depth.

"David is not available just at the moment."

"Aiden, don't." Naomi's voice was quiet and she shook her head at the horror of seeing David's body but hearing Aiden's voice. "What have you done with David?"

"He's in here, with me. He doesn't feel very well, but he'll be fine. I just need to teach him a lesson."

Aiden stood David up like a badly controlled puppet and made for the door. Naomi grabbed at him, but was thrown off his arm. "Leave me alone, Naomi. Leave me alone." His voice was bitter, twisted and full of hate.

Aiden was looking for car keys in jacket pockets hanging up in the hall way, throwing them behind him as he rummaged carelessly. He flinched as if he was punched in the face and took a step back. David was fighting back now. The body stopped moving for a moment whilst both souls left it unattended to continue the fight.

"Aiden, bring him back, NOW!" Naomi screamed at him and took hold of David's arm.

Aiden had won the second round. He span David's head round and peered lifelessly into her eyes. "We're going for a little drive. I feel he may be some time."

The pure hatred in the voice coming from David's mouth left Naomi chilled to the core, and terrified for her lover's life. Aiden took hold of Naomi's hand and removed it roughly from David's arm. He turned to leave.

Naomi was feeling utterly helpless now, and was crying hard, the panic overwhelming her. "Where are you going? Come back here, now. David, fight him!" The friends and Darryl had to hold Naomi back. "David, fight him, please fight him!"

"Let him go for now, Naomi, we'll call the police to find the car." Peter said.

From the front door, Aiden turned David and looked up

the stairs. The blank, lifeless shark-like eyes of David under Aiden's control looked back up to the friends in the darkness. He pointed at Naomi, and opened the door

"And then, I'm coming back for you."

They left.

-|-

Charon arrived at the cathedral shortly after the Principium Angeli had summoned him. His mood was as black as ever it could be and he brought with him the stench of the river and the temper of all the fires in hell.

He stamped down the nave with his pole banging the floor, echoing round the darkened rows of chairs. He strode purposefully towards the light beneath the dome.

"What do you call me here for?" he called as he approached. "I have work to do."

Di Yi felt nervous looking upon the giant of a beast pounding towards him. He looked like he would kill anything in his path. The smell of death and the river preceded him, stinging the nostrils of those iaround. He stopped short of the column of light and glared in from beneath his hood.

"Do not take that tone with us, Charon. It is not welcome here. We have word of Aiden." Uriel had spoken first.

"Where is he? I've been looking for him for five days. I cannot find him anywhere in this Godforsaken city."

"Di Yi, tell Charon what you know." Gabriel finished Uriel's speech for him.

The old Chinese man looked at the Principium, pleading not to have to speak to this beast of death, but they remained silent. "He was hiding from you, Charon. I found him when his friends asked me to be their guide when using a ouija board. I took him to them." He cowered down, almost bowing and not daring to make eye contact.

Charon swung his pole into the light and picked the old man up and pulled him into the darkness where he stood. He drew the end of the pole, the crook, closer to his face. The stagnant smell making Di Yi gag on top of the strangulation of the crook round his neck. He held on to the slippery wood as best he could to tease the strain away from his neck.

"Charon! That is enough. Di Yi is not to be harmed. Use him to find Aiden, an nothing more. He is to be returned to us unharmed when you find him."

Charon growled. He wanted to take his annoyance out on someone, but had to obey the Principium. "As you wish." He bowed to the angels and turned to Di Yi. "Where did you leave him?"

-|-

Peter had run after David and Aiden but had to watch as the car drove off northward into the driving rain, splashing through puddles as it haphazardly sped away. David presumably fighting back as Aiden was trying to drive. It had hit two cars as it pulled away.

Back upstairs, Peter dried himself off on a towel Naomi had given him.

"What are we going to do, Peter?" Naomi and Jane had asked.

Peter spoke through his towel, drying his face. "I have no idea. File a missing persons report?"

"No, we can't do that yet." Darryl was looking out of the window. "He's not technically missing unless he's been gone for twenty four hours. Best thing we can do is report the car as stolen."

"But David owns that car, so technically, it's not stolen, is it?" Peter suggested.

Jane added "True, but it is Aiden driving it, is it not?"

"Are the Police really going to believe that Aiden is driving the car by controlling David's body? No, of course they're bloody not! Shit!" Peter was losing patience and sat down hard on the sofa. He shivered and noticed that his breath was steaming in the air again. He looked at the table and the cut up paper letters. They were arranging themselves and jumping up from the floor. "Oh, dear God, look at this!"

The friends and Darryl turned slowly, also feeling the chill and their hairs stuck up as hard as they good as the icy cold touched bare skin. "What's happening?" Naomi's voice quivering in the deepening cold.

Darryl touched her arm. "I've never seen anything like this

before. The board seems to be reforming."

-|-

Di Yi looked at Charon as he picked up the letters off the floor. Charon was standing inside the window, his head just below the curtain pole. "Spell it out, now."

"Yes, of course. One moment." Di Yi was scared. He didn't trust Charon one bit to adhere to what the Principium had told him.

"I want to know where Aiden is. Spell it."

"I am, I am. Please, have patience. There are not enough letters for this. This is the best I can do."

-|-

W H R

S

A I D E N

Naomi, shivering hard looked at the message on the table in front of her. "What does that mean?"

"Shouldn't we be holding hands or something for this to work, Darryl?" Jane was dumbfounded by what she was seeing. Darryl looked blankly at the letters and then back to her, confused.

"I think it is asking where Aiden is." Said Peter.

"Should we speak, Darryl?"

Suddenly, the 'YES' piece of paper sprang off the floor and landed on top of the other letters.

"Oh God. It wants us to speak to it. Darryl, you do it."

"Eh? OK." He came closer to the table and kneeling beside the letters explained what had happened. "So we don't know where Aiden has taken David. All we know is that drove off. He could be anywhere. Can you help find him?"

"Tell him I only want Aiden." Charon was adamant.

Di Yi looked at Charon. *"Do you not want to find their friend also?"*

"Unless he's dead, no. Just Aiden."

Di Yi found the letters and rearranged them.

O N L Y

AIDEN

"Who are you?" Darryl asked.

"Why do you want to know who he is?" Naomi was confused.

"Because whoever can move these letters by themselves is extremely powerful. I've never seen anything like this before."

Charon looked at the group. *"Tell them who I am."*

"Yes, of course."

C H A R O N the letters moved together and slowly formed the word. Darryl looked astonished as the pieces of paper stopped moving.

"Charon? Who is Charon?" Peter was confused as what he saw.

Darryl rubbed his chin with his hands, eyes fixed on the word in front of him. "This is incredible." He whispered. "Charon is the Ferryman across the river Styx. He is the mythological being who takes souls to Hell."

"Di Yi, time to go. I'll start searching. You stay with these souls. If they find anything out, summon me with this." He gave Di Yi an article that looked like a lantern. Quite small with glass sides and an iron structure. *"Just light the candle and I will come."*

"Yes, of course." Di Yi looked at the lantern and then to Charon. *"I will, as soon as I hear something."*

"So this spirit wants to take Aiden to hell?" Peter sounded almost excited.

"It looks like it, yes."

Charon waved his pole over their heads, sending a draft of cold air around, mixing up the pieces of paper. They all looked around to see if the windows or the door had blown open. When they returned to the table, the temperature had gone back to normal, but the letters had been rearranged again.

B A C K
T O
H E L

24th November

Aiden drove for hours whilst suppressing David from taking control of his body back. Eventually, David had become so weak that he had no choice but to sit at the back of his own mind and see what was happening as if he were dreaming. He could not see where he was going. He could hear the miles passing by though, the rain on the windscreen and the flap, flap, flap of the wipers. He was trapped. A prisoner in his own head.

All along the M6 towards Birmingham, Aiden had driven, mentally kicking his host every-so-often and abusing him for even daring to think of touching Naomi.

Abandoning the car at the Stafford motorway services and leaving all forms of identification in the car, Aiden had hitched a lift to Liverpool with a Polish truck driver. He figured the language barrier would mean there would be no awkward conversation to contend with.

The journey had been uninterrupted and the driver dropped Aiden off at Albert Dock just after dawn. Thanking the driver, he had just jumped out of the cab and started to walk through the cold and the rain along the A565 through Bootle and out towards Waterloo.

He turned left onto South Road and stopped for a moment on the bridge across the railway by Waterloo Station. Aiden considered jumping and finishing David off once and for all, but decided not to, instead preferring to make David suffer some more.

Further along South Road, Aiden turned right onto Marine Crescent and further along to Adelaide Terrace and finally left onto Blucher Street. He left the impressive terraced houses and the street lights behind him and walked down to the beach.

Standing in the water and on the sand were tens of statues all the same height and facing out to sea. These were the Anthony Gormley sculptures called 'Another Place'. Aiden felt that this was the place that he should leave David alone.

The tide was turning, beginning to come in. Aiden saw his chance. He could feel that David's body was weak with fatigue and cold. It had little energy left to continue walking. Half tripping through the dunes towards one of the statues, David began to wake, sensing Aiden's thoughts of what to do with the body.

Aiden felt the awakening and started to mentally hammer David back again, his body stumbling into the wet sand. They both tried to gain control of the body again, each being able to use an arm and a leg. The dual control made the body look drunk as it stumbled up and down the dunes towards to freezing sea and the statues, just a few metres away now.

David was quickly losing his ability to fight. Aiden was too strong, but he was weakening too. Having to control both the body and the thoughts of David for so many hours was draining. He had to get out.

Finding the nearest statue with the incoming tide lapping over its feet, Aiden stumbled towards it, and grabbed it like a drowning man a piece of driftwood. A new squall of rain started chilling David's body again.

Aiden had to ensure David had no memory of what had happened to him, or even who he actually was.

The tide crept rapidly higher as Aiden began to repeatedly beat David's head against the iron chest of the statue. He could feel the pain too. He felt the skin split on his forehead and the warm gush of blood down David's face. He'd not felt any physical pain since before he had died. It was strangely refreshing to feel the pain of a body and not just that of a mind.

After just a couple of impacts, David's brain lost all consciousness and slumped heavily to the ground, twisting as it sank to the sand and allowed the waves to wash the sand from under him. He sat facing the sea, resting on the rusty legs of the Gormley statue.

Ensuring David was as bad as he had energy for, Aiden pushed his way out of the body and stood next to him, looking pitifully down at him as the rain washed the seeping blood away from the cut above his left eye. His breathing was shallow, his skin white and his lips were turning blue.

Aiden turned and left him to the rain and the tide. He now had to get back, as promised, for Naomi.

-|-

Naomi hadn't slept all night. She had sat in the kitchen with the phone in her hand, hoping for David to call and wondering if she should call the police and report him as missing, or kidnapped or possessed. She didn't know what to say.

She couldn't believe what had happened the night before. She had never experienced anything so terrifying in her life. Darryl had been useless after his experience had run out, and now poor David was somewhere under the control of her bastard late boyfriend. She now understood how close love and hate could actually be. She still loved Aiden for who he was, but hated him now for what he had become. She wanted him gone, but not to have taken David with him. She wanted David now. She wanted to hold him and for him to make her feel safe.

It hadn't stopped raining all night, and with the fight going on inside David's head, Naomi hoped to God that nothing terrible had happened with the car.

Jane and Peter had gone to bed after sitting and feeling as bemused as Darryl and Naomi were for nearly two hours. Naomi had given them her bed, excusing herself from it, suggesting that she wouldn't be able to sleep anyway. She wasn't wrong either. Darryl had helped himself to a blanket from the airing cupboard and settled uncomfortably on the sofa whilst

Naomi just watched out the kitchen window all night, through the driving rain, hoping David would come back to her.

She had felt so alone in those few hours. Alone and vulnerable. She had begun to feel sick too. He stomach feeling light and airy, like going over a humpback bridge several times in a row. She had rubbed it until it calmed down, but even this morning it felt funny. She took some indigestion tablets to help calm it down. Too many cups of tea and coffee on top of last nights wine, she guessed.

Darryl shuffled into the kitchen. He had slept on the sofa next to the table they had left untouched from the night before. They thought they might need it as evidence if the police became involved.

Flicking on the kettle to help himself to a cup of coffee, Darryl put his hand on Naomi's. She was cold and tired. "Any word?" Naomi shook her head. "I think we can call the police now, then." Said Darryl.

"What do I say? I sure as hell can't tell them the truth, can I?"

Darryl smiled at her. "Of course not. Just report him as missing. Strictly speaking, it is him you are reporting missing. Aiden's dead remember. It was David who drove off in the car, irrespective who was in control of him. It'll be David's physical form they'll be looking for." He didn't want to use the word 'body' because they didn't know if he was dead or not.

"OK, I guess so." she said, picking up the phone and dialling the police station.

"Are you sure you know what to say?" Naomi held up her hand to silence him. Darryl stopped what he was saying.

"Hello? I would like to report a missing person please." She paused, listening to instructions.

"The details, yes. Um. David Holestead. Yes, he went missing last night at about half passed ten. Yes, of course I've tried to contact him at his home. No, I haven't been there to check. He was so angry he wouldn't have gone home. Can I meet you there? Yes, of course."

Naomi gave the desk sergeant all the details he requested and agreed to meet an officer at David's flat before lunch.

"There, done." She said, looking at Darryl for some kind of support. "I hope we're doing the right thing by not telling them the truth."

"Of course we are, Naomi. Do you really think they'll believe a story like the one we have to tell?"

"No, I guess not."

-|-

A springer spaniel charged along the sodden sand of the beach, winding its way round the statues and splashing in the incoming tide. It didn't care that it was raining, his lush thick coat, although sodden was keeping him warm. His owner, Mary had had to wrap up warm against the bitter chill of the wind and the piercing icy rain. Her hood up and pulled tight with it's drawstring left just her eyes and nose poking from behind the fake fur round the edge. She felt warm enough on top, but her legs were stiff with the cold.

Behind her, and equally wrapped up with a warm coat was her son, James. He was a scrawny ten year old and spent the entire time protesting about having to take the dog for a walk on a Saturday morning. He should have been left at home to watch the telly or play his games. It was too cold and the beach was boring despite the waves now beginning to crash ashore as the wind became stronger.

David was close to death. He had regained some form of consciousness and was sitting with the waves crashing over him. He was already waist deep in the surging tide. His arms felt heavy and there was a taste of blood in his mouth. Trying to open his eyes, they were immediately stung closed again with sea water as it crashed onto his chest.

The dog had run round him a couple of times, barking at this strange decrepit half sunken man in the water. He had licked his cheek too and had now run off. David heard a voice in the wind coming from behind him.

A thick Liverpudlian accent was calling the dog. It was the boy James. David tried hard to lift his left hand to wave, but could only manage a a little way out of the water before it dropped again, the effort to keep it up was too much. The dog returned, and the boy's voice was getting louder.

"Mam, mam! I think Silas has found something!" James

sounded excited now as he approached the slouched figure in the sea.

David responded to the voice. It gave him some strength. From where he didn't know. He looked over his left shoulder, and through the mist of the rain, the wind and crash of the waves, he saw the figure of the boy running towards him. Rolling himself over into the sea, he tried to push himself up, to take his face out of the water. The cut above his eye stung badly and the sea went up his nose. He coughed up the water, but his strength ran out and he fell face first into the water again.

With all the strength he could muster, David reached his arms out in front of him and clawed at the sand, desperately trying to get some traction to haul himself out of the bitter sea that was engulfing him.

"Mam! Mam! It's a man, in the water! Help!" The boy's voice was closer and within seconds David felt two gloved hands grab his wrists and start to pull hard. He lifted his head up for a breath and saw the face of James straining to pull him up the beach. Flapping his legs in the water, David tried all he could to help, but they were so numb, he could hardly feel anything.

From behind James, he could see his mother come running down the beach, hands in front of her, calling for an ambulance. "James, take the phone and get an ambulance here, now. Do it." She instructed him whilst taking over the pulling of the heavy David out of the water.

Mary dragged him as far up the beach as she could towards to car park, but had to give up half way. She propped David up against her, she held him closely, trying to give him as much warmth from her own body as she could. "What's your name, pet?" she asked, sounding almost as cold as David.

David couldn't speak. He just mouthed something to her. His head couldn't focus on anything. He had been mentally beaten so badly that he couldn't even speak. His eyes, crazed with fear and cold looked up. He was shivering uncontrollably, despite the efforts of his rescuer to keep him warm. Looking down, and taking her gloves off, Mary cradled his face, trying to warm up his bitter and salty skin with her hands.

"My name is Mary. There's an ambulance coming. It will

be here soon. Just you hold on, love. You'll be alright." She started rocking him like a baby, as if to comfort him. Her voice sounded ethereal, calming but reassuringly honest.

The bleak beach David could see through his painful and bloody eyes lost what colour there was, and his vision darkened from the edges until the last thing he saw was Mary's face looking round for the ambulance. Then everything went black. The last thing he heard was James' voice saying something, then the crash of a wave, and then silence.

25th November

Back at the flat in London, Naomi had noticed that it had been colder than usual despite the heating being up higher than normal. She was wearing a large woollen jumper and leggings, plus her boots. Not flattering, but at least she felt a little warmer. All the windows were closed and the air was beginning to smell stale.

Di Yi had followed Charon's instructions carefully. He had stayed with Naomi, ensuring that the lantern Charon had given him was always close at hand, in case, or rather when, Aiden came back.

He admired Naomi from his side of the veil for her courage in her situation. He had listened to conversations with her friends when they came round to see her and on the telephone too. The police were being as helpful as they could, and were on the phone again this morning. They had found David's car abandoned on the M6 motorway. All of his identification and money was inside.

"Really?" Naomi sounded hopeful and doubtful at the same time. "What do you think I should do?...Nothing?... Really? I have to do something, I feel so helpless."

The voice on the other end of the phone apparently was

being as comforting as possible. They now had something solid they could follow-up. They could check the CCTV footage at the service station and try to find a likeness for the people there that night. Thankfully, being so early in the morning, the service station wasn't very busy, so they were sure they would be able to find something of use.

Naomi ended the call and sent Peter and Jane a text with the news.

-|-

Aiden had taken his time coming back to the flat. He was sure that Charon would be searching for him, so he had to make sure that the coast was clear before he went in.

He had had time to think a lot about what to do when he got back to Naomi and was still unsure now he had arrived. Should he just sit back and watch what she does? Or should he express how angry he was at her. He was possessed with the idea of not leaving her. He just couldn't, no matter how hard he tried to come to terms with the scenario, the idea of being without her was torturous. It was too painful, and even when he had tried to go the other way and make his way to St Paul's to find the Principium and beg forgiveness, he was not able to bring himself to do it.

Now he was standing outside the flat, on the opposite side of the road, looking up at the kitchen window. There was no-one there. All the windows were closed. He waited. He didn't have to be anywhere else other than here. Eternity was a long time away, and if he had to wait that long, he felt he could.

He had arrived back a couple of hours previously. It was early in the morning, but now the day was brightening up. It was still dull, a hangover of clouds from the yesterday's rain storms that whipped the country loitered in the sky.

What about David? Who cares? But Aiden was curious what had happened to. He felt a twinge of guilt that he had hurt his best friend so badly. He loved David, after all. But he quickly supposed that that was in life, but in death, Aiden was jealous of the attention he and Naomi were paying each other, and after catching them in bed together that day, Aiden couldn't care less if David was dead or dying.

The kitchen light flicked on and Aiden saw Naomi walk

in, presumably about to make breakfast.

A car pulled up outside the front door. It was Jane. Damn, why did she have to turn up now? That was all that Aiden needed. He would have to deal with them both now.

Remembering how easy it was to take over David's body, he ran across the road and grabbed hold of Jane's head before climbing straight into her body. Jane was overcome with surprise, she had no chance to react or properly defend herself. She didn't know how.

The world around her turned quickly black as Aiden took over her movements and thoughts. She cursed him and tried as best she could, but Aiden just pushed her hard back into the recesses of her mind. There she sat, scared of what would happen next. She could hear everything, but not see.

Aiden, feeling empowered with a new body to play with, talked to himself for a moment, trying to make sure he used Jane's voice and not his own.

"Hello, Naomi." He said. No, too deep.

Loosening his mental grip on Jane, he tried again. "Hello, Naomi." The voice was higher. Better. He loosened the grip further. "Hello, Naomi." Perfect.

He knocked loudly on the door.

In the kitchen, Naomi finished buttering her toast, licked the knife and went downstairs.

Opening the door, Aiden lost his grip on control of Jane for a moment and her body wobbled as it was briefly under no-one's control.

"Hi, Jane. My God, are you alright?"

Regaining control and shoving Jane back into her mind, he looked and smiled at Naomi. "Hi, Naomi, yes, I'm fine. Just lost my balance on the step. Sorry." Aiden guided Jane in to the flat and up the stairs, straight to the living room.

"Can I get you a cup of tea, Jane?" Naomi went to the kitchen to put the kettle on and called through to her.

The living room had been cleaned and tidied since Aiden took David away. Chairs were back in place, sofa cushions replaced and there was no sign of the candles. "Yes, please." He sat down in his old spot on the sofa and crossed his legs as he used to. Not very ladylike.

Naomi brought the tea in to Jane and noticed where and how she was sitting. She stopped in her tracks. Could it be? No, of course not. An image of Aiden sitting there flicked quickly into her mind. Suddenly feeling very nervous she sat down on the armchair opposite Jane.

"Have you heard anything from David?" Aiden enquired, noticing how he was sitting and adjusted himself, trying to remember how Jane sat.

Naomi looked concerned. "I spoke to the police this morning. They found his car at a service station on the M6. His wallet and stuff was left inside. I'm really worried about him, Jane. He hasn't tried to contact you has he?"

"Me? No. He is much more likely to contact you first, don't you think?"

Di Yi was watching intently. Something was not right here. Naomi surely wouldn't be so nervous around her friend would she? He noticed her shivering in the chair opposite Jane. The temperature had dropped a bit further. He reached for the lantern.

"I guess so. I'll never forgive Aiden for this. I don't care if we are supposed to be destined to be together. I would rather be with David now. He has no right to come back and haunt us like this." Naomi was sounding melancholy and lost.

Jane's fingers twitched at the sound of this. Aiden couldn't understand what he was hearing. He began grinding her teeth together and clenched a fist. "Maybe he wants to be with you, Naomi. I think it's quite romantic, really."

Naomi threw a filthy look at Jane. "Romantic? How the hell can you say that? That bastard terrorised me, scared the life out of you and Peter and has possessed David. There's nothing romantic about that at all?"

Without thinking, but blind with feelings of betrayal, Jane's body was out of the seat and across the living room before Naomi could react. She pinned Naomi to the chair by the arms, and with her nose to Naomi's, Aiden brought his own voice forward. Naomi, too fearful to let out a sound, looked at her, deeply into her eyes. Somewhere in there, she thought she could see Aiden. She tried to loosen Jane's grip on her arms.

"All I ever wanted was you, Naomi. Just you and me forever. And you go off with David."

"Aiden?"

"Hello, Naomi. I said I would come back for you, didn't I?"

"Aiden, no. You mustn't do this. Give Jane back."

Di Yi immediately lit the lantern on hearing this and the temperature in the room dropped further. *"Aiden, leave her alone. Come out of her body, now."* The old Chinese man reached in to the back of Jane's head to try and take a grip of Aiden, but he flung the head round to refuse him entry.

Calmly, Jane loosened the grip on Naomi's arms. "Do you not understand that I have come back to look after you? I have literally been to hell and back, my love for you is so strong."

"You are dead, act like it!" Naomi was struggling harder now.

Jane was spitting anger, the sting of the tears and the rage too much for Aiden to control. "You ungrateful bitch! I have fought death itself, the angels and the ferryman to be with you, and you refuse me? I can't leave you, Naomi."

"Just die will you!"

"Don't you get it? I am already dead, and I have nowhere to go without you."

"Oh yes you do, Aiden!" The voice came from behind. Aiden span Jane's body round to see the imposing figure of Charon and his pole standing tall in the middle of the living room. *"Don't make me hurt the woman to get you out."*

"You'll have to kill her to get me out, Charon." He stood up, confronting him. But Naomi could see nothing, just Jane arguing with thin air.

Charon? That name was familiar. Darryl had mentioned it on Friday night. He was the ferryman to hell. He was here? Oh, shit, this was going to get bad. Getting out of the chair, Naomi got up and grabbed Jane round the arms in a bear-hug. "Take him, Charon, get the bastard out of her."

"You see, she doesn't want you, Aiden." Charon stepped

forwards and reached inside Jane's chest, fishing for Aiden. Naomi could feel her arms turning beyond icy cold as they held on tight. Jane started to struggle to get free. Aiden was holding on tightly.

"I'm not leaving, Charon." He struggled more as Charon used both hands inside Jane now. One in her chest and the other in her head. Naomi lost her grip and Jane fell onto the table, breaking it.

Inside her mind, Jane was doing her best to keep away from the fighting. She could feel her physical body in pain as Aiden threw it round the room, trying to shake loose the grip of Charon. She could hear Naomi trying to catch a hold of her, calling to her, reassuring her.

Finally, a sharp bang on the head knocked Jane out and her body bumped heavily to the floor, the television wobbled on its stand where she had hit it. Inside, Charon grabbed the stunned Aiden and hauled him out of Jane's twisted body. Her limbs twitched as Aiden lost control of them.

Charon locked the crook of his pole around Aiden's neck and dragged the exhausted spirit out of the flat. Di Yi looked back at the two women on the floor, smiled regretfully at them, and blessing them both, and he left too.

Quickly, the room became warm again with Naomi nursing Jane back to consciousness.

26th November

The shackles around Aiden's wrists held him tightly to the railings along the river by Tower Bridge. They had already started to wear through the skin. No matter how he positioned himself, they dug in deeply, cutting him. The blood ran along his arms and into his shirt. It had dried a crispy brown colour, and the drying puddle of blood he sat in was slowly spreading out-wards. He had no physical blood to run out, so the spiritual blood he was dripping would continue to flow until when? He had no idea.

He was wasted, exhausted and trapped as he tried to make himself as comfortable in the queue for the ferry as possible. Charon had beaten him all the way to the bridge. His battered spirit numbed and dumbed by the brutality he had only seen on the other side of the river. His moans of grief now joined those who had been chained there before him.

Through the veil, he could see the living walking by, taking their photographs and having fun by the river, the famous bridge across the Thames making the perfect backdrop to countless photographs. The happy people he could see grated on him and he looked on with jealousy. He had gone so wrong, and he knew it. This misery was just the tip of the iceberg as far as his eternity of despair was concerned. This really was just the beginning. He was certain that Charon would do anything he could to prevent Aiden from escaping hell again, perhaps even tipping him overboard into the river Styx to join the fetid remains of those dead at sea and his short lived friend, Duncan.

Newcomers arrived in a steady stream and were chained up along the railings by the demons from the other side of the river. They too were shackled, but by long chains and to each other, with one end welded to the very first pillar of the railings by the bridge. Charon though, had shackled Aiden personally, making sure the iron was tight enough to break the skin and never be remotely comfortable.

Did it always rain on this side of the veil, and in this place in particular? The drizzle rusted the shackles of the thousands of souls locked up on the railings. The oxidised iron staining the skin and poisoning the blood. It never killed any of them though. It would take so much more for a soul to die a second death.

Enveloped by misery, Aiden tried to figure out a way to escape from Charon before he was taken aboard that hideous ferry again.

-|-

The man in the bed in a private room at the Royal Liverpool University Hospital was a mystery to the nursing staff. He had been brought in after being found on Crosby Beach two days earlier. He had not regained consciousness since he lost it on the beach. The paramedics had nearly lost him a couple of times to cardiac failure and hypothermia on the beach and on the way to the hospital. He was luck to be alive.

With his head wounds dressed and body temperature slowly brought back to normal, the stranger was connected to various monitors in his room. He was checked every thirty minutes whilst staff and police made efforts to find out who he was.

Inside the mind of the stranger, he was trying to piece together what had happened. He was in the dark. He had lost the memory of who he was or where he came from. His head hurt. It was throbbing so badly that he didn't couldn't open his eyes and his mind was not in a state good enough to allow itself back to consciousness just yet.

Only every-so-often did he hear anything other than the steady hum of the machines around him. There was an ache in the back of one of his hands. What was going on?

There were the familiar voices again. They sounded young. One a northern voice and the other foreign. They felt his arms and moved something on his head. They spoke to each other about what they had done at the weekend. Their boyfriends had gone out together and left the two of them home alone with a baby.

One of them was very strong, the northern sounding one. She cradled his head and shoulders whilst the other one did something behind him, then he was laid down again. He felt more comfortable now. Ahhh, some pillows had been plumped up.

Now a man's voice entered the room.

"Good news. Meet David Holestead. He was reported missing from London two days ago."

"Hello David." Said the foreign nurse.

"His girlfriend is being contacted. Hopefully, she will come to be with him."

28th November

Waking up hot and sweaty, Naomi didn't feel very well. Her stomach felt knotty and weak and her skin was tender to the touch. She felt exhausted too, like she hadn't slept at all. She was just really, really tired. She got up and, ignoring the kitchen, went straight to the bathroom for a shower. She felt clammy and her hair was oily.

She didn't feel like her usual 'first thing in the morning coffee'. There was a funny taste in her mouth, it was a bit tinny. She brushed as much of it away she she could whilst the shower was warming up. She didn't feel right at all. Thinking about it, she hadn't felt right for a few days now. This had crept up on her a little each day, but today was by far the most noticeable.

The water felt too hot on her sensitive skin. She turned the temperature down as she got in. 'Strange,' she thought 'I don't normally have to adjust the temperature.' She didn't think about it again until she started washing herself. Her breasts felt sore. She examined them and couldn't see any difference in them. They just felt different to usual. Her hair felt different too. In fact, there was something very different about her completely. He tummy felt odd, but not sick, she was tired but not under-slept, her boobs hurt and her hair was oily.

With an overwhelming sinking sense of worry, she stepped out of the shower and dried herself off, her mind running through a hundred different scenarios as to why she felt the way she did. She hunted for her diary in her dressing gown. Where had she put it? First there was David still missing, and now this. What else could go wrong?

She searched through her handbag, not there; the living room, the diary was nowhere to be seen; Kitchen? No. Hallway? No. Bedroom? She emptied the drawers, cursing and, with a sense of rising fear, she reached for her phone to text Jane.

'Jane. Can I come and see you this morning? Love, N. X.'

She threw the phone on the bed and got dressed quickly.

Ding, dong, ding, dong. Her phone went off. *'Sure. When?'* Asked Jane via text.

'Now?' Naomi typed straight back, hoping her friend wasn't doing anything this morning.

A moment or two passed. Naomi looked at the screen, willing a response to come sooner rather than in thirty seconds time. Even ten seconds was too long.

It came. *'OK. See you in a minute.'*

Slipping on some trainers, Naomi looked in the full length mirror in the hall. Not great, but she wasn't going out to impress anyone. Old shoes, dirty jeans, t-shirt and jumper wasn't exactly flattering, but she felt the urgency of getting to Jane's was much more important than how she looked. She was so nervous.

Jumping into her little car in the resident's parking area, she pulled straight into the quiet Saturday morning traffic. Thankfully, there was nothing coming. She turned on the radio, hoping to hear something jolly for her journey. The news came on straight away with news about something disturbing happening in the middle east. "I'm not listening to that!" she said and flicked it off. She would have to be content with her thoughts until she got to Jane. She would put her straight. She always did.

-|-

Jane ushered the worried looking Naomi into the house. It was tidy and clean. Peter had gone out for the morning and wouldn't be back till after lunch. The place was their's for now.

"Coffee, Naomi? You look dreadful, what is it?"

"Coffee? No thanks. Tea please. I don't know."

As prepared as always, Jane had the kettle boiling just in time for Naomi to arrive so the tea was ready quickly.

They sat across the breakfast bar from each other, nursing their drinks like they had cold hands. The mirrored each other very well without even noticing they were doing it. Peter and Aiden had commented on it in the past. They joked that Jane and Naomi were like bookends, their body language was so similar.

"What's up, Naomi?" Jane was concerned and looked at Naomi who was stirring her tea, trying to find the words to explain how she was feeling. "Naomi? You OK?"

"You and Peter are trying for a baby, aren't you?"

"Yes, but we are having problems. Why?"

Naomi looked at Jane, her teary eyes looked ashamed. "Have you got a pregnancy test I can use? I'm late."

Jane looked shocked. Her friend had always been careful, always. She couldn't quite believe what she was hearing. "Shit, Naomi, really? How late?"

"I don't know. A week, maybe two. I've lost my diary."

"When did you last have it?"

Naomi shook her head, knowing it had gone. "It never leaves the flat. I must have thrown it away by accident when I was clearing out Aiden's things. I'm scared, Jane."

"Oh, God, Naomi. I'll get you one." Jane stood up and went to the medicine cupboard above the kettle. Rummaging around in the disorganised pile of pills, bandages and little cardboard boxes, she pulled out a pregnancy test and slid it in front on Naomi. "There you go. Have you done a wee this morning?"

Naomi put a hand on it. Too scared to look. "Yes, only once."

"It may not give you an accurate reading then. It's best to use it first thing. When was your last period?" Jane was concerned. "Do you remember?"

"Thanks. No, I don't. With everything that has been going on, I'm lost without my diary. It had everything in it. All my due dates." She shook her head and looked out the window. She wiped a tear from her eye.

Jane tried to cheer Naomi up. "Come on, go and wee on it, then you'll know." She smiled. Naomi didn't. She got up and went upstairs to the bathroom.

The minutes passed and Jane waited in the kitchen for Naomi to return. She had heard the toilet flush what seemed like and hour ago. She was genuinely worried for her friend, jealous too. Her and Peter had been trying for a baby for three years without any success. A miscarriage not long after they were married was all the luck they had had. Peter wasn't producing particularly strong sperm and her body didn't seem to want any of them to reach their goal. And now Naomi was more than likely pregnant, the thought hurt. She had to hide it though, Naomi needed her to be strong at the moment.

Naomi's handbag started ringing, the phone inside demanding to be answered. Jane thought she ought to call Naomi down, but decided to leave it. The phone stopped. A moment later it rang again.

Feeling that she shouldn't be doing this, Jane reached into the bag and pulled out the phone. "Hello, Naomi's phone." The voice on the end of other end introduced herself as PC Andrew Mason.

Jane's heart fluttered. "Hi." Said Jane "how can I help? No, Naomi is not available just at the moment. She's with me, but she is out of the room. Can I take a message?" She listened to what the officer had to say "...Really? That's such good news, Naomi will be there as soon as possible. Where is he again?... Liverpool? Right, I'll tell her."

Putting down the phone, Jane realised that today could be a very good day for Naomi as well as a really bad one.

Standing at the bottom of the stairs, Jane called up excitedly to Naomi who was still in the bathroom. "Hey, Naomi! They've found David! Come down!"

Naomi was sitting on the toilet, her jeans and knickers round her ankles staring at the pregnancy test with a handful of tissues up to her nose and mouth. Her mind was suddenly an avalanche of emotions. Her eyes were fixed on the pale blue cross that she had watched appear in the tiny window of the test. She was utterly dismayed to discover that she was pregnant, and now, from nowhere, overjoyed that David had been found. Whose baby was it? Was it David's or Aiden's? The last thing she would want is Aiden's baby now. Not after what he had done to her and her friends. She was not at all religious, but she silently hoped to God that it was David's.

Pulling herself together, she went downstairs. Her eyes were bloodshot from her tears, but Jane didn't seem to notice straight away. "David is at the Royal Liverpool University Hospital, Naomi. He was found on a beach four days ago. That's great isn't it?"

Naomi smiled a fake smile. She wanted it to be real, of course she did, but at the moment, she was somewhat lost as to how to feel.

Jane frowned at her. "What is it? Are you OK?" she knew exactly what was coming, but refused to believe it until she heard it.

"I'm pregnant, Jane. What do I do?"

-|-

The darkness David had been facing was beginning to clear now. There was light entering his vision and he could make out vague shapes through the insides of his eyelids. The shapes turned from black to a deep red as the light of his room filtered through the blood in the veins. He could feel the numbness disappearing from his limbs and he started to ache, like he had been fighting.

He flickered his eyes open and was dazzled by the light and it took him a few moments to get used to it. Looking around he was lost. He didn't know where he was. The drip in his hand had left a little bruise round the needle and it and hurt like hell. He coughed and pulled the short oxygen tubes out of his nose. The machine next to him showed a steady blipping line. His heart rate presumably, judging by the pads on his chest.

Reaching up to his head, he felt a bandage wrapped round several times. Then he noticed his incredible headache. Oh, boy, this was a good one. What had happened to him? He couldn't remember very much and his brain hurt to think about it. He lay back and hoped a nurse would be in to see him soon.

-|-

Jane had put Naomi back at the breakfast bar and topped up her tea.

"What did you say about David?" Naomi asked.

"He's safe and warm in hospital in Liverpool. You can go and see him when you like. He's not conscious at the moment though. They suggest you go tomorrow." Jane slid Naomi's tea over the table to her.

Naomi wasn't concentrating properly. "Right. OK. I'll do that then. I think I need to see a doctor myself actually."

"I guessed you were pregnant, Naomi. How do you feel?"

"I don't know. A bit numb I suppose. Shocked. Angry at myself for being so stupid. I don't even know whose it is, Jane." She broke down and Jane came round the bar and grabbed her friend's shoulders, hugging her tightly. "What am I going to do, Jane?"

Jane felt jealous of her friend. There is nothing in the world she wanted more than a baby at the moment. She and Peter had been trying and trying, and now for her friend to be pregnant by one of two men just added insult to injury. "Calm down, first. Sit there, pull yourself together and go and see David. You've got time to work things out."

"But what if it's Aiden's? I can't have Aiden's baby. I hate him, and I don't want to look at his child and be reminded of him all the time."

Jane was shocked. "You can't say that, Naomi! And what if the baby is David's?"

"Sorry, Jane. I don't know. I'm not thinking straight. I need to think about this. Knowing David is OK is fantastic. I'll go and see him tomorrow. It's too late to go now, isn't Liverpool a good five hour drive?"

"It's not even lunch time yet. If you go now, you'll get there in time for dinner. Why don't you ring the police and hospital and see what they suggest. And then ring your own doctor and get an appointment for yourself."

"Hmm. Good idea. I'll do that."

-|-

Doctor Bobeck, a Polish gentleman came to see David who was now sitting up but still slightly dazed by where he was and how he managed to get from his home in London to Liverpool without remembering anything about it. He had his blood pressure taken and his pupil dilation checked whilst the doctor asked him various questions about how he felt, and his memory.

Luckily, he could remember more now about himself than when he had first woken up. He could remember his name, address, phone numbers and car registration, but was still blank about the events leading up to his discovery on a beach in Liverpool. He did, however remember being at Naomi's, and that was where his memory ended before waking up in the hospital.

Doctor Bobeck seemed to be pleased with this result, assuring David that this memory loss would be temporary and it would likely return in a few days. He encouraged David to eat and drink something little and often as he had been unconscious for four days which was a fact that surprised David.

"How could I have been unconscious for four days, doctor?"

"You were hypothermic when you were found by a mother, her son and their dog, plus you have two large cuts to your head, presumably from where you head butted one of the statues on Crosby Beach. It is not unusual for people to be unconscious for that long when suffering a trauma like that. You're on the mend now, so don't dwell on it. It'll give you a headache." The doctor smiled at David and patted him on the shoulder. "I'm just pleased we know who you are. We had no idea until your car was found on the M6, then the police worked out the rest."

The doctors' humour had not gone unnoticed by David who laughed at the head ache joke, and then wished he hadn't as it made his head hurt beneath the bandages. "I vaguely remember hearing the nurses talking about that. I wasn't quite awake, I don't think. But I do remember it."

"Good. I'm pleased. Now, I must continue. You rest-up and I'm sure someone will come along to see you later or tomorrow."

-|-

Spending most of the rest of the day with Jane, Naomi had calmed down from both the good news and the not so good news of earlier. Although wanting to go and see David in Liverpool, she was advised by the hospital that she should come tomorrow. He had only woken up that day and was still a little confused as to his whereabouts and how he came to be there. Despite Naomi's protestations that she could help him with his memory, Doctor Bobeck was adamant that she should not come until tomorrow.

Disappointed, Naomi went home from Jane's early in the evening after sharing some dinner with Jane and Peter. She felt exhausted, and after sitting alone in silence on the sofa staring at the pale blue cross in the window of the pregnancy test, she went to bed. She hadn't thought of anything in particular. The blue cross held her attention. This first indicator of a new life inside of her was so clinical, she found it surreal.

Naomi was half excited and half worried about David and completely worried about the child she was now carrying. She didn't know who the father was. She had no idea at all, and she couldn't work it out from the dates of her monthly cycle because her diary had gone missing. Had she come on between Aiden dying and making love with David or not? If she had, then the baby would be Davids, if not, then the baby would likely be Aiden's and that would be the greater of two evils.

The long and short of it was that she did not know what happened to her body between the day Aiden died and today. With the stress and emotion of everything that had gone on, she had completely neglected to keep track of what was happening. She felt guilty and confused by it all.

As she lay staring at the green figures on the alarm clock, the room began to brighten. A warm white glow come from the foot of the bed. She didn't feel threatened by it, but did feel it was a bit odd. Perhaps there was some work going on in the buildings across the road and it was a halogen lamp shining in. She remained still.

The voice of the angel drifted calmly over the duvet to her ears. She shut her eyes tightly to it, hoping to be dreaming. "Naomi. I have a message for you. Do not be afraid."

The angel sat on the end of the bed and reached towards the covers and laid a hand on them. Naomi felt instantly calm and very much at peace. She moved a hand to push the duvet slowly away from her face to see who, or what was sitting on the bed with her.

"Who...who are you?"

"I am Michael. I believe I once met your aunty Esther. She has told you about us, hasn't she?"

"Yes, she has. You're one of the Principium Angeli, aren't you?"

"Yes, I am. I have a message for you."

Naomi sat up and looked at the most peaceful face she had ever seen. Michael's eyes were beautiful, and his touch on the duvet was warm and comforting. The glow coming from his clothing bathed her with the most amazing feeling of being at one with herself. She felt like crying at the sensation of incredible that came over her body. "OK. What is your message. There have been lots of things going on recently, and I really don't need any more bad news."

"You are safe now, Naomi. Aiden has gone. He can't come back to harm you any more. David will be fine, and the baby..." he smiled and paused for a moment.

"What about the baby, Michael? What about the baby?" instinctively, she rubbed her tummy, as if protecting her precious cargo. She felt an overwhelming sense of love for it now. She didn't have that before Michael came to her. It was an incredible feeling. Her voice sounded worried.

"Nothing, Naomi. I cannot tell you anything about your baby. You must discover how precious it is for yourself, and you and David must love it as much as you will discover you love each other tomorrow."

"Why can't you tell me anything more about the baby? Surely you know."

"We do know, Naomi. But if we tell you, then your life would no longer have any mystery to it, would it? Isn't that what keeps the human race going, the mystery and trying to solve it?"

"I guess so."

"Well, there you are then, my child. My message has been delivered. Gabriel requested me to visit you, to reassure you, comfort you, if you will."

"Thank you, I think. But what about..."

Michael held up his hand to silence her. "I will see you again, Naomi. Not for many years though. You were right when you had a life to lead. Now is the time to lead it. Go to David, love him, and love the baby."

"I will, Michael."

The light faded and once again Naomi was left in the darkness. Putting her head down on the pillow, she fell swiftly and soundly to sleep.

30th November

Doctor Bobeck had told Naomi, when she arrived that David spends a lot of time asleep but was getting better at staying awake. The painkillers David was on were now being reduced in dose so his conversations were had become more lucid and allowed his memories to come back to him.

When Naomi had arrived at the hospital, she had sat with David all night and watched him sleep. She had managed a couple of hours of shut eye in the chair next to him. It certainly wasn't proper sleep. She was astonished at how noisy the hospital was, even at in the night. There were people walking by, beds bing pushed, trolleys, orderlies and patients getting up to go to the toilet. There seemed to be a never ending stream of traffic outside the door of David's room. Even on the inside there was noise from the monitors he was connected to. Nevertheless though, Naomi did her best to rest as much as she could.

After breakfast and his medication, David was helped to sit up by Naomi and the nurse. He was a bit dizzy as the blood left his brain and his head wobbled little before his neck caught it and held it still.

"Naomi?" David was sleepy, woozy on his pain killers.

"Yes, David. What is it?" She looked at David with a kindness in her eyes that made David's heart melt.

He smiled a crooked, tired smile. "Your eyes are so beautiful. I could look at them forever."

"Thank you, David. That's very sweet." Naomi blushed.

"I want to be looking into your eyes, when I die, Naomi. I'm not frightened of anything when I look into them." David was suddenly incredibly coherent. The slurring had gone from his speech and his own eyes seemed to be able to focus completely on Naomi's now. She had never heard anything like this before, and she took hold of David's hand as the enormity of what he said settled in. She saw a tear run from his eye and she realised right then that he wanted to spend the rest of his life with her.

"David, you don't need to talk like that. You're not going to die. At least, not any time soon." She tried to lighten David's mood, but she wasn't entirely sure if his mood needed to be lightened. What he had said was incredibly romantic. It was possibly the most romantic thing she had ever heard, and the tears in his eyes were truthful enough, so what was she trying to lighten? David tear was one of happiness, surely, despite the pain he was in. She wasn't sure how to react. A faithful and truthful kiss would have to suffice for the moment until she could fathom what to say. A wrong reaction could be perceived as a criticism, and that was one thing she did not want to happen. She loved what he was saying. It was perhaps a bit early, but never-the-less, it had been said now and she found herself touched by the devotion of the statement.

"No, you're right, Naomi, I won't be dieing for quite some time. But wouldn't it be good if we were together at the end?" David was testing the water about marriage, with a smile. Although he was still dopey on his medication, he was alert enough now to ask a veiled question and decipher the answer.

Naomi could see where the conversation was going, and she was not going to be lead along this path by her drugged-up, beaten-up boyfriend. Not now anyway, she had more important things to tell him. Like the fact she was pregnant and wasn't sure if he was the father or not. She had to change the subject before he did something silly like tell her that he loved her. "We'll see, David. Shall we get you better first before we talk about anything more serious?"

"Good idea, darling." David was nodding off back to sleep again.

Doctor Bobeck walked into the room after a gentle knock on the door and a peak through the window. "Everything alright?" he asked quietly, noting David's closed eyes.

"Just fine Doctor. Thank you. When do you think I may be able to take him home?"

"I was coming to talk to you about that." Dr Bobeck smiled broadly, obviously pleased to about to be delivering some good news. "David is showing rapid signs of improvement. His memory of getting here is slowly coming back and we are happy with all of his other memory and physical functions. If he feels well enough, he can go home with you tomorrow. But he must be kept rested."

"Of course I'll keep him rested, Doctor. Thank you so much for looking after him for me."

Doctor Bobeck smiled and left the room. Naomi took David's hand in hers and looked at his bandaged head. She could feel a sickness rise inside her like she had never felt before. It wasn't the kind of sickness you'd feel if you had not eaten, or even eaten too much, it was just, there, an urge to want to be sick for no real reason. Morning sickness, she supposed.

How was she going to tell David she was pregnant? The poor man had been possessed by her late boyfriend and beaten half to death because of her. She could see how much he was falling in love with her. It was so obvious, and sooner rather than later she was going to have to tell him something that would just add to his stress. If only she knew if the baby inside her was his or Aiden's, it would be so much easier to tell him. But she didn't know and she would have to find the right time to tell David the truth. She would need few days to find that moment and to work out what to say to him and think of some answers to some of the questions and reactions he might have.

David stirred in the bed and rolled over towards her. She kissed the back of his hand and lay her forehead on his fingers. His thumb stroked her cheek. Even in his sleep he could feel her presence and wanted her to feel safe.

-|-

Naomi sat up quickly and looked at David. She rubbed her eyes and yawned loudly, forgetting for a moment where she was. She must have fallen asleep herself as there was a fresh jug of water on the bedside table and the flowers she had brought with her had been moved. The shadows on the bed covers had almost moved. How long she had slept, she had no idea. But she had woken up with a start as if her chair had been kicked. She felt wide awake and very clear headed.

Her confusion before she had fallen asleep had vanished and now there was absolutely no doubt in her mind what she was going to do about the baby was the right thing to do.

She looked at David who was still lying asleep with his hand where she had left it. She examined his face, his features, his arms and hands. She stroked his hair above his bandages. He was a good man. He was a very good man to her; he had tried to protected her as best he could and God only know what he went through for her when he was possessed by Aiden. He had been honest and truthful at dinner that evening before they first made love, and she did rather fancy him and perhaps the scars on his forehead would make him look even more rough round the edges. She smiled at him as she rested a hand on his chest, feeling him breathe peacefully in his sleep.

The more she looked at him, the more it dawned on her that sometime in the last month she had actually fallen in love with him. She knew what she felt was true because the thought of ever being without him again was too much to handle. Even the thought of leaving him alone to find something to eat left her with a bitter taste in her mouth. She shook her head with a smile. She had always been so aware of her feelings that for this feeling of love for David to creep up on her like it had done was quite a surprise. She pecked David on the cheek and went to find the cafeteria. She was starving but at least the sickness had gone for the moment.

10th December

David had been made to feel very welcome at Naomi's flat whilst he got over the worst of his injuries since he left hospital. Naomi had looked after him and he was now able to move around easily and even drive his car. His parents had gone to fetch it from the motorway service station for him and bring it to the flat for him so he could go home in when he felt he could.

The problem was that now he was here, he didn't want to leave. He loved being around Naomi so much that to leave her now would be gut wrenching. He felt that he could be very wrong in feeling so comfortable because Naomi had become slowly more on edge as the days had gone on. She seemed to be fine with him, but there was something on her mind that he didn't know anything about. She became snappy when he mentioned anything about it and she would frequently make excuses to be somewhere else and not in the same room as him.

Naomi was in a terrible quandary. She had a wonderful man staying with her and she was loving every second nursing him. It gave her a sense of purpose, but as the days wore on, she felt that she was beginning to live a lie with him. She was withholding a terrible secret from David, and she did not have the first idea on how to tell him about it. She had sensed that he knew something was wrong. He wasn't stupid after all, and her mood swings just added to the friction in her head. She decided that she just had to do it and deal with it however it happened to turn out.

David was sitting in the living room, bandages off his head now, and a neat line of stitches were ready to be removed. Naomi could see how sore they looked as she sat down next to him. She turned to him, her hands shaking as she took his. She gave him a kiss on the cheek.

"What's up, darling?" David looked into the eyes he adored so much and saw they looked pained. He smiled.

"David," she gulped and looked down to her and David's intertwined fingers. "There's something important I need to talk to you about."

"When you were in hospital, I found something out that I've not been able to tell you about until now." Naomi said as bravely as she could. David turned to face her on the sofa. "I didn't want to tell you before now because of how you were feeling..." She fell quiet.

With a smile and a chuckle, David took her chin in his hand and lifted her face to his and kissed her gently on the lips. "What? Are you going to tell me that you're pregnant?"

Naomi didn't change her expression. Her eyes remained locked to his, the tears welling up from beneath them. "Yes, David, I am." She gave him a half smile and sucked her lips between her teeth and bit them to try to stem the tears. David could almost feel his adrenal gland squeeze dry of adrenaline. It flowed easily into his blood and made him feel light headed. Naomi looked as terrified as he felt. Her eyes were wide and her chin was trembling. He pulled her close and wrapped his arms around her to comfort her. His heart was pounding from the news "What's the problem, Naomi? It's good news isn't it?" Deep inside though, David was terrified.

"Good news, David? How can you say its good news?" Naomi sounded angry and worried.

David tried to sound cheerful to hide his own fears. "You and me and a baby. That's good news, surely?"

"It would be lovely news, David, if I only I knew who the

father was. You or Aiden."

Silence. David's grip loosened on Naomi's shoulders. He pushed her carefully away from him, his eyes suddenly stabbing with pain at what she had just said.

"You don't know who the father is?"

"No, I don't. I'm sorry David. I've lost my diary with all my dates in and stuff. If I had it, I could work it out." Naomi was starting to panic. She looked completely lost. "I have an appointment at the hospital on the eighteenth for a scan. They'll be able to let me know then."

"So, there is a chance it could be mine then?"

"It most likely is yours David, yes. You were the last person I made love with."

David felt a great sense of relief. He took a deep breath to help disperse the huge urge to walk away.

"But, David. It also might not be. I really want it to be yours. I would have trouble with it, if it were Aiden's after what he's done recently." Naomi stroked David's face.

"Really? How sure are you?"

"I'm not sure at all, to be really honest with you." Naomi was calming down too. The fact that David hadn't run away when she told him was a relief and she was beginning to relax.

David took a deep breath. If he wanted to stay with Naomi, he had to prepare himself to possibly bring up someone else's baby. Yes, the baby could be his best mate's, but it wouldn't be biologically his would it? That is something David felt he would have to get over. He would have to accept the baby as being his long before the birth.

"You're not sure? OK. Great. Well, not that great." David was losing track of this thoughts. He coughed, trying not to lose his composure too. "Let's get to the scan and see what happens shall we? And then take it from there."

18th December

Naomi lay on the propped up bed in the ultrasound room with David next to her holding her hand. His scars on his forehead were the only reminder to them both of what had happened that night with Aiden nearly a month previously. Nothing had happened since Michael had been to visit Naomi. The flat had been quiet and unnaturally peaceful even though David had been there recuperating.

Lucy, the sonographer lifted up Naomi's jumper and t-shirt and cheerfully went about putting some cold gel onto her tummy, chatting all the time about how this scan would tell Naomi how old the baby would be.

Both David and Naomi were nervous and David held her hand as they looked at the ultrasound screen.

Placing the device onto Naomi's tummy, Lucy moved it around, smearing the gel down towards the top of her jeans.

"Ooh, look, there!" Lucy pointed to the screen with her free hand. "Just there look. There's your baby."

Naomi choked with tears at seeing the tiny life inside of her. David squeezed her hands as he tried to keep hold of his manliness, but failed.

"Everything looks fine with him so far. Let me just measure him and we can see when he was conceived."

Their pulses raced whilst Lucy changed some settings on the ultrasound machine, Naomi and David looked at each other. He gave her a kiss and a reassuring stroke of the head. "It's OK. Don't worry."

"Everything alright, Naomi?" The bubbly Lucy was suddenly sounding a little worried. Naomi nodded. "You sure, love?"

"Yes, I'm sure."

Lucy beamed at the couple. "Right then, your little Prune is one point one inches long now, which gives us a conception date of between..."

David interrupted. "Wait." Naomi threw him a look. "How accurate is this measurement."

"David!" Naomi snapped quietly.

"It's within a blip of a percent, David. Nothing to worry about, unless...oh!" Suddenly the realisation that David may not be the father dawned on all three of them. The mood in the room soured.

"It's alright David, really. It is." Naomi tightened her grip on his hand.

"Shall I continue?" Lucy just wanted to get this scan over and done with now. She was feeling very awkward.

"Sorry." Said David. "Please, go on."

"As I was saying." Lucy smiled again. "Your little prune, who is one point one inches long, weighing about 14 ounces was conceived between the first and sixth of October. And that gives you a due date of ninth of July next year."

David hung his head down. The dates didn't match up when he and Naomi made love. She squeezed his hand tightly. He had so wanted the baby to be his. It was Aiden's after all.

When Naomi had told him she was pregnant, she had told him that there was a chance it might not be his, but that didn't put him off the idea. He wanted to share this with her, but now they knew the baby couldn't possibly be his, David felt deflated and let down. He had wound himself up over the last few days to the point that he had convinced himself that the baby was his, and now that feeling of the proud father-to-be had left him.

Lucy cleaned up Naomi's belly after giving her some information about what would happen next with midwives, appointments and the like, but David heard none of it. Naomi didn't take much notice either.

Lucy had been kind enough to print off some pictures of the scan for them to take home. She glossed over the fact that this lovely couple appeared to be heartbroken at some of the news she had given them. She wished them well and sent them on their way home.

22nd December

St Paul's Cathedral had been busy all day with the pre-Christmas preparations for services and and celebrations. Wardens and priests and volunteers had decorated the expansive nave and transepts with bouquets of holly and ivy. The Christmas tree was a gigantic Norwegian Spruce similar to that in Trafalgar Square, and this stood proudly in Paternoster Square, outside the main door to the cathedral.

Long after dark, the cathedral was silent and the shadows crept around the seats, the pillars and round the traditional nativity scene. The noise of the traffic outside was quietening down now the bulk of the Christmas shoppers had gone home. The traffic was mostly taxis, minicabs and buses moving business parties and people celebrating early from bar to bar and home again.

Charon stalked down the aisle towards the dome high above the marble circle. He didn't like the cathedral at the best of times, and now he appeared to be alone there. He had been summoned to appear before Gabriel alone. For what reason, he did not know. He was just told to be at the cathedral tonight. Dutifully he had come. There was no light coming from the dome tonight, it was as dark as the rest of the cathedral, lit solely by the street lights outside.

Although glorious by day and when illuminated by the interior lights, at night, it was a forbidding place. Too many shadows for things to hide in; too many echos to be afraid of.

Gabriel stepped out of the shadows of the north transept and approached Charon, his robes emitting a little light.

"Charon. Welcome." The angels arms were outstretched, as if offering a place for Charon to receive a blessing.

"Gabriel. Good to see you. Why have you brought me here tonight?"

Charon could see a severe look on Gabriel's face. "Do you still have Aiden on this side of the Styx?"

"Yes, I do." The gravelly voice of Charon echoed the severity of Gabriel's mood.

"You must get him across and as far away from the edge of the veil as you can. He must not be able to break through again. Do you understand?"

"Yes. But why? I had planned on keeping here for a hundred years because he has no fare to pay me."

"Naomi is pregnant and he must not be allowed anywhere near her ever again. We cannot trust his anger and jealousy. We did once, and it was a mistake and nearly cost Naomi her destiny."

"But were they not destined to be together, Gabriel?"

"They were, but she now despises him for what his jealousy has done to her and to David. She has changed her destiny."

"So they will never be together again?"

"No. An eternity separated."

"I'll see that it is done, my Lord."

"Make sure that you do. We do not need a repeat of recent events, Charon."

"It will be, Gabriel, I can assure you it will be." Charon backed off into the shadows, affording Gabriel a long graceful bow "And whose baby is it?"

"Aiden is the father."

"Thank you, Gabriel." Charon then slipped back into the

darkness, smiling almost as darkly.

-|-

Walking down the main steps into Paternoster Square, Charon looked up at the huge Christmas tree in front of him. The icy blue lights smothering it shone brightly and the clear night beyond them exuded peace and a sense of hope. Christmas Day was in three days time, and as Charon flicked back his hood and breathed in the chill in the air, the realisation dawned on him how he could ensure Aiden would never come back, or attempt to come back across the veil.

-|-

The comforting and familiar tunes of the same Christmas CD that virtually every house in the country had, filled the living room as David and Naomi decorated her flat for the festive season. Neither were feeling particularly festive. They were both thinking about the news they were given a few days ago.

Since leaving the hospital, they had barely spoken to one another. What should have been a wonderful early Christmas present had turned out to be a bit of a disappointment, if they were honest with each other. Neither of them wanted the baby to be Aiden's. He had betrayed them both so much that they both agreed that he did not deserve to be remembered like that. In flesh and blood.

But now, a few days on from the scan, both David and Naomi had had deep thoughts to themselves about what to do. Naomi had remembered what the Angel Michael had said about the baby, and how they must both love it. She had not mentioned that to David at all. She didn't quite know how to. He may not believe her for a start, and, looking at the scars across his forehead as he brought in a cardboard box full of tinsel and baubles from the car, she thought it best to be the only secret she would keep from him.

Michael had been right. They had fallen in love when she went to see David in the Liverpool hospital. And he had fallen for her too, or rather, his love for her had been reciprocated.

She had spent several days with him whilst he built his strength back up again before he was strong enough to leave. She had even come up with a believable story for the police about how his car was abandoned half way up the M6 to Liverpool. She had told them that they had had an argument at her flat in London and he had walked out on her in anger. She hadn't heard from him for a few hours when she called to speak to him. He was at the service station. He decided to disappear for a few days, and when he arrived in Liverpool he walked to visit his favourite sculpture on Crosby Beach when he was set upon by a couple of drunks and left by the statue. The police found the story to be plausible and had said nothing further about it, to both Naomi and David's relief.

The Christmas Tree was in the corner of the room as it had been every year and the television had been evicted to a spot in front of the windows.

After some discussion about the colour scheme of the tree, gold and red, silver and gold or red, silver *and* green, the tree was finished, just the fairy to go on the top and the lights to be switched on.

David put his hands on Naomi's shoulders and turned her round to face the corner with the tree.

"Naomi?" He peered into her, searching out the deepest part of her soul.

"Yes, David." She sounded gushing, but didn't mean to

"About the baby." Naomi frowned and went to chastise David for bringing it up now. He touched a finger to her lips to silence her before she could speak. He took a deep breath. "I think it would be a great idea if the two of us were to bring up the baby completely as our own and try to forget the events on the run-up to you finding out. What do you think?"

Naomi beamed at him, but with a questioning look on her brow. "That's great David. But what about you? How do you feel?"

"To be honest with you, Naomi, I couldn't be happier. I've thought a lot about it over the last few days and I know that I can do this for you, and for the baby. It would be a privilege to be his or her father. On one condition though..." he paused for dramatic affect and to gauge Naomi's response.

"What?" she said sternly.

David beamed back at Naomi. He leaned closer to her and put his mouth next to her ear and began to whisper.

"Provided everything goes alright, shall we have a baby of our own in a year or two? What do you think?"

Naomi leaned back and looked at David's face. There wasn't a trace of nerves to be seen. He looked strong, confident and ready. "That sounds like it could just work David." She touched the side of his face with her hand, feeling the stubble beginning to come through from the morning's shave.

"Are you going to put the fairy on top of the tree?" he kissed her neck. She nuzzled into it.

"Why don't you do it?"

"Because it's your tree and your flat. That's why. It's your honour."

Suddenly she became like a little girl, all giggly and gooey. "OK," she said "Lift me up, I can't reach."

David gave her a huge beaming, loving smile and handed her the fairy that had graced the top of every tree in her homes since she was a child. She had made it at school years and years ago.

The little cardboard fairy now only had one wing and more than half the glitter had been rubbed off, but it was one thing that connected Naomi to the magic of Christmas as a child. She loved that fairy and treasured it.

As David lifted her up under the arms, Naomi gave the fairy a kiss and wished it a Merry Christmas and placed it carefully on the point of the crown of the tree.

Letting her down gently, Naomi turned to David, put her arms around his neck and kissed him. "Merry Christmas, David. You going to switch the lights on?"

"Merry Christmas, Naomi. Yes, I will."

He kissed Naomi back with his hands cupping her face, the warm feeling of her lips running through him, filling him with happiness.

Kneeling down and prickling himself on the needles of the tree, David reached for the plug switch.

"Ready?" he said "Drum roll, please!"

"OK" Naomi made a rough impersonation of a badly played drum roll.

David flicked the switch.

Nothing.

"Bugger." He said from beneath the tree.

24th December

"AIDEN WILLIAMSON! WHERE ARE YOU?" Charon was calling out along the railings on the banks of the river not far from Tower Bridge. The others chained there cowered away from the swinging stick that the ferryman wielded as he beat them on his way passed. "Merry Christmas to you too!" He tormented them as the drizzle fell on them, dampening them down and mixing with their miserable tears.

It wasn't raining on the living side of the veil, and the joyful happy laughter of those going home to sleep the night off and wake up to present echoed through the veil and tormented those trapped on the railings be Charons shackles.

"AIDEN!"

Some way off down the bank, Aiden heard his name being called. He tried to stand to grab Charon's attention, but the shackles and chains were too short and as he stood, they dug into his wrists and pulled him back down again.

"I'm here Charon!" he called out into the wet dark of Christmas Eve.

Charon span round at the sound of his name and through the bleak drizzle saw Aiden trying to stand. He strode over toward him, smiling broadly. This would be a superb

Christmas in Hell for this man, Charon thought to himself.

Standing tall over Aiden, Charon clapped the crook of his pole round Aiden's neck, released his shackles from the chain and railings but left them round his wrists and picked him up to his own eye level.

Charon's breath was stagnant in Aiden's face. "Merry Christmas, Aiden. Want to come for a little walk?" Not waiting for an answer, he dropped the end of the pole to the ground and began to drag Aiden along the paving westward towards Waterloo.

Aiden struggled to stand by making his his legs catch up with his body to gain some kind of balance so he half staggered, half slid across the ground. "What do you want, Charon?"

"You'll see, you'll see."

-|-

Naomi yawned loudly and propped herself up off of David's chest where she had been dozing for a few hours. She looked at her watch. Half past ten. David had nodded off too. The large glass of whiskey he had started was not finished and sat on the table. The ice melted and it was warm now. There was a rubbish film on the television. Lazily Naomi switched it off and made to stand up.

She looked at the tree in the corner of the living room. It's lights were glowing brightly and the little fairy on the top sat proudly. It looked peaceful standing there. She looked at David, rubbed his chest and kissed his cheek. "Merry Christmas, David." She whispered into his ear.

David stirred and sleepily pulled her back down onto his chest, holding her tightly. "Hmm, yeah." He snuggled her down into his jumper. "Merry Christmas to you too." He kissed the top of her head.

"Come on, bed time." With a smile, Naomi pushed herself of his chest again and tried to haul him up off the sofa by one hand. "Come...on" she pulled hard, making him uncomfortable.

David grunted and hazily stood up.

"Doesn't the tree look lovely, David? We did a good job of it, didn't we?"

David half opened his eyes, the glowing bulbs making him blink, then focus. "Yeah, we did." He kissed her again and followed her to the bedroom.

25th December

Aiden and Charon walked into Naomi's bedroom. She was lying with David cuddled up behind her with his face on her long hair and arm over her, holding her close, protecting her.

"Why have you brought me here?" Aiden was choked and angry at what he saw before him.

The bells of the nearby church clock chimed midnight. Aiden looked towards the window. Suddenly he felt low. As low as he had ever felt since his death. He loved Christmas and waking up on Christmas morning with Naomi was the best feeling he ever had. They had always had a long lie-in exchanging presents and having breakfast in bed. Then they would perhaps get up for a late lunch with one set of parents or the other.

"I'm going to make you an offer, Aiden. A Christmas present, if you like." Charon spoke slowly, making his point as clear as he could and waved his hand towards the sleeping couple, pointing at neither in particular. "One soul in exchange for yours."

"What? Really?" Aiden brightened up with excitement.

Charon was sounding as black as he ever had. Even when

he was calling across the river when Aiden had escaped hell did he not sound this sinister. "Which one is it going to be, Aiden?"

What sort of a question was that? The decision was so easy to make. It was a Christmas present indeed. Aiden laughed out loud at Charon's foolishness. He couldn't believe that this monster from Hell would offer him something so simple. "David's. Take David's soul in place of mine."

"No, I don't want David's. You don't understand, Aiden. Perhaps I didn't make myself clear enough."

Aiden looked confused. He screwed his face up and looked into Charon's eyes.

Charon smile "I want the baby's soul in exchange for yours. You can do what you want with David's soul, he won't care after you've killed the unborn."

"Baby? What baby?" Aiden took a sharp step back. His eyes widened as they welled with tears. He looked hard at Naomi. He could feel the familiar fierce, burning, agonising rage brewing inside him. He sank to his knees, the anger exhausting him quickly. It was so powerful that he didn't know how to deal with it. It weighed heavily upon him and pushed him down to the floor. "Naomi's pregnant? No."

Charon smiled widely at his captive. "It's your baby, Aiden. Yours."

Aiden could not believe what he was hearing. "THIS CAN'T BE HAPPENING TO ME! DEAR GOD, NO!" He yelled out at the top of his voice. "You want me to choose between my unborn child's life and my own happiness and time with Naomi?"

Nodding, Charon laughed out loud, mocking the situation he had formulated for Aiden.

Stunned, Aiden turned to lash out at Charon for suggesting such a barbaric thing, but the crook around his neck was just far enough away that he could not reach to punch nor kick his captor. Instead, Charon easily pinned him to the floor with it and looked at him from the shadows beneath his hood and the smile on his face suggested he knew the choice was an impossible one. Aiden was flailing to stand up again, struggling to exact some kind of harm, but it was no use, Charon was too strong.

"Think about it Aiden. I'm willing to give Naomi back to you. All you have to do is give me your last living part: Your baby's soul, that's all, and then I'll leave you here to take care of David as you place. You can be with Naomi after all, in David's body."

Aiden slowly got to his knees as Charon lessened the pressure on the pole and then he continued "You can be together forever, Aiden. Is this not what you have been fighting for these last few months?"

"Not like this, No. This is so unfair." Aiden was falling apart, just as Naomi had done at his funeral. He looked at her sleeping so peacefully in the loving arms of his best friend. His love for her was doubling over and over again. All he ever wanted was for her to be happy.

A crushing realisation brought Aiden's head down to his chest. All he had managed to do was hurt them both since he would not accept the fact that he was dead.

He knew and felt that he really was dead now. He was dead to himself, and he was dead to his friends too. Why could he not have accepted that in the beginning?

Above that though, he had gone against the will of all those more powerful than himself and he had nearly killed his best friend through his jealousy of those still alive.

Sitting on his haunches at the side of the bed like he had done when he had first been allowed to return by the Principium, Aiden sobbed. The realisation of his own failures broke all over him with each new wave of tears. He held his face in his hands in the deepest of regret. Charon could feel the most intense feeling of loss spread throughout Aiden's soul. He knew he had won.

The crook pulled Aiden's head back up to look into the sleeping face of Naomi. "Merry Christmas, Aiden." The Ferryman smiled "What's your choice?" he whispered, the darkness of his voice ensuring Aiden knew precisely what he knew the answer would be.

Every ounce of hope had evaporated from his soul now, and Aiden felt like he was already in hell. He was heavy with loneliness, despair and regret. There was no other choice to make.

With all the love he had ever felt for Naomi, and no matter how much he hated David now, he couldn't wish any pain on his unborn child. There was no fight left in him, he was spent and he had no right to decide on the life or death of his child. He looked up, helpless and hopeless at Charon, his eyes burning as if already in hell, but with tears instead of fire. "Take me, Charon. I don't want to be here any more. Let me burn for what I've done."

Charon smiled, took a tight grip on the pole and pushed Aiden out of the door, and back to the ferry.

Naomi and David slept on.

> *'...and I thy guide*
> *Will lead thee hence through an eternal space,*
> *Where thou shalt hear despairing shrieks,*
> *and see Spirits of old tormented,*
> *who invoke*
> *A second death; and those next view,*
> *who dwell Content in fire...'*

Dante Alighieri, 'Inferno', 1314

Notes

Principium Angeli

I wanted to have a group of Angels in the book that could be bound by a group name. I wasn't keen on calling them the Archangels, because they are not all Archangels. I therefore came up with the name on Principium Angeli which loosely (literally) translated from Latin means *Principal Angels*. You can do your own research into the individuals, but here are the ones that feature in The Veil: **Michael** (translation: *who is like God?*),kindness of God, **Gabriel** (archangel) (translation: *the strength of God*), performs acts of justice and power, **Uriel** (translation: *God is my light*), leads us to destiny, **Samael** (translation: *the severity of God*), angel of death.

Darryl Cowling

Darryl Cowling is the minor character that comes to assist the friends with the Ouija Board on 23rd November. I wanted Darryl to use some kind of protection charm when everything goes wrong for him and his experience runs out, his fall back position, if you like. When it does all fall apart, he says: *"Vitae est nunc extincta, Et effugare ab hoc loco reditum de quo egressus es, Spiritus ergo noster est fortius quam tuus, Ergo iam non estis suscipit mi. Vade ad spiritum deorum."*

This is pigeon Latin for "Your life is now extinct, Be gone from this place and return from whence you came. Our spirit is stronger than yours. You are no longer welcome here. Be gone, back to the Gods."

For the translation from English to Latin, I used Google Translate. I am aware that it is probably not completely accurate, but for the sake of artistic license, I believe it is close enough!

London, Liverpool and Locations

For the sections where streets are named and you can follow the action along, you can actually use mapping software on the internet to follow the action and see the buildings described. This is particularly so in the chase through London when Aiden escapes from Hell and when he possesses David and forces him to drive to Liverpool.

Some of the locations too, such as Mr Gorshani's shop and Agostini's Coffee shop are based on actual places I know and like to visit on occasion.

Errors...

Nobody is perfect, and you may have found some errors in the text of this book. If you have, I am really sorry. If you let me know where they are, I will correct them for you. If there are enough errors to warrant either a second edit and a release of a second edition, I will be certain to do it, so you will be able to have a correct copy of your book.

Contact and Coming Next...

Becoming a writer is also becoming very social! Why not drop the author a line and join in the social side of his work? Check out his website, blog and Facebook page or follow him on Twitter. Here's how:

Web: www.msabansmith.com
Facebook: www.facebook.com/msabansmith
Twitter: @msabansmith

Keep an eye out in Spring 2014 for M. Saban-Smith's second book. It will be a chilling exploration into how a collection of cursed puppets can affect their owner.

The Punch and Judy Man.